KU-098-729

SEASON OF SACRIFICE

Recent titles by Bharti Kirchner from Severn House

GODDESS OF FIRE

The Maya Mallick series

SEASON OF SACRIFICE

Bharti Kirchner is the author of seven critically acclaimed novels, four cookbooks and hundreds of short pieces which were published in magazines and newspapers. Bharti has written for *Food & Wine, Writer's Digest, The Writer, Fitness Plus, San Francisco Chronicle* and *The Seattle Times*. Her essays have appeared in ten anthologies. She has won numerous awards for her writing, including a Virginia Center for the Creative Arts Fellowship. Prior to becoming a writer, Bharti worked as a systems engineer for IBM and as a systems manager for Bank of America, San Francisco. She has also worked in Europe and other continents as a computer systems consultant. Bharti lives in the US with her husband. Visit www.bhartikirchner.com for more details.

SEASON OF SACRIFICE

A Maya Mallick Mystery

Bharti Kirchner

This first world edition published 2017
in Great Britain and the USA by
SEVERN HOUSE PUBLISHERS LTD of
19 Cedar Road, Sutton, Surrey, England, SM2 5DA.
Trade paperback edition first published
in Great Britain and the USA 2017 by
SEVERN HOUSE PUBLISHERS LTD

British Library Cataloguing in Publication Data
A CIP catalogue record for this title is available from the British Library.

ISBN-13: 978-0-7278-8724-5 (cased)
ISBN-13: 978-1-84751-831-6 (trade paper)
ISBN-13: 978-1-78010-899-5 (e-book)

All Severn House titles are printed on acid-free paper.

Severn House Publishers support the Forest Stewardship Council™ [FSC™],
the leading international forest certification organisation.
All our titles that are printed on FSC certified paper carry the FSC logo.

Typeset by Palimpsest Book Production Ltd.,
Falkirk, Stirlingshire, Scotland.
Printed and bound in Great Britain by
TJ International, Padstow, Cornwall.

For Didi, Rinku, Tinni, and Tom
How fortunate I am to have you in my life

ACKNOWLEDGMENTS

Warm thanks go to those who stood by me during the creation of this book. Their names (in no particular order) are: Kimberly Ito, Debra Borchert, Elena Hartwell, Tami Euliano, Christine Mason, and Gail Kretchmer. Their optimism and suggestions have helped give life to this project.

I am also fortunate to have a stellar publishing team. Priya Doraswamy, agent nonpareil, is always supportive and always a pleasure to work with. Everyone at Severn House has given enormous care and thought to this task. I'll forever be grateful to all of you.

I am deeply appreciative of my scientist friends whose knowledge has informed the premise of my story. Special thanks go to Mike Hawley, who patiently answered my questions about police procedures. And to 4Culture for a grant that partially supported this project.

To those not directly connected with my efforts, but who have sustained me over the years, I say thank you. Shau-lee Chow for the trips to the shows and for always having a spirit of joy. Rekha Sood and Santosh Wahi for leisurely lunches and sisterhood. Lakshmi Gaur for wide-ranging conversations that kept me centered whenever we could catch a few moments. Lalitha Uppala for being there. Elizabeth George for somehow managing to find time for tea and shop talk. Deepa Banerjee, Librarian at the University of Washington, for her confidence in me.

And, finally, to my husband Tom for his love, support and encouragement. You ultimately made this possible.

'Truth exists, only falsehood has to be invented.'

Georges Braque

'We do not live an equal life, but one of contrasts and patchwork; now a little joy, then a sorrow, now a sin, then a generous or brave action.'

Ralph Waldo Emerson

ONE

With the early morning summer breeze tickling the back of her neck, Maya Mallick hurried toward the neighborhood bakery for pastries and a jolt of caffeine. She needed the energy to finish a project she'd acquired in her previous job as a nutritionist.

Her eyes took in the well-kept Tudors, Dutch Colonials, Craftsman bungalows and occasional modern mansions that typified the Green Lake district of Seattle. Rounding the corner, from half a block away, she spied a crowd of ten or so people. Eyes closed and dressed in white, they overflowed the sidewalk in front of an imposing oyster-gray house that loomed over the intersection. A rally of some sort? Her instinct as a private investigator demanded to know. Or a benefit event? No – they emitted a loud, throaty, harsh and almost spooky chant in an unfamiliar tongue.

Although she knew she had to get going, Maya approached and stood a respectful distance behind the group. Wearing her white top and matching pants, she blended in; nobody would notice her, or so she hoped.

A petite young woman stepped forward from the group, turning briefly to face the crowd. Her full body except her eyes was shielded by a dazzling white shroud; a garland of white lilies encircled her neck. Chests vibrating, arms linked, the group arranged itself around her in a tight semicircle and continued chanting.

An olive-skinned man of medium height with a hat slanted across his forehead nudged the woman forward. He wore a white jacket and dark, wraparound sunglasses, even though the sunlight was feeble. There was something sinister about him. His middle finger sported a wide silver band.

Watch him, a feeling in her gut insisted. Maya stood on her toes and glanced at him, trying not to be obvious.

The young woman sank to her knees, whispered a few words

to Sunglasses Man and sent him a longing look as he bent over her like an executioner.

The chanting continued, the chorus ascending and then dramatically descending, sounding cruel and evil. A second woman came forward, pivoted and faced the assembly. Taller than the first, she was also dressed in a white shroud, with a similar garland around her neck. Maya saw only the woman's bright eyes above her veil, eyes that looked familiar. They reminded her of Sylvie, a dedicated malaria research scientist and the sister of Maya's best friend. Sylvie had been adopted from a Tibetan refugee camp in Darjeeling, India, when she was still a baby. Her bloodline could be traced to a Tibetan royal family. But Sylvie, who didn't have a political bone, wouldn't come to a street rally. She'd rather be cooped up in her research lab for a twelve-hour day.

And yet, Maya's chest tightened. She called out, 'Sylvie?'

The chanting stopped for an anxious moment.

With a sweep of his hand, Sunglasses Man gave the second woman the go-ahead. She took a few shuffling, mechanical steps, unsteadily assumed her place beside her companion and gazed up at the mansion.

With his thumbnail, Sunglasses Man ignited a pair of red-tipped wooden matches and handed one to each woman. After uttering a few instructions, he backed away to a safe distance. The women accepted the tiny, playful sparks as if in a trance.

'Don't!' Maya screamed.

In delicate, graceful strokes, the women drew the flickering matchsticks along their clothing, which must had been doused with gasoline or another combustible fluid. Flames, accompanied by an audible whooshing sound, billowed, tattooed and engulfed them, burned a dark, malevolent red and shriveled the lilies. Sunglasses Man stood still at a distance.

'No!' Maya shouted and blinked, still paying close attention.

Both women screamed; the sound pierced Maya to the bone. She shoved through the human shield but a man pushed her back, nearly knocking her to the ground. A bitter odor settled in the air.

'Stop!' she yelled. A surge of panic welled up within her, crushing her chest like a vise.

Her plea brought no reaction. She'd left her cellphone in the car; she couldn't call 911. She tried to tear the jacket off a mustachioed man in front of her but he shook her off.

'This is a sacred ceremony, miss,' he said in an edgy voice.

She'd seen him before but she couldn't remember where – this sixtyish, ruddy-skinned man with a boxer's nose and a neatly trimmed mustachio. 'Ceremony?' she asked, but received no reply.

Still screaming, the taller woman tugged an ornament from her forearm. Fingers curling, tongues of blue-streaked flame dancing over her body and showing their rage, she flung it to the ground, the item of evidence. The inch-wide, solid gold bracelet rolled away, hit the edge of the pavement and came to a halt.

Her mind in a whirl, Maya stared at the burning women and again tried to get closer, only to be shoved back. The air, now thick with a nauseating odor of burning flesh, made her gag.

Arms extended, the women slumped forward. Sunglasses Man motioned the members of the prayer group to move farther away. The group chanted louder now, a distraction from the women, their white clothes appearing yellow in the glow of the flames.

A blue Nissan cruised up the side street and slowed. Maya sprinted to the car, frantically waved at the driver and pounded on his rear window. 'Call an ambulance. Quick!'

The driver accelerated, as though he hadn't heard her or noticed the macabre scene.

'What's the matter with you?' Maya shrieked. 'We've got to save them!'

Her eyes filled with tears, her ears rang and her heart threatened to push up into her throat. In her thirty-three years she'd never seen anything remotely like this. Ritualistic suicides? They only occurred in places like Tunisia or Tibet, not in this sleepy Seattle hood. She stumbled back and stood behind the chanters. Chest heaving, she gasped for breath, a putrid breeze around her. The air boomed with the sound of prayer. A few neighbors trotted out of their houses, perhaps to see what the hullabaloo was about.

The tall woman toppled onto her right; her companion slumped forward. Mouth tasting bitter, her insides churning, Maya imagined how they must feel: dizzy, confused and craving oxygen, with unbearable heat gnawing on their flesh, their hope stolen. The prayer group's eerie chanting rose to a crescendo, as though inviting more destruction. With her arm outstretched, Maya again tried to get close to the women, to hear their last words, to say or do anything to help ease their suffering, but the wave of heat pushed her back. Then there was a crackling sound.

Sunglasses Man glared at Maya and yelled a warning – '*Nyet!*' – to a person who now stood next to her.

A silver stick sliced the air, struck her elbow and lower back with a sickening sound of metal on flesh and bone. Maya bit her lip, recoiled from the shooting pain and turned to face the attacker, but tripped and lost her balance.

She stumbled against a maple tree on the sidewalk and grasped at a rough branch. The bark scraped her back, her ankle twisting beneath her, and she slid to a sitting position at the base of the tree.

A dour, compact, middle-aged man, with a deep mahogany complexion and droopy eyelids, stood over her. *Jerk!* She wanted to kick him. Clean-shaven, balanced on a pair of metal crutches, he was clad in a crisp white shirt and shorts, his right leg encased in a toe-to-hip cast.

Damn you! More curses welled up in her throat as she rose but Maya didn't utter them, only managed to squeak out in her flustered state, 'Why?'

The man stood before her like a stern disciplinarian. 'What the hell do you think you're doing, miss?' She noted the rapid delivery and the lilting Indian accent of a fellow countryman, a *desi*. 'You mustn't go any closer. Hear me? Those two ladies sacrificed themselves to protest the Chinese atrocities in Tibet.'

Maya rubbed her elbow with her free hand, her twisted ankle now throbbing dully as she cast him a fierce look.

'I knew the taller one.' He looked around nervously. 'We were members of the same meditation group. She sent me a text early this morning. It was her wish.'

Should she believe this man? Maya's voice rose above the

chanting. 'This is insane. You're asking me to mind my own business? I'm a private investigator.'

The whining of a siren cut through the air. Maya looked up and took several steps back along the sidewalk. The chanting voices faded; the prayer group dispersed. The gathering pedestrians quickly stepped aside as a fire truck pulled up next to the flaming bodies. Sunglasses Man had slipped away from the crowd. Maya focused on the street, saw his back fast disappearing.

Firemen in full gear charged from the truck. Several crouched over the bodies, extinguished the few lingering flames and checked for vital signs. An ambulance screeched to a halt by the truck. So did two blue-and-white police squad cars, their lights pulsing.

'I am Officer Rand from the city,' a uniformed policeman, displaying his badge, announced to the onlookers. 'Please move back.' He sealed off the area with yellow crime-scene tape.

Maya crossed the street to the opposite sidewalk. The man on crutches was also there. He stared at her and she could read his unspoken thought: *You're from India, too?* It would be natural for him to reach this conclusion since Maya had typical Indian features: dark eyes dominating a honey-colored, round face, a small forehead and bushy eyebrows. She was five foot four and wore a mid-length, layered haircut like many modern Indian women.

'You know about the Chinese foreign minister Hui Yu's visit, don't you?' said the man in a strained voice, pointing at the oyster-gray mansion across the street. 'The criminal is staying there – his son's home – instead of at the Chinese consulate. The limo parked in front is his official car. It's all in today's daily.'

Maya peered up at the modern mansion, the tallest building in sight. The Chinese national flag, red strewn with gold stars, fluttered above its roof. She was aware that the Chinese used red to symbolize passion, happiness and revolution as well as sacrifice. The black limousine parked in front had two small Chinese flags fluttering on short poles affixed to the mirrors. Those flags in the car indicated it was, indeed, the temporary home of a dignitary from Beijing.

Paramedics wrapped the blackened bodies in white sheets, loaded them onto a pair of gurneys, slid them into the back of the ambulance and sped away. A few people stepped forward, bent down and touched the ashen dust in a gesture of respect.

'Our two sisters are so brave,' the man on crutches mumbled.

Were so brave. They were no longer brave. They were no longer anything at all. The unbearable stench and thick smoke were proof. Several bystanders wiped their eyes, as did Maya. Somewhere a bird made an intermittent chirping noise.

It couldn't have been Sylvie.

A light of devotion in his gaze, the veins of his throat bulging, the man on crutches said out loud, 'May our beloved sisters find peace. May we keep them in our hearts forever. May we all be kind to one another.'

Maya sensed movement around her. With gloved hands, a police officer started taking measurements of the area. Another officer had begun gathering bystanders for interviews. He didn't notice Maya standing off to the side.

A second look at him and Maya turned to stone. Detective Justin Stevenson of the Seattle Police Department. The cool cop – tall, lanky and handsome, blue eyes turning indigo in the intensity of the situation – was a former lover who had come close to being Mr Right. Until he'd ditched her.

As an eyewitness, shouldn't she speak with him about this bizarre and violent incident? Then, as she glanced at her watch, an alarm bell went off in her head. She had already cancelled an appointment with her client once before due to a schedule mix-up. She couldn't afford to cancel again; she needed the funds. Bending to touch her swollen ankle, burning with pain, she felt the need to sit down. Another glance at Justin Stevenson and she decided to call him from the privacy of her car, when her senses would be sharper.

Heads low, steps heavy, keys jingling, part of the crowd melted away. Others took pictures and conversed in low voices. Video camera in hand, a journalist arrived. Thank heavens the bodies were already on their way to the hospital. Maya started walking, the ache of her ankle overwhelmed by the discomfort in her gut.

An obviously stoned teenager, wearing frayed jeans, stared vacantly from the opposite corner. Crows joined in a cacophony overhead. The wind howled and made a door rattle. Maya took a few steps, disturbed by the sight of a patch of half-dead purple petunias. She tried to draw in a steadying breath, only to have her hair caught by the swaying branch of a pear tree. She untangled her hair and kept walking. A baby burst out crying in a nearby house.

The man on crutches caught up with her. 'My name's Atul Biswas. I'm an accountant. Friends call me Atticus.'

'Maya Mallick.'

'Sorry – I almost hit you with my crutch.'

Weirdo. Maya could press charges against him for assaulting her. Except, given the enormity of the situation and the fact that the authorities had graver matters to handle, she would rather not. 'Not almost. You hit me; my elbow hurts. Why did you do that?'

'Nothing intentional. Please, I'm a basket case. Didn't have the foggiest what I was doing.' His eyes rounded in sorrow. 'My sincerest apology. May I give you a ride somewhere, Maya?'

She shook her head. 'One question. What's the name of the place where you meditate?'

'Padmaraja Meditation Center.' He pivoted and hobbled away.

After taking another glance at Detective Justin Stevenson, busy talking with witnesses, Maya walked away from the grisly scene and soon reached her car. Before sliding into the driver's seat, she twisted her head once to see if anyone was following her.

Leash in hand, a determined dog-walker strode past. The menacing-looking dog held itself stiff, stared at Maya, jumped and growled.

After steadying herself, she dug out her cellphone from the glove compartment and punched in her landline number. Hopefully her mother, Uma, visiting from Kolkata, would answer in her gentle manner. She badly needed to hear that voice just now. It rang, rang and rang, then the call clicked into voicemail.

'No pastries today, Ma. Something's happened.'

TWO

Cellphone still in hand, Maya placed the call to Justin, her heart thumping wildly as she listened to the ringing. Voicemail. She left him a message in a duller tone than she'd hoped for. She had just witnessed two self-immolations in the Green Lake neighborhood and asked him to call her back, without mentioning how deeply she'd been affected. After disengaging, she tried not to replay the message in her mind, tried not to criticize the sound of her own voice or to mull over how *he* would think she sounded, tried not to worry that she might have sounded hurt or needy or pathetic.

A man in business clothes, walking past her car, fired off a mean look in her direction. She swallowed, a brief walls-closing-in moment, and wondered if he might have noticed her in the crowd.

A long truck rumbled past, fouling the air with coils of diesel, its clatter assaulting Maya's ears like a dull hammer. Once the noise abated, she called her best friend Veen and recorded a brief, 'Hi, call me,' message. She needed to make sure that Sylvie wasn't one of the two women. Sylvie had never talked about Tibet, her ancestral homeland, much less hinted at a desire to be a freedom activist.

The same age as Maya, olive-skinned with velvety-black hair and delicate features, Sylvie was softly spoken and energetic, reminiscent of a sparrow flitting from one tree branch to another. Her shining eyes always revealed that she had much to say, although she kept most of it to herself. Maya found it hard to believe that a young bio-med scientist like Sylvie, so passionate about her work, so invested in helping others and for whom a shining future awaited, would kill herself in such a violent way.

Maya set off into the traffic. Upon her arrival at a modern, three-story building on Woodlawn Avenue called Future Space, she parked in the underground garage. Emerging from the elevator, she strode down the hall to number 106, her new abode as a private investigator. Most of her savings from her previous career had gone into the renting and refurbishing of this office. Now she half-noticed the lack of any sign on her door and frowned. The vendor should have delivered the brass plaque by now.

She unlocked the door and walked into the two-room workplace. The front room had a carpeted wood floor, an antique black executive desk, a matching swivel chair, three straight-backed visitors' chairs, two secure file cabinets and a painting on one wall of a riverside Indian village, all organized just the way she liked it. Yet, on this day, the room seemed empty. The sound of a lawnmower coming through a half-open window overlooking a manicured courtyard jarred her.

'Hi, Maya!' Hank, her investigative assistant, called from the back room.

Maya took in a deep breath, returned the greeting and still nearly tripped as she joined him in the back room. It was equipped with a desk, a coffee-maker and a portable refrigerator. Hank Anderson, a skinny, blond, bright-faced, twenty-three-year-old MFA student sat in front of an open laptop. When not busy with his thesis of a short story collection, Hank worked for her part-time as the first line of communication. He fielded phone calls and emails, employed search tools and linking technology, dug into professional-grade databases and also maintained Maya's website. Softly spoken, he used his fiction-writing acumen to his advantage. 'Characters are everything, fucked-up as they often are,' he'd argue as he dissected the words, actions and motivations of a prospective client.

With his clear gaze, gentle enough to put people at ease, but also perceptive, Hank surveyed her closely. 'Is everything OK?'

Maya shook her head and narrated this morning's gruesome happenings. Hank remained rooted in his chair and, when she'd finished, let out a low whistle from seemingly holding his breath and finally exhaling. 'Beyond bizarre – terribly sad too. Worst thing that could have happened.' He tried to rise, then sat down again. 'I'm sorry, Maya, I don't know how to process it. You're limping?'

'A minor injury. I'll let it go.'

'Do you see yourself getting involved as a P.I.?'

'I have no reason to. The police showed up and I assume they gathered all the obvious clues, although they could have missed some subtleties.'

'Such as the subtext and deeper motivations?'

Maya nodded. 'Any calls or emails?'

'Yes and yes. A Japanese woman called to whine about her granny missing. It's a referral from Ms Pillai, a lawyer acquaintance of yours. Something didn't sound right, so I called Sophie. She got the scoop from the community. The feisty old granny has secretly flown to Las Vegas with a young man – arm candy, from what I hear – for a little fun of her own.'

Maya smiled, caught up in Hank's enthusiasm. 'So the case is closed, at least for now? I doubly appreciate your effort, Hank, knowing how you feel about Sophie.'

Sophie was Hank's ex-girlfriend, an Australian-Japanese who he was still on speaking terms with. It was clear to Maya from the sheepish expression on Hank's face that he'd like to get back with her.

'She and I had a thing.' Hank's voice turned heavy. 'I'll get her back from that asshole dude and I'll get her cuffed.' He diverted his gaze to the screen. 'Here's an email asking you to do an undercover investigation of an office theft. Again, it's a referral from a former nutrition client of yours. I've asked for more input. Also, your mother called to see if you were here yet. She must have been cooking. I could hear the sounds of pots and pans. I could almost smell the curry.'

Oh, Mother. She always had to check to see where her daughter was. 'She loves to cook.'

'Mine had a Ph.D. in Chinese carry-outs.' Hank's gaze flitted over Maya's in a mock look of envy. 'Lastly, an Indian man called from a blocked number. Mumbled he met you this morning. I get that he's nervous. Hashtag old-school. I'm like, "Speak up, man." He said he'd try back later and hung up.'

Maya stood still for a second. Must be Atticus. Given that he knew she was a private detective, he'd found her on the Internet. What did he want?

She had half-turned when Hank said, 'Do you have a gun, Maya?'

She gave a start. 'No, I don't have a firearm permit. Why do you ask?'

'There's a bookish saying.' Hank's lips parted in a smile. "If there's a gun on the mantelpiece, it must go off before the story is over."'

Maya laughed; she needed a light moment. 'I'll wrap up my last nutritionist gig and check with you about what's going on.'

'Totally, boss. Now I can call Sophie back. Tell her you were pleased with my sleuthing. Maybe even offer to take her out for a green-tea shake.'

Maya rose and smiled. 'It's worth a shot.'

On her way to the client, she noticed a blue sedan passing her too close, adding to the anxious feeling still gripping her chest.

Several hours later, after finishing the client consultation, Maya decided to check out the meditation center; the place was a common element between Atticus and one of the self-immolators. She drove north, passing by a tent encampment for the homeless, reached her destination, parked and scoped out the surroundings. In this renovation-ready neighborhood filled with creeping shadows and boarded-up storefronts, the sidewalks were chipped and the exteriors of a few aged buildings showed mold growth. Pedestrians strolled by; an occasional car wheezed past. The meditation center stood out, an unobtrusive, single-story, flat-roofed building freshly coated with lotus-white paint. Why this neighborhood? Cheap rent? Desire for privacy?

Emblazoned in flowing black calligraphy across the top of the entrance was the name of the establishment: *Padmaraja Meditation Center.*

The door was locked and the lights inside were not on. The center must be closed at this hour. Still, Maya rang the doorbell. No answer. She stood and absorbed the strange silence that permeated the immediate area, then drove home.

As she hopped out of her Honda, her gaze fell on her house, a small, single-story, two-bedroom Craftsman bungalow. It was all she could afford. Painted a muted blue, it had squared columns, a large front porch and deep eaves. Clean, simple lines – her favorite. Even more so after this morning's horror.

Sunlight illuminated a section of her front yard, highlighting a sweet-smelling honeysuckle bush that spilled over a long fence. Next to that, a bank of daisies bloomed, each white flower with an inviting yellow cushion at its center. Daisies, a sign that summer was at its peak, also indicated that the season would soon disappear. And the flowers would die.

She picked up the mail from the mailbox and opened the front door. The aroma of sizzling oil wafted from the kitchen, as did a hip-thrusting Bollywood soundtrack from the CD player. Her mother, Umaratna, must be at the stove, preparing wickedly delicious snacks for their tea break, as she'd done every afternoon since her arrival from Kolkata a month ago. In no time, Uma had become 'Auntie' to Maya's friends; she solved their problems. They fawned over her and brought her truffles, candles, scarves and show tickets. Maya never hoped to be as popular as her mother.

Should she tell Uma about the self-immolations? Perhaps not yet.

Uma peeked out from the kitchen, a petite woman swathed in a white sari with a rosebud border, her hair done up in a neat bun. 'Oh, you're back.' Her large eyes shone, the music of her Bengali words hung in the air and she turned off the soundtrack. 'You said you'd be back by eleven and it's now close to two.'

'When will you stop worrying about me, Ma?' Though she tried to make her voice reasonable, Maya failed to conceal the edge of irritation, having already had too much to deal with today. 'For heaven's sake, I'm almost thirty-three. I can take care of myself.'

'Cool it, dear child,' Uma said in English. She'd been picking up slang and colloquial expressions and relished using them. 'Did you know that the Chinese foreign minister is visiting? Big deal. Yesterday's news said the activists were planning to march their boots off to protest the Chinese rule of Tibet. Being from Kolkata – they call it the City of Processions, you might remember – I know how those demonstrations can turn ugly. Huh! What I don't understand is why the protesters only concern themselves with Tibet. They obviously don't know, or care, that the Chinese have been holding the citizens of our beloved state of Arunachal Pradesh under their fists since Nehru's time. Talk about an expropriation! Talk about a dance between a dragon and an elephant. To me, it seems more like the dragon is strangling the elephant.'

'Have you watched any demonstrations—?'

'No, I didn't bother to turn on the television. I took a long walk through this neighborhood instead.'

Thank God Uma hadn't viewed the media hype that likely dominated the television and the Internet by now. Even a fleeting shot of a flaming body would have undone her habitual state of equanimity.

A troubling thought wiggled in Maya's mind: Uma, alone in the house all day. She rubbed her face with a hand to hide her expression of distress.

The kettle whistled, startling her.

'There goes the attention-getter. Be right back.' Uma hurried to the kitchen.

Maya sank into a sofa in her uncluttered living room and kicked off her shoes, surrounded by the warm scent of sandalwood coming from an incense burner on a sideboard. Her gaze swept the room: ivory walls adorned with batik paintings and a smattering of furniture – another solid off-white sofa like this one, an armchair near the fireplace and a sideboard, all in place, yet harmony was somehow lacking. The opposite wall featured a picture window where Maya caught a sliver of a washed-out denim sky mottled with patches of darkening cloud peeking through the open curtains.

She sorted through the mail, discarded the advertisements and opened a brown package airmailed from Kolkata by Simi Sen, her new employer. With pleasure, she fished out a large box of business cards. Done in white linen paper with black lettering, the logo-free cards boldly proclaimed her name.

Detectives Unlimited of Kolkata
Maya Mallick
Private Investigator

Her business number and email address for the Seattle branch followed. Maya put the box on the coffee table, closed her eyes and listened to the rattling of pans. The comforting scent of Uma's cooking wafted into the room through the kitchen door. How could she ever thank her mother, who could always discern what she needed even before she opened her mouth, such as her need for a higher income? To pay the mortgage. To have a savings account. Also, as the sole proprietor of a nutrition consultation business, she'd run out of challenges. Four months ago, Uma, through her network back home, had made the initial contact with the Kolkata-based detective agency.

'Although you make good money, you're tired of your whining clients, acting as food police and raiding people's refrigerators,' Uma had said over the phone. 'I don't blame you. With your energy, smartness and toughness, you can do so much more. Your eyes are sharp and searching and you're mostly level-headed. You want more in your life; you can't wait to get it. Why not fly back here and have a chat with this company? They're successful and they pay well. A gut feeling – you'd like the high-adrenaline work of a P.I.'

'But Ma, isn't it a little unusual for a company in India to branch out into other countries?'

'Such practice is becoming increasingly common. Maybe the news hasn't reached you there yet? India is growing at an alarming rate and many businesses here are trying to get a foothold abroad. All that cash on hand. Look, it would mean working for an international outfit – you'd have loads of opportunities that you currently lack.'

'Seattle does have a large Indian population,' Maya had said. 'But crimes? There aren't that many in our community, or for that matter in the Asian neighborhoods.'

'Give it time, dear. Crimes involving Asians could become a growth industry,' Uma had said jokingly. 'And yes, they want to see you in person.'

So Maya had flown to Kolkata for an interview with the agency, which turned out to be a well-decorated operation in a high-rise building. There she'd met with the owner, Simi Sen, who preferred being called Sen. Fit, well-groomed and elegant, dressed in a yellow silk sari and pearl earrings, the fifty-something Sen was reputed to be a tough investigator. Behind her back, industry insiders called her the 'Iron Lady in Soft Silk.'

'We're an all-women boutique agency, discreet, confidential and private,' Sen had said, sitting behind her high-gloss, executive desk. A strong presence lifted her to beyond-pretty level. 'When we first started this operation, a few pompous male detectives made fun of us. "Those ladies in saris would beat the streets and chase gun-wielding gangsters? They have no place for their cameras." Look at us now. We recently celebrated our tenth anniversary. Women are better at it. We have our intuition and people skills. Nobody can beat us when it comes to pre- and post-matrimonial investigations and cheating spouse cases. "Wedding detectives," they call us, and we've expanded to nine cities. Now I want to branch out to Indian communities in the U.S. You know better than I do that Indians are one of the most successful minority groups there. They must also have plenty of headaches. My guess is our Indian people will go to another *desi* for help, if one is available.'

Maya had nodded while Sen adjusted her sari at her shoulder.

'Detecting must also be in your genes. Your late father, Subir Mallick, the legendary detective with the Kolkata Police Department – who hasn't heard of him?'

Maya had lowered her face. Sen hadn't needed to remind her of her father's brutal murder decades ago, when Maya was only nine years old. It would remain an unsolved case.

'I'm sorry,' Sen had paused as a bearer served them each a glass of amber tea. 'Here's a hypothetical situation. A bride's family requests us to find out if the groom smokes or not. Smoking is a big no-no in the bride's family. The groom claims he's never touched nicotine, although that raised some eyebrows. How would you prove or disprove him, if you were to handle the case?'

Maya had thought for an instant. 'Oh, I'd shadow him and catch him off-guard. Disguised as a man, I'd videotape him in a latrine, lighting up and humming.'

Sen had given a rare laugh. She'd concentrated on Maya's résumé in front of her. 'You paid for your college tuition by working part-time as an office assistant to a private detective? Now I see why that might have worked. You took criminology classes in college? That shows real interest. Even earlier, you helped your mom when a burglar broke into your flat in Kolkata and stole all your possessions. You gave a testimony to the police and helped indict the criminal. That was in the *Statesman* newspaper. You were only twelve then?'

Maya had nodded.

'It's obvious you're an independent soul. If you work for us, you'll have autonomy as far as the cases you wish to look into.'

How will I learn the trade so fast? Maya had wondered. *You don't exactly inherit those qualities from your father, do you?* And as far as her former lover, Detective Justin went . . . In their two-year history, she'd watched how he operated. Even with the support of a whole department, it hadn't been easy for him. 'How will I do it all by myself?' she'd asked Sen.

'You'd laugh if I told you who we used as operatives – our eyes and ears, our sixth sense – when we first started out: cabbies, servants, street vendors, friends and relatives, and neighborhood busybodies. The point is, Maya, mainly we talk to people. Research and surveillance are our other tools.'

Maya had held her back straight. She'd always considered herself a good researcher and interviewer, someone who could listen between the lines. People generally did confide in her about their feelings. And she had the ability to jump into action – she kept her purse by the front door – when necessary. But could it really be that easy? 'What's your success rate?'

'We're hitting sixty to seventy percent. Our competitors think they're doing well if they come close to the fifty percent mark.' Sen had smiled. 'You're interviewing me? Good, good.'

After a lengthy conversation, she'd offered Maya a position as a private investigator based in Seattle. 'We'll give you all the support you need from here. We have informers and plenty of databases at our fingertips. When can you start?'

Maya had hesitated. Working long distance for a foreign company in a line of work that was new to her . . . She could be trapped, stabbed, kicked or shot at without her boss knowing about it. Yet, she could also view herself on the street, excited to be chasing a lead and identifying a culprit, wherever that might be. One good break and you're made, as they say. And from what little she could remember of her father – a tall, slender man with a light of mischief in his eyes – he'd enjoyed his chases. Once, coming home late and bending over her, he'd said, 'What do I do all day, my darling? I give bad guys a run for their lives.'

How fortunate also that she'd picked up so many investigative tips from her relationship with Detective Justin: do your legwork. See, hear and smell. Read the client, hoard the facts and lie if you have to. And Justin, with ample law enforcement resources at his disposal, might help her crack a case, if only as a friend. At that moment, she'd experienced a sudden burst of happiness, silently thanked her mother and replied to Sen. 'It'll take about a month to get background checks done and get licensed by the Washington State Business Licensing Services. Another week or so to obtain a liability insurance policy. I should be able to start within a couple of months.'

'Hire a smart assistant. And build a business website.' Sen had offered Maya a joining bonus to help pay for both.

In the following weeks, with the official papers in her hand, Maya had formally opened the Seattle branch of Detectives Unlimited for her employer.

A car door slammed; Maya looked out through the window. Her closest friend, Veen Burton, came around the front of her Toyota on the driveway. Face pinched and the edges of her mouth downcast, she walked up the stone pathway leading to the front porch. Normally at this hour, Veen, a dedicated architect, would still be at her job, her 'green game.'

A woman of ample proportions, Veen, who had an American father and an Indian mother, boasted a creamy complexion and eyes the color of a perfect cup of tea. Her reassuring manner usually declared: *Everything will be all right.* Maya hurried to the front door and yanked it open.

'Maya!' A cry of pain escaped Veen's lips.

'Hey, come in.' Maya led the way to the living room and gestured to her friend to sit. 'You all right?'

Veen slumped onto the sofa. Maya, feeling Veen's agitation, seated herself next to her.

Eyes raw, Veen could only say, 'I got your message.' After another moment of heavy silence, she whimpered in a teary voice, 'Oh my God . . . Sylvie . . . Oh, Maya . . . Sylvie's dead. Dead. She set herself on fire. She's dead.'

'What? *What?*' It took Maya a few seconds for the facts to sink in. Her blood chilled, insides churning, mind a blur, she closed her eyes for a moment and absorbed the honking of a passing car. 'Some sort of a religious ceremony was going on. Sylvie, a scientist. No, I can't imagine that.' She gasped, touched Veen's hand. 'The police must be wrong.'

'I can't believe it, either. For the life of me, I never would have thought . . . My sis. How could she? God, what got into her? What could possibly get into her?'

This morning's blazing scene played before Maya's moist eyes. A scream, a painful blast, almost escaped her throat. Her stomach turned. She'd done nothing to stop that traumatic incident. 'Sylvie? It was really Sylvie?'

Uma bustled into the room. She balanced a fragrant tea service on a tray, complete with several antique teacups, a platter of snacks and a blue-flowered teapot. Maya wiped her eyes with a hand, stumbled to her feet and helped Uma lower the tray to the coffee table.

'I heard your voice,' Uma said to Veen, warmly.

'Auntie!' Veen rose, smothered her face in her hands and dissolved into sobs.

Uma put her arms around Veen's shoulder, almost standing on her toes. 'What in heaven's name's happened, my dear child?'

Veen's shoulders were rigid but, as Uma held her, she melted and softened and rested her tear-streaked face on Uma's shoulder. In a minute, Veen raised her head and said, 'Sylvie's dead.'

'Good Lord.' Uma's face went ashen. 'What happened? What could possibly happen? A sweet young girl like her? Impossible.'

'I can't take it, Auntie. I can't take it anymore. I wish I was dead.' Speaking in fits and starts, Veen repeated the story she'd told Maya, then dropped back on the sofa.

'I can't believe it.' Uma brought the armchair closer to Veen and watched her guest carefully. 'No way could it have happened. Sylvie practically saved my life when I caught malaria. She got the news from Maya and recommended the best doctor in Kolkata, someone she'd heard about.' She paused. 'How did you . . .?'

'The police called me this morning before nine,' Veen said. 'I was like, "Shit," still half-asleep. My alarm was set for nine-thirty because I had the morning off – I'd worked my ass off the last four nights. The officer asked me to go over to the Harborview Medical Center.' Veen covered her face with her hand.

Maya held her breath and put a hand on Veen's shoulder.

'My sis . . .' Veen inhaled deeply, her eyes shining with tears. 'She was the youngest – it was our duty to look after her. She burned herself to death. Can you fucking imagine?'

Uma, also clearly distraught, lifted the teapot and, almost mechanically, poured Veen a cup. Then she poured one for Maya and one for herself and gently encouraged Veen to eat. A few restless sips brought color back to Veen's face. She served herself a piece of samosa; Maya helped herself to a fudgy-white, tender *sandesh*. To distract herself, she silently thanked Uma, who still followed the Indian tradition of balancing the pungency of tea with a combination of savory and sweet bites.

'I'd planned on calling Sylvie yesterday but never got round to it. I'm sorry, I'm so sorry, Sylvie!' Veen cried out. 'If only I had known. I'd have rushed there to stop her madness. Even if I had to catch on fire myself, I'd have jumped in and dragged her away. Even if I had to burn to death, I'd have—'

'I . . . I was there, right there, by chance . . . on the way to the bakery,' Maya said to both Veen and Uma.

'You were there?' Veen said in a voice rising high with reproach. 'Why didn't you stop her? Why didn't you, Maya?'

Maya shifted her position and felt that same burning ache she'd experienced at the scene of suicides. 'I was half a block away when I first noticed it. When I got closer . . . well, the crowd wouldn't let me get too close, nor could I see the faces of the two women. I was dumbfounded that they'd do this – but Sylvie?'

Uma rose, patted her tummy and asked Maya, 'Why didn't you tell me this?'

If only Uma would resume her understanding, forgiving and placid posture. If only she would stop scrutinizing Maya's actions so minutely. 'Oh, Ma, I didn't want to upset you.'

'Upset me? Am I so old or what?' Uma shuffled over to the sideboard and fussed with the dahlias placed in a vase. She returned, her face pale, and picked up her *chai*, but didn't take a sip.

'You didn't at all suspect what Sylvie was up to?' Maya asked Veen.

A slight irritation showed in Veen's voice. 'I'll always hate myself for that. She lived only three miles from me but we didn't hang together. Lately, she hadn't been acting like herself. Something changed. I haven't seen her in over two months.'

'Of course, as a malaria scientist, she must have worked her butt off,' Uma said.

'Yes, malaria research, and only that, got her juices flowing. She was so fucking dedicated – pardon my French. And we had a few issues between us. She didn't share much with me, except to say a month or so ago that her cat, Augustine, had died. She'd already buried her.' Reaching down to put her teacup on the coffee table, Veen missed. The cup fell to the floor and shattered into pieces; a trickle of liquid smeared the rug. 'Oh, no, I'm so sorry, Maya, I broke . . .' Veen, appearing mortified, tried to reach down to the floor.

'You sit still.' Maya looked at the pink-and-white demitasse, a favorite of hers, now reduced to jagged pieces and shimmering on the floor. She paid no attention to her tender feelings, fetched a dustpan, a small vacuum cleaner and a wet cloth, and cleaned up the mess. She slipped into the kitchen, her investigative self newly awakened to the reality of the situation. Belatedly, she noted the death of Sylvie's cat, Augustine. And the fact that Sylvie 'hadn't been acting like herself.'

Standing by the kitchen window, Maya checked her cell-phone. No message from Justin. An email from Hank said that the Indian gentleman had called back, again from a blocked number, and again refused to give out how to get in touch with him.

'He clammed up with me,' Hank had added. 'Shall I get rid of him?'

She sent a text to Hank saying she'd look into the matter.

Back in the living room, Maya settled into her seat, heard

the screech of brakes outside and asked Veen, 'Do you know anything about Sylvie's meditation group?'

'Meditation? No. That seems to fit. Sylvie was the quiet, dreamy type, an "Om girl" who kept to herself. But how do you know about her group? She never told me. Did she tell you?'

'No, a man in the crowd did.'

'What? A man in the crowd? Who the hell is he? Tell me what you heard. Tell me!'

Maya repeated the little that Atticus had revealed: he and Sylvie went to the same meditation center. Sylvie had texted him early this morning.

'I didn't get a text. Why didn't I? And meditation? I don't think even my mom knows about that.' Veen checked her watch. 'Mom hasn't heard. She's coming home this afternoon – she's been in India for the last four months teaching post-colonial studies as a visiting lecturer at Delhi University. I have to pick her up from the airport shortly. She's been traveling for almost a day, with layovers in Bangkok and Los Angeles. How in the world can I break the news to her?'

Maya sighed and leaned toward Veen. 'Should I come with you?'

Veen shook her head and turned to Uma. 'Sylvie was Mom's princess. To her, she glowed like precious gold. She grew up classy, chic and beautiful. I could never match her in style or popularity. Mom will question why I didn't look after Sylvie in her absence. But how can you look after a thirty-one-year-old who keeps to herself, and who has no time for you?'

'Dear me,' Uma said to Veen. 'It'll be difficult. Did Sylvie have a boyfriend?'

'Yes. Eight or so months ago, she met a guy at her research lab, a junior scientist. His name is Ivan Dunn. I saw her even less after they became an item.'

'Did you ever meet this guy?' Maya asked. 'I sure didn't.'

Cheeks blushing copper, Veen looked down at the floor and said in a low voice, 'Yes.'

'I suppose Sylvie's emails would further point to—'

'The police detective has taken her laptop and all of her documents, Maya. No one is allowed in her apartment.'

'But how did the detective connect her with you so quickly?' Maya asked.

'Apparently Sylvie was wearing a gold bracelet that she threw on the ground once the fire began.' Veen pressed her shaking hand to her mouth. Both Uma and Maya placed consoling hands on her shoulders.

'I saw that,' Maya said softly. 'I saw her throw it onto the ground. What did the bracelet look like?'

'It was a wide band made of genuine gold, in a swirl pattern, studded with pearl, and with intricate markings inside, including Sylvie's full name in a stylized Bengali script. Mom gave it to her on her eighteenth birthday. We'd all gone to Kolkata to celebrate with our extended family, some sixty or so people. Our family jeweler made that bracelet to commemorate the event. I think Sylvie wanted to pass the family heirloom on to Mom and me before fire melted it.'

'It's quite a coincidence that the detective would know how to read Bengali.'

'No, Maya, he couldn't read it. A crime-scene officer did a walk-through of the street corner and collected all the physical evidence he could find, including the bracelet. The detective who was also there later asked an Indian colleague. He deciphered the name in English. Made it easy for the detective to Google that name and get the link to Sylvie's website.' Veen laid her snack plate gently on the table. 'Sylvie had my website link on her site and that led the police to get in touch with me.'

Pretty good work, given the possibility that the bystanders might not have known Sylvie's real name. And DNA identification was pending. 'I wonder why Sylvie threw the bracelet away like that,' Maya said.

'So it'd go to us, her family. I just explained that.'

'You have an overactive mind, Maya,' Uma said. 'You tend to overanalyze.'

'Auntie's right,' Veen said. 'An experienced police detective has taken charge.'

That was Veen. She could be cruel. Maya lowered her head, realizing she'd irritated both of them. Perhaps she should keep her mouth shut for now. Yet an insistent inner voice worked on her.

'No doubt the detective is sharp,' Maya said to Veen, trying to smooth over any annoyance she might have caused her friend. 'Did you get his name? Don't you suppose I should speak with him?'

'Are you sure you want to?' Veen sighed. 'It's Justin Stevenson.'

THREE

After Veen's departure, Maya lingered in the side yard. Her feelings about Justin had never fully gone into remission, not after being intimate for almost two years. How long had it been since they broke up? *OK, let's stop pretending. Five months and twenty-one days.*

Then why did it seem like they'd been together yesterday? She stared at the scraggly lilac tree at the back fence, long past its blooming time, as if it might have the answer. She could so easily imagine the good-looking, muscular man who stood just over five foot eleven, quite a few inches taller than her, and who could never 'uncop.' One image dissolved into another and soon she pictured a leisurely dinner on a soft summer evening, their second date at Chowder House.

He'd talked about a young dude beating up a teenager walking the Green Lake trails, beating him up bad. 'By the time our men arrived, the guy had taken all his clothes off and jumped into the lake. We had questions. Does he have a criminal record? What does he do for a living? What's his home situation? Where there are questions, there usually are leads. We eventually got him.'

Maya had given a warm look to the tough cop with intense eyes and a quiet demeanor. *Where there are questions, there usually are leads.*

Over the next few weeks after they'd met, as the basil in her garden spread its leaves and the plums turned a fierce red, Maya saw her quick-on-his-toes new man almost daily – dining, jogging, catching midnight shows – and basked in his attention. Here was a caring friend and a considerate lover, so easy to be with, even though he saw the 'worst of the worst.' She'd never expected to be so fascinated by a cop, one she could trust, one so thorough and conscientious. He'd been raised partly by his grandmother who had taught him to be that way.

All seemed fine until the day when Veen spoiled Maya's ecstatic state. Seated at Café Trieste, Veen, ever the blunt person, suggested to Maya that she'd lost both her head and her heart. 'Really, Maya, what do you see in him?'

What did she see? A galaxy, complete with sun, moon, stars, planets and a golden halo. All she could hope for. And a steady, dependable pattern, too. Justin wasn't full of himself like so many other dates she'd had. She'd decided not to challenge Veen quite yet and replied instead, 'A cop makes a girl feel secure, you know.' Justin carried a ready-to-fire gun both to work and when off-duty, and had at least one rifle in his house. He saw violence in the streets and in people's homes every day and knew how to handle himself. In Maya's presence, he was patient, gentle, and caring – most of the time.

Veen had eyed her with concern. 'What if someone shoots at him, trying to settle a score? Here's something else. Don't cops mess with women of questionable repute? You know what I mean? Hookers? Thieves? Drug addicts? Petty criminals?'

'What are you talking about?'

Veen's eyes had flashed a flame of warning. 'I saw a news item about a cop using his position to have his way with vulnerable women. He was caught in bed with a teenage hooker.'

'Why are you telling me about a creep like that? Justin isn't that kind of man. You don't know him at all.'

A shade of contemplation had fallen over Veen's face. Following more probing, she'd admitted that the excerpt didn't specify Justin's name or any name at all.

Then Annette, a friend of Veen's and an ex-police officer – tall, slender, high heels, purple blazer, strawberry-blonde hair and Dior perfume – had dropped by. They'd lost the thread of their conversation. When Annette left, Maya had asked Veen, 'Hey, what about Annette? You're friends with her and she's ex-police. So obviously not all cops are bad.'

Veen had changed the subject. She must have realized that the topic of dirty cops was inappropriate and that if she wanted to have a splendid time that evening with her friend she'd better not go there again, her negativity toward Justin never explained.

A plane flew overhead; the sound shook Maya back to the present. She strode back into the house and was greeted by the sounds of her mother tidying up in the kitchen. In the living room, her gaze settled on the iPad resting on a side table. She plopped down on a chair, logged onto the Internet and studied the screaming headlines:

Self-Immolation in Seattle
Two female Tibet activists set fire to themselves

The headline jumped to a pair of color photographs, each portraying a covered body lying on the sidewalk. Maya couldn't look at the familiar scene without feeling the same alarm and revulsion she'd experienced only a few hours before. She squinted incredulously at the screen and skimmed through the narrative that followed, which characterized the suicides as an isolated incident protesting the Chinese suppression of Tibet. No involvement of a 'Dalai Lama clique' had been suspected. And no other violent demonstrations had taken place anywhere else in the city. *Thank God*. Nevertheless, the authorities were on high alert. A link to an unofficial video had been provided.

Uma stepped into the living room and fluffed up the throw pillows, patting them a little harder than usual. 'There isn't much in this world I haven't seen or read about in my life, but two girls setting themselves on fire publicly in an American city?' she said. 'It's an outrage beyond my comprehension. In the East, it's different. We come from a land used to the notion of sacrificing one's life if the occasion calls for it, but not here. Why would Sylvie . . .?'

'Don't have it figured out, Ma.' Maya gripped the arm of her chair. For the sake of Veen and her family, and for her own reasons, she needed to trace the events that had led to Sylvie's death. Indeed, a plan of action began to hum in her mind. 'I've left messages for Justin. He might help me get to the bottom of this.'

'Never met the man and not sure I want to.' Uma studied her face the way mothers do, examining every pore and intensely trying to probe into her interior. 'But to think you'll go to him? After how he treated you?'

'I know, Ma, I know,' Maya said quickly, not wanting to rehash the painful, humiliating memory. 'It didn't work out but we're still on good terms.' She gulped, realizing that the last bit might only be a delusion on her part. She hadn't seen him since they'd split.

'Veen didn't seem to approve of him.' Uma always paid attention, never forgetting what she'd seen or heard, even in passing. Usually, this was a boon.

'Oh, girlfriends. You know how protective they can be.' Maya waved her hand in dismissal of anything Veen had said about Justin. 'It took me a little time after we split but I've gotten back on my feet.'

'So you say.' Uma walked toward the kitchen and hesitated at the doorway. She looked back at her daughter, her dark eyes even darker in warning. 'I'm afraid you're fooling yourself.'

'Ma, really,' Maya began, shaking her head with a forced chuckle.

'Give yourself a break, dear,' Uma said with unexpected tenderness. 'Don't head for the house of pain.'

Maya didn't answer. She stood and scooped up her cellphone. Not for the first time, she would ignore her mother's advice.

She shoved the cellphone into her purse and said a hurried goodbye to Uma. If Justin did call – and it would be interesting to see how quickly he got back to her – she would like to answer. He might wait until after work. By then, her heartbeat would slow and she would see him as just another cop, a faint shadow from her past, a house plant that had stopped flowering and now sat outside on her porch, orphaned.

A few minutes after six p.m., she found herself cruising through Justin Stevenson's neighborhood, one she'd religiously avoided over the past few months. She turned the radio on and listened to a snippet of news.

'The Chinese foreign minister, Hui Yao, has immediately cancelled all of his public appearances. A spokesperson for the minister says he wants to stop any more demonstrations or further violence from taking place. He offers his condolences to the families affected and wishes peace to our city. He has left for Beijing.'

Good for him. Maya made a right turn to get to Justin's street, a hawthorn-lined thoroughfare with single-family dwellings on either side. She steered around a curve, slowed and glimpsed the single-level, pale yellow twenties' Craftsman house. Although she couldn't see the yard, she knew every inch of it; she'd tinkered there for countless hours, planting, staking, weeding, watering and pruning in the two or so years of their relationship. Justin never had the time to do those chores, although, surprisingly, he always noticed the gentle beauty of the flowers she'd helped bloom.

Should she take a peek to see how her plants were doing? Maybe she shouldn't. Why wade through old memories, experience the emotional see-sawing? They hadn't had any contact since the day he left, without much explanation. No phone calls, no accidental meetings – it had been a clean break.

He wouldn't be home quite yet if his old habits were unchanged. He'd have dinner somewhere first, then he'd cozy up to his favorite ice-cream parlor for a scoop of coconut gelato. He would have no idea that Maya was now a certified P.I. That the inspiration had come partly from him. That she'd gleaned much from him about detective work.

Maybe just a peek? What if a neighbor saw her loitering on his property and reported her for trespassing? She pulled up to the curb and picked up an envelope from the passenger seat – a utilities bill ready to be mailed. She stepped out and sprinted up the front stoop, acting as though she had to deliver this envelope to Justin's mailbox, not sure in her heart if she should be doing this.

The weeds were having a field day. The crew-cut grass was veiled in a layer of summer dust. The daisies moped, shrunken and brown. Even the prolific candytuft, jutting out from nooks and crannies, sported only a few reluctant blooms; they obviously hadn't been watered. A trashcan, filled to the brim, was topped with crumpled newspaper pages. Somewhere a crow made a racket.

About to pull a patch of grass that had made its home among the creeping rock rose, she heard footsteps pounding up the front stoop. She stood up, a cold wash running down her neck.

A bright male voice, one she would know anywhere, filled with surprise, called out, 'Maya!' The tenor of that voice still had the power to cause a quake in her body. 'Really? You?'

Justin, dressed in jeans and a plaid shirt, stared at her. She took in his tall frame, fine-cut facial bones, full mane of dense blond hair and confidence as solid as crystal, the man who once could make her forget time. 'Oh, I was passing by and wanted to have a peek at your garden.'

He fumbled for words, then said in a wavering tone, 'Total surprise. Didn't expect to see you here.' He moved nearer, an eager light in his eyes, as though wishing to embrace her. Then he thought the better of it and positioned himself at a respectable distance. In that big blank space, she witnessed their shared history disappearing.

Cheeks flaming from her embarrassment at being there, she replied, 'Did you get my messages?'

'Yes, I did. Since it was on my way, I stopped by your house. Your mom said you were out. Hope I didn't disturb her. She seemed, oh, a little distracted.'

Maya forced a pleasant expression. Uma, with her motherly instinct and all she'd heard about Justin, hadn't been as welcoming as she'd normally be, offering tea and chatting up a minor storm. Even so, it cheered Maya that Justin had taken the trouble to pop up at her place. 'Oh, mom was just busy. She's quite social, actually.'

He leaned toward her as he listened to her response; there were changes in him. He appeared happier and boyish, not the cool, mysterious man he'd been in the last few months of their relationship. He also sported a beer belly, something unexpected. And no, it didn't seem like he was trying to get back with her, although he might have some regrets about their uncoupling, made evident by a brief, worried look at her, followed by a short sigh that escaped him.

She looked toward the yard for a plant, a flower, even a weed to catch her eye and distract her from this letdown, and finally spoke. 'I wanted to talk with you about what happened today, Justin. I was there at the scene.'

'You were probably spooked. We'd expected demonstrations

against the Chinese foreign minister but this type of violence is a first. Of course, we're going to do a death investigation and, in conjunction with the fire department, a fatal fire investigation.' He paused. 'I'm sorry for your loss. I know how close you are to Veen. But Maya, we've spoken to a lot of people, which has given us a good picture of what went on today. The crowd was cooperative and I got a number of eyewitness accounts. Our technicians have walked the scene. They've collected all physical and biological evidence they could get their hands on – hairs, fibers, footprints, fire remains, nature of the accelerant used. Our forensics unit is doing the lab analysis. An odontologist will check the dental details.'

'But wouldn't you like to hear another first-hand report?'

'I think you should wait a day or so when you're more rational.' He gave her a glance of concern. 'But I can offer you a glass of iced tea.'

He was treating her like a crime victim in need of solace. No, she wanted to tell him, she wasn't a casualty, she stood on her own strong feet. 'I'm perfectly rational and ready to give you a statement.'

'Of course, of course. I want it in writing.' He was about to say more when a noise from across the street momentarily claimed his attention. Maya turned to see a workman wearing a hard hat, safety goggles and denim overalls attacking a bigleaf maple with a chainsaw. At least ten feet off the ground, he stood on the very branch he was about to dismember.

Maya gave the tree-cutter a stunned look. 'Shouldn't we—?'

'He's an expert, knows what he's doing. That's his kamikaze style.' Justin gestured with a hand. 'Let's get away from the noise.'

He led her along a brick walkway to his fenced backyard dominated by a pine tree. A round, wrought-iron table and a set of wicker chairs stood in the middle of the patio, canopied by a garden umbrella. He disappeared through the back door into the house, fetched a pad and a pen and placed them before her. He asked her to jot down her impressions, then drifted back into the house.

He had guns in his bedroom.

She didn't know why she was reminded of that. Her palms were wet.

She reconstructed the suicide scene in her mind. As she finished her narrative account and put down the pen, he popped up with two tall glasses of red rooibos tea. He took the opposite chair. For one glimmering moment, Maya basked in the warm glow of connection to the past, noticing how the cuff of his shirt closed around his slender wrist. She pushed the notepad across the table toward him. He glanced at it.

'What you might not know is this.' Elbows on the table, Justin proceeded in the cool, detached manner of a professional. 'The women had released a joint written statement to selected press members minutes before they took their lives. Marked confidential, it said no one was responsible for their deaths. They chose this particular fate of their own volition.' He paused. 'Insane – that's all.'

'I've known Sylvie. She was a top scientist, highly respected in her field. This doesn't—'

'We're going to get both the signatures verified,' Justin rushed ahead. 'We'll also study the coroner's report when it's delivered.' He glanced at her. 'Are you all right?'

Reluctantly, Maya pictured Sylvie's burned flesh lying on a wheeled, stainless-steel table in the chilled, windowless morgue. She could almost smell the stench of a horrible death. 'Well, no, I haven't quite settled down yet.'

Justin tapped his fingers lightly on the table. 'We'll all need a few days, maybe even a few weeks.'

'Did you listen to the latest news?' She informed him of the Chinese foreign minister's departure.

'Yes, I heard. That's a relief for us, even though we've increased patrols in public areas. Until things return to normal, which, I trust, will be soon.'

Maya studied the tall, stable pine tree. There wasn't the slightest breeze to sway its branches. It crystalized in her brain now: Justin was advising her to erase the episode from her mind.

She raised her voice to be heard above the chainsaw's racket. 'But the real issue remains.'

'The whole Tibetan conundrum, you mean?'

'Yes. Protesters give their lives to raise attention to the plight of their people, to get their country free again from China's clutch, but then it's back to normal.'

'I've kept up with the news from Tibet ever since I dug into the murder of a local Tibetan community leader,' Justin said. 'Despite his family's fears, there was no Chinese involvement – none.'

'This is an entirely different situation, wouldn't you say?'

Maya heard a crack. A gunshot? Her heart leaped. She heard a snap and couldn't breathe.

Then it came to her: it was only a branch falling from the tree-trimming activities across the street. Arms crossed, Maya sat back as Justin ignored her question and stared into space. Again, she observed how the atmosphere between them had cooled. She was beginning to get a headache, a throbbing in her temples from the tree-cutting noise and Justin's non-cooperation. Not about to give up, she asked, 'Who was the second woman, by the way?'

'Her identity has been released. Anna Kamala, another Asian-American.'

Maya weighed this fact. 'I don't suppose you know what Anna Kamala did for a living?'

'She was a candy-maker, worked for Spices and Sweets located on Sandpoint Way.'

'Oh, that place.' An odd sensation ran over Maya. She glanced at Justin. A craving for Indian *mithai*, sweet concoctions reminiscent of her younger days in Kolkata, had led her to make multiple visits to that confectionary, although she didn't recall ever meeting an Asian-American worker there. Justin had developed a taste for those sweet treats as well; he relished the rush of milky sugar. She recalled bringing a box home and presenting it to him one evening when he came to see her. He put a piece of the killer *raj bhog* into his mouth, washed it down with a sip of *chai*, closed his eyes, drew her closer and planted kisses on her lips.

The tree-killer from across the street must have turned his chainsaw off. For a split second, a stiff silence prevailed. 'Here's another point I'd like to make,' Maya began. 'Neither Veen nor I had any inkling that Sylvie was so gung-ho about Tibet. There were no signs she cared one bit about her motherland.'

Justin rubbed his eyes, either to remove the day's tension

or as a cue to cut this conversation short, and said off-handedly, 'Well, she could have been mum for any number of reasons. My guess is you've watched too many cop shows on TV. Just let us handle it. We know what we're doing, Maya, believe me.' He paused. 'I know you're concerned about Veen's well-being. The best thing you can do is stick with her, provide emotional support and maybe even arrange for her to see a therapist.'

He flicked his gaze at his watch, making it obvious he wanted to terminate the conversation. It had also become clear that she wouldn't be able to depend on police resources, if necessary, and certainly not Justin's division.

She pushed herself to her feet. 'Better be going – dinner with my mom. And, oh, on another topic – the coroner's report?'

'I'll call Veen when I get it.'

The evening had begun to thicken around the pine tree and the fence. They stood facing each other for a moment. His voice curled around an unexpressed emotion as he said, 'Good to see you, Maya.'

Could she make a similar response in return? No, she couldn't. She hadn't expected to be thrust back to the rosy days of their courtship but she'd wanted a bit more than she'd gotten from him, such as taking her concerns seriously. That hadn't happened.

'Thanks for the tea,' she said and turned away.

FOUR

The next day, watering her yard in the early afternoon, Maya felt a sharp twinge in her elbow. She rolled up the sleeve of her blouse, examined her arm and rubbed the aching area gently, only to find it still red and swollen. Once again, the image of Atticus popped into her mind, the strange man who'd called her office several times, who might be a potential informant. He was, after all, her countryman, a *desi*. Although India had more languages than you could count with the fingers of your hand, she figured from his last name that they came from the same state.

How would she get hold of Atticus, whose real name was Atul? She only had his full name and his occupation, that of an accountant.

OK, Atticus Biswas wasn't a common name in Seattle, if it was a common name anywhere. Within minutes of sitting down at her iPad, Maya found a website: www.AtticusBiswas.com. The homepage announced: It's a numbers game! We're @ your service to help you with all your accounting needs. Come to us for care, precision and friendly service.

Directly below the headline was a headshot of Atticus, a gaunt-faced, serious-looking accountant in his late forties, the same man who'd prevented her from assisting Sylvie. His lips were slightly parted in a smile but the rest of his visage refused to cooperate; his eyes and forehead remained stubbornly gloomy.

Maya clicked on the Contact Us @ button. A number flashed before her, which she punched into her cellphone. It came as a surprise when the man himself answered. She identified herself by her first name only.

'Oh, Maya. So sorry. Hope your elbow is feeling better. Is there a way I can make it up to you?'

'Yes, I'd like to speak with you. Sylvie Burton was my best friend Veen's sister. Veen won't be at peace until she finds out what really happened. When I put myself in her shoes, I feel her terrible desperation. And I knew Sylvie. I want to help Veen by piecing together the last few months of Sylvie's life.'

'Oh, you knew Sylvie. What a surprise. I dearly loved her, gentle soul. I, too, am in the dark, and having the worst time, but please come over. We can commiserate. My condo is situated right across from the Green Lake.'

It gave Maya pause, the notion of visiting a stranger in his condo, a man she didn't trust. 'Any chance we could meet in a coffee shop?'

'With my leg fucked-up like this – pardon my language – I haven't been out of the condo much in the last several weeks. A friend has been doing the grocery shopping for me or else I'd starve. I overdid it yesterday by going to the demonstration – been in pain ever since. Now I'm waiting for a client call on my landline. You'll be safe. I don't bite and I promise not to hit you again.'

She replied to his outpouring with a caustic laugh. 'Thanks.'

'You're a Bengali, aren't you? You have that glow about you—'

'When can we talk?'

'Right now. By the time you get here, I'll have coffee and homemade cupcakes ready. Come to think of it, I haven't eaten much since yesterday – haven't felt like it. I'm single, but I cook and bake. My ex-wife – ex as far as I'm concerned – used to say real men don't make cupcakes, but I'm a real man and I do. I follow a recipe like it's a mathematical puzzle and, if I may say so, my cranberry cupcakes are delicious raised to the power of two.'

He seemed a bit too much, this lonely guy. Should Maya call on an overeager bachelor in his lair?

'I can provide personal references, if you like,' Atticus said in a light tone.

Maya smiled bitterly to herself. This undertaking might be worth it if she could get some sort of a hint from Atticus, a reaction that slipped out of his mouth, one that pertained to Sylvie. If Maya sensed any threat, she'd run out of his place. And surely she could outrun a man on crutches. 'What is your address, Mr Biswas?'

'Atticus,' he said. 'Please call me Atticus.' He recited his address, which turned out to be less than ten minutes from her home.

'I'll be there in fifteen. By the way, have you been calling my office?'

He mumbled something, which could be either a yes or no, but she knew the answer.

After rustling through her purse for her car keys, she walked into the kitchen. Her gaze alighted on the tall, glass-fronted cabinet on the opposite wall that displayed her antique teacup-and-saucer collection. Missing was the pink-and-white demitasse, broken and discarded. To the right, hunched over the sink, Uma rinsed a stack of dishes. A basket of purple plums, stationed on the counter, exuded a rich, ripe smell. Uma would keep busy baking a tart, Maya assumed. Still, the thought of leaving her alone worried Maya.

Amidst the sound of running water and the clattering of dishes, Maya announced that she'd be gone for a while.

Uma turned. 'Running off again? Will you be home for dinner?'

Maya nodded. Before Uma could say more – her eager open mouth and widened eyes a clear sign that she was ready to do that – Maya waved and marched out the door.

She jerked at the sound of a leaf-blower from a neighbor's sidewalk. Her eyes rested on a snapdragon patch in front of her house bursting with flaming red, dragon-mouthed blossoms, and she shivered. Might it be the suggestion of a dragon? A reminder of the red flag fluttering over the Chinese foreign minister's temporary residence? The shock of the frightfully red blaze over Sylvie's body?

Before climbing into the car, Maya halted and considered again whether she should visit Atticus.

It'll be all right, she said to herself, her hands unsteady on the steering wheel.

FIVE

Ten minutes later, Maya gazed at the upscale, five-story condominium complex before her, which had taken on a saffron hue in the lazy afternoon light. From each unit a private balcony jutted out, complete with grillwork for the railing. An identical building stood across from it.

Once inside, she rode the elevator to the second floor, listened to the prattle of children down the hallway and knocked on the door of number 207, stirred by the twang of a sitar striking a sad-sweet melody.

Atticus opened the door, balancing on his fiberglass crutches. His ears stuck out, creating an impression of constant alertness. 'Please come in,' he oozed. 'You got here in only ten minutes. Do you live nearby?'

'You play a musical instrument?'

'Only for myself.' Keys jangling, he locked the door from inside.

'Why did you have to—?'

'That's the way this lock has been designed.'

She drew closer, snatched the key from his hand and took a pace back, saying, 'I'll keep this for the duration of my visit, if you don't mind.'

Although appearing to be taken aback, he nodded and ushered her into the living room, which extended into a dining area. Maya's gaze swept over a snug, luxurious flat, which had bamboo flooring, an ivory rug, a stylishly neutral palette and matching modern furnishings. Large windows let in a wealth of sunlight, as well as a wink of the lake.

'I've always wanted to live like Mahatma Gandhi.' Atticus invited her to a seat at one end of an oval dining table. 'Haven't quite made it. Gandhi would probably look at all this and say, "Still too many possessions, young fellow."'

Maya smiled. 'He'd say the same to me.'

While waiting for him to sit down, Maya checked the rest of the room. A chess set had fallen off an end table. A sitar case reclined in a far corner, surrounded by a haphazard arrangement of cushions. The wall on the left was taken up by a large bookcase laden with books, photographs and CD cases, some items overflowing. Dust had collected on a brass figurine of Goddess Saraswati, the goddess of learning, standing on the same bookcase. The sense of the place was one of culture and learning, being uprooted and not being cared for.

Atticus stowed his crutches neatly against the far wall, wobbled for a second and perched on a chair at the other end of the table, elevating his leg onto a stool. 'Imagine an accountant losing his balance! I can't wait to get rid of these. It kills me, you know, the potholes on the sidewalk, getting into and out of the elevator and, oh, the strain on my shoulders. Normally I relax in a legs-up-the-wall stance, but I can't quite get into that position anymore. Have to wait a few more days.'

'Were you in an accident?'

The ceiling light accentuated Atticus' grave features. 'Long story. Yes, you might call it an accident.'

'Anything to do with Sylvie?' Maya spotted the lines of distress on his face. She'd get back to that topic later. 'I'm still trying to make sense of what happened yesterday.'

She followed his eyes to a coffee pot and a platter of cupcakes placed at the center of the table. Could she really trust the food? 'Thanks, but I'll pass.' She made an excuse about having a queasy stomach.

Atticus served himself, made a sound of satisfaction, soon demolished the cupcake on his plate and looked at her with mournful brown eyes. 'My wife left me – no warning. I got home one afternoon and all her personal belongings were gone. She'd wiped out my bank account too. She even had the nerve to move into an apartment building across from mine. Never another Ukrainian woman again.'

Maya shook her head. He had a Ukrainian wife, who perhaps spoke Russian as one of her languages. She remembered the *nyet* from Sunglasses Man, an ominous sound.

'So why were you at the demonstration?' She noticed a change in Atticus' expression. 'It seemed so unreal, like a setup, like I'd walked into the last act of a play with you in it. Nobody would let me help Sylvie. Thinking back, I can't put two and two together. Might you, as an accountant, be able to do that?'

'What's two and two? Whatever the tax code says it is. Did you know that two is both even and prime?'

'Oh, cool, but to get back to the urgent matter at hand – I assume you were part of the prayer group who shielded Sylvie?'

'No. I know zilch about them. Never seen them before. Never heard that type of chanting. They don't belong to our center.'

Really? Maya would have to track down one of the chanters, the mustachioed man with a boxer's nose whom she'd seen in her neighborhood. For now, she resorted to a different question. 'Do you mind telling me how long ago you first met Sylvie and where?'

'Two years ago. At our weekly meditation session.'

'I suppose you clicked?'

'Yes, she was a neat woman.' His eyes were misty. 'We became fast friends, even though I'm older by more than ten years. Our guru asked me to be Sylvie's spiritual brother and get her oriented to the practice. That brought us closer together. We'd usually have eight or so people show up for meditation – Sylvie one of them. Once the session was over, we'd all go to the Bodhi Teahouse a block away, then a gang of us would head out to sup.'

'Sounds like a friendly bunch.'

If only for a second, Atticus' eyes focused intently on his empty plate. 'Quite. I've been with that group for over a decade, although my attendance did fall off for a period when I got married.'

He looked up at Maya and, though she'd met him only yesterday, she sensed that he would pour out more of his marital woes at the slightest cue from her. But the mention of the meditation practice had given Maya a pinprick of discomfort. She wasn't sure why. And the fact that he was Sylvie's spiritual brother. Maya's own efforts at meditation had not been successful. She could never set herself in the full lotus position. Nonetheless, she wanted to exhaust the topic.

'Would I be interested in a group like yours?' she asked.

He sat back in his chair and spoke in a lofty manner. 'We don't speak about our practice. It's not a religion, only a discipline for maintaining a healthy mind and body, and we don't proselytize.'

She kept her face open and friendly as she ventured, 'Even if someone is eager to give your discipline a try, you don't welcome them?'

'I'm afraid not. Ours is a closed group. We have strict rules for joining as was dictated by our master. He's ascended to the afterlife, but his disciple – who goes by one name, Padmaraja – is now our guru. Padmaraja channels his wisdom weekly to us, his disciples.' He gestured toward a silver-framed studio photo on the wall of an elderly, slightly smiling, distinguished East-Asian man. 'Our beloved master.'

Weird. A disciple, an earthling, who bridged the material world to the afterlife? In heaven, or wherever the master resided, he came up with a weekly lesson plan for the group? *Get real.*

She thought out loud. 'I wonder why Sylvie, a medical researcher who worked in the scientific community, would be drawn to this practice.'

His face had shut down; must be to do with her insensitive remark. Still, she couldn't help but say, 'So far you haven't suggested any ties between your meditation group and the immolations.'

He stared at the photo on the wall and said emphatically, 'There are absolutely no ties. Our guru had nothing to do with it.'

She decided to try another tack. 'You know, Atticus, that guy in sunglasses used the word *nyet*. Remember? Russian accent. Was he giving you a warning to back off?'

He expelled a sigh. 'I'm not a good judge of accents. Nor do I like to overanalyze. I like order and perfection. For me, numbers have to add up right. I find myself in a situation where nothing adds up.'

'Do you have any Russian speakers in your meditation group?'

'None. Except for Sylvie and me, our group is all born and raised here.'

'You told me about the final text Sylvie sent you. Her sister Veen didn't get a text. I'm sure she would like to know what it said.'

His face became taut with an unreadable expression. 'I couldn't make heads or tails out of that text, which freaked the hell out of me. I had to erase it.'

You want me to believe that? She'd learned from Detective Justin that people lie to the authorities, sometimes for no reason at all, and also lie by omission.

'Please think hard—'

Atticus interrupted, one hand extended as though unable to listen to her anymore. 'My leg hurts if I sit too long.'

'Can I get you anything?'

He squeezed his eyes shut, as though in pain.

'Sorry to have bothered you.' She rose heavily. 'May I call you at a better time – tomorrow, perhaps?'

He opened his eyes. 'I'll have to check my schedule.'

Maya took up her purse, pulled out her new calling card and slid it across the table toward him. 'Give me a call when your leg doesn't hurt and you're willing to help a grieving family.'

He checked the card. 'I did hear you say this morning you were a private investigator. I didn't realize you worked for Detectives Unlimited of Kolkata. I've heard of them. My niece in Kolkata, whose cheating husband was found dead, used the services of D.U. and was extremely satisfied. Please, sit down, Srimati Maya.'

Maya nodded and regained her seat. Srimati was a term attributed to young women in India. She made a note of his reverence for his motherland. 'I'll stay only if you tell me your long story. Mind if I take notes?' At his nod, she took a pen and notepad from her purse and clicked the ballpoint.

'A gang beat me up because of Sylvie.'

Yeah? Maya gestured for him to elaborate. Faced with silence, she said, 'If confidentiality is a factor here, I can fully appreciate that. After all, I'm a stranger. But the same gang could go after your guru and try to harm him. What will happen then?'

'Oh, no, I wouldn't be able to bear that. In his absence, our meditation center will have to shut down. We'll be orphaned. The very thought makes me want to throw up.'

'Another possibility. If the police ever find out Sylvie regularly went to that meditation center, they could become suspicious. They might arrest the guru. What then?'

'OK, I'll tell you my story. You see, I enjoy a midnight snack, a terribly unhealthy habit, you might say. On one night three weeks ago, my cupboard was empty. I drove to the grocery store, parked my car in an almost empty lot and bought a packet of cheese crackers – I'm addicted to that stuff. I was about to get back into my car when two heavyset men wearing ski masks grabbed me from behind and dragged me into the trees at the edge of the lot. One of them had a thick, heavy stick with him.

'"Stop hanging around Sylvie, old man," one of them shouted at me in a heavy accent that I couldn't place. "Sylvie and I are just friends," I told them. I didn't say the rest: don't be ridiculous, I'm much older than her and I'm no prince charming, I'm her spiritual brother. And, in any case, my preference is for women with big breasts. They began punching me.'

Atticus went quiet for a moment. Maya watched him intently for any sign of deception: body rigid, fingers shaking, eyes moving right and gripped with the horror of the memory. His voice rang with honesty. Most likely, he wasn't making this up.

'Go on, Atticus,' Maya said, almost in a whisper.

'Well, Maya, I've never dealt with gangster types in my life but I could tell these guys were amateurs. They seemed nervous and constantly looked around; maybe someone had paid them. "Hey, Sylvie and I only talk about mantras and sutras," I said. I begged them not to twist my arm so hard.'

'Did they say anything?' Maya asked, still looking to find any holes in his story.

'Yes, one of them told me that Sylvie was trouble and that I should stay away from her. I had no idea what they meant. Sylvie was the last person on earth I'd describe as "trouble."'

'I share your feelings,' Maya said.

'I told them that Sylvie and I were worlds apart. That they'd obviously made a mistake. I must have made them madder. One of them raised his stick. I was trembling, practically peeing in my pants. All day long, Maya, I help people with their tax issues, troubles they didn't know they had. Or I ponder the new largest prime number. Or I do games to cross-train my brain. Those are all I'm good for. The excitement was too much for me.'

'And then?'

Atticus looked down at his shaking hands. 'The guy struck me at an angle and smashed my leg. Oh, the pain that zinged through me! All the lights went out before my eyes. I screamed, slipped and hit the ground. "You motor-mouth, you S-O-B," the guy said. "Shut the hell up. Don't let the story get out or we'll be back and the next time we'll kill you." They took off, got into an SUV and sped away. I somehow willed myself to drive to the hospital. And here I am, with a broken leg and a broken spirit, wondering who was behind all this.' He paused. 'By the way, you're the only one I've shared the full story with.'

'You didn't talk to the police?'

'No. Couldn't make myself go to the precinct and offer a statement. I feared those thugs and didn't want any negative publicity. I have a small business; reputation means a lot in my field. If my ex-wife, Klara, that mad woman, found out, she'd join in my character assassination. I'd have to move to Bora Bora or some such faraway place.'

'You probably didn't say anything to Sylvie, either.'

'Didn't get the chance. I returned to meditation after a week just to see her but she didn't show up. Not for the next several weeks, either. I tried calling her. Couldn't get her on the line. I feel terrible for not trying harder.' Atticus gave a hiss of frustration. 'This might seem abrupt, but suppose I made an offer to retain you for your services. Would you consider taking on my case? Find out who was behind what I went through and why and, more importantly, what happened to Sylvie? I'm on thin ice. I could use some help. I won't get much from the police, I know that for sure.'

Startled, Maya sat back. In the last several months she'd successfully worked on cases that included background checks, recurrent office theft, accident reconstruction and a missing child. This would be the first homicide for her to deal with, an order of magnitude more difficult and perhaps a bit out of her league. In trying to hunt down the criminals, she could get herself in trouble. Then came a small voice from within: she hadn't thrown herself fully into saving Sylvie. She owed it to her. And she was already involved in the case, if privately.

Still, she asked, 'Why do you think I can help you?'

Atticus, leaning forward, met her eyes. 'I met you only yesterday but I can see that you're sharp, committed and intuitive. You're a *desi*. You won't screw me over. Pardon my language. You pay attention to details. I can tell from the way you questioned me and how you took my keys that you'll make a fine P.I. Besides, this is a personal issue for you as well, isn't it? I can see in your face how much you're grieving. You might be the only one who can—'

'If protection is what you're concerned with, then why not hire a professional bodyguard?'

'No, no, a muscular armed man would attract too much attention, which I don't want. I would rather you looked into this whole tragedy, working privately for me, find out the identity of those goddamned goons and clear up what both you and I are puzzling through. As Sylvie's spiritual brother, I feel responsible.'

'Could it also be that you're concerned about the safety of someone close to you?'

He sighed. 'Yes, my guru's. That's uppermost in my mind.

He wouldn't hear of having a bodyguard. Being a spiritual being, he doesn't worry about himself.'

'Is there any way I could meet with him?'

'He's in mourning for Sylvie and not receiving any visitors. But I'll do my best to make sure you get the chance at some point. What's your fee structure?'

Maya named an amount, discussed terms and conditions and sized Atticus up. Obviously he was well-off and would be able to pay. He got his cellphone out from his pocket and made a few notes.

With a glance at the keys in her hand, she asked, 'I'm still wondering about the locked door.'

'Oh, it's a precautionary move, so my ex doesn't get in.' Atticus wiped under his eyes with a hand. 'I've been a mess since she left. She said I was the oddest duck she'd ever been with. So what's new? I don't fit in, I have some quirks. I'm ugly. I'm boring. She also said she married me for my bank account but realized eventually that it couldn't make up for my lack of charm. Didn't it buy her a most comfortable six months? I'd also have liked to ask her where she buys charm. But she was gone.'

'Join the club. My relationship with a cop broke up too.' Maya regretted the words that had flown out of her mouth.

'Maybe we can cry together.'

'I'd rather that we talked more about—'

'My leg hurts if I listen too long.'

Here we go again.

A truck rumbled by on the street below, causing the windowpanes to tremble. Atticus' face became distorted by dread. 'You know, Maya, I think you should leave. You might have brought trouble for yourself by visiting me. You could be the gang's next target, now that you have a Sylvie connection.'

'How would anyone know I visited you, Atticus? Or that you're employing me? Do you suppose someone is watching your place?'

Atticus stirred and looked toward the window. 'Quite so. Maybe I'm paranoid, but sometimes I sense that I'm on a watch list. Bad people waiting in dark places, ready to clobber me again. Bad people breaking in here, going through my stuff. Bad people waking me up at night, shaking me, staring at me.'

'Why didn't you warn me ahead of time?'

'If you'd rather not engage in this case, I can understand.'

'Look, I already am involved.' She popped up to her feet and grabbed her purse, wondering what she'd locked herself into. Worse yet, she might have involved Uma. How much she loved her mother. Her well-being . . . Maya couldn't process any further. 'Perhaps we'll touch base another time?' she said to Atticus. 'At least over the phone?'

Eyes darkened with apology, he uncoiled himself from the chair and moved slowly to the door on his crutches. 'Yes, do keep in touch, but not a word to anyone.'

'My assistant will draw up a contract.' She stepped up to the door, twisted the key in one of the locks and turned it. 'You're really scared, aren't you, locking up tight like that?'

He kept his chin down, pulled open the door and stood aside. Maya offered a word of thanks and returned his keys.

'Let me escort you to the elevator,' he said in a fatherly fashion.

'Not necessary.' Even as she waved, he maintained a deeply disturbing silence. She heard him relock the door.

Out on the street, Maya looked up toward the roof of the building across the street and up and down at the street itself, scanning the doorways and balconies to determine if any surveillance was going on. She detected the movement of a shadow on a lower balcony. She raced to her car, plopped into the driver's seat and locked the door.

SIX

The following morning, at 9 a.m., Maya sat in her office, a cup of homemade *chai* and an iPad in front her. She keyed in a link to a news item in her iPad, which continued to churn out details about the fiery protest and eventually landed on an analysis titled 'Tibetan Spring.'

Hank strode into the office, said hello and took a chair opposite her.

'Have you heard of Tibetan Spring?' Maya asked.

At Hank's headshake, Maya turned the iPad around so both of them could read the screen. The analysis stressed that the two Seattle suicides were isolated incidents. Harold J. Francis, a local psychotherapist who'd been interviewed, was quoted as saying, 'Suicide is an iconic expression for those who feel helpless against a powerful, oppressive force.' Francis further insisted that people who had no outlet for expressing their grievances often used self-harm as a tactic, considering it an effective form of protest. 'I might die but I'll make a point.'

Maya raised her eyes. 'No, no,' she said angrily. 'Sylvie was too smart for that.'

They went back to reading the screen. Further down, Francis expressed his fear that a wave of politically motivated, copycat immolations could follow, the 'porous human psyche being susceptible to contamination.'

'We don't want that,' Maya said, and Hank concurred.

Next they studied a brief profile of Sylvie that appeared in a side column. Titled *A Trailblazer*, it contained mostly routine material about her academic history, including graduate degrees from the University of California and scientific papers she'd published, along with a few tidbits of personal data. Sylvie's Tibetan birthparents had given her the name Silver at her birth on a full moon night, which was changed to Sylvie by her adoptive parents.

'Silver.' Hank looked away from the iPad. 'A person by that name has to be fascinating.'

'She used that name in signing cards and letters. She had a large, loopy, memorable signature. The last birthday card I got from her even had a brief, handwritten note. Her penmanship was exquisite.'

'Something you'll keep forever, I'm sure.' Hank paused. 'Can I ask you more? If Sylvie was a big Tibetan activist, why didn't she turn to her sister or anyone else for support?'

'This is what I'm guessing.' Maya enumerated the reasons. 'Sylvie might not have felt her family would approve of her advocacy. Or she might have been the kind of person who compartmentalized her life. Or it might have had to do with her being an adopted offspring; her ancestry was so sacred to her that she didn't want to share it with anyone. It could also have been that Sylvie and Veen had serious issues between them and a dialogue wasn't possible.' Maya concluded by saying, 'Regardless, how could we all have missed the signs?'

Several hours later, after answering her emails and doing some research on the Internet, Maya left the office and drove home. As she parked her car on the driveway, she watched her neighbor's black-and-white cat run across the street and that, once again, reminded her of Sylvie. One evening, months ago, she and Sylvie had been talking in Veen's kitchen when Veen's cat, Pearl – silvery, with black markings, practically a fur pillow – had slipped into the room, sniffed at Sylvie's ankle and meowed at her. Sylvie had scooped up the cat, held it to her chest and stroked its head. 'I have a calico at home,' she'd said to Maya, her eyes shining. 'Her name is Augustine.'

Those images faded from Maya's mind when she entered her living room, sat on the sofa and booted her iPad.

A sandal-footed Uma swept in from the kitchen. Fresh-faced, with a flash of silver-gray in her hairline, she looked smart in a sky-blue sari and a chain necklace. 'I thought I heard you.'

Maya pointed to the Sylvie article on her iPad. 'Have you seen this?'

Uma sank down on a chair and glanced at the screen. 'Yes, it disturbed me so much I burned my breakfast. I hope people have sense enough not to engage in copycat acts. And, oh, Veen called late last night after you went to bed. She sounded terrible. Poor Veen. I want to hug her, sit with her, lend her a helping hand.'

Uma, the sharp one, could help Maya with the investigation. 'Would you consider extending your stay, Ma?'

'Oh, I don't know.' Uma smiled; her eyes sparkled. 'I got a letter from Neel, my friend and neighbor, the tall, fair one. Do you remember him? Retired professor. He asked me to come back soon. His afternoon tea tastes bitter because I'm not there to share it. He also said our neighbor's boys missed the beautiful stories I read to them. And, apparently, the building potluck last week was so dull without me and my squash sauté that Neel left early.'

'You're blushing beautifully, Ma.'

'Me? I'm not a spring chicken.'

'Romance can happen at any age, Ma. But you're also needed here. You have an open ticket, don't you?'

'Let me have a think.'

Maya peered at Uma, expecting to see her smile – a woman who liked being useful to others. Instead, Uma peered at the street outside the window, blazing under the sun. Her forehead tightened into wrinkles and her face became clouded, as though a sense of dread trembled her insides.

'What is it, Ma?'

'Since yesterday . . . I've been getting the strange feeling we're under observation. Have you noticed a blue sedan that parks across the street? It passed by only moments ago. I know what your neighbors' cars look like. It's not one of them. Last night someone sat in that parked car and watched our house for at least fifteen minutes.'

Maya's neck prickled, like cold fingers were grabbing her, but she kept her expression unperturbed. She rose, went over to the window and saw only an empty street, its monotony dissipated by the lush foliage of a pear tree. She returned to her chair. 'Did the driver have sunglasses on?'

'He might have. Let me check next time. I might even speak with him.'

'No, Ma, don't. He could have a firearm. If you ever see someone loitering, call Justin immediately.'

'Justin, that sleazebag? Even if I was being stalked, he'd be the last person I'd get in touch with.' Uma looked away for a second. 'I'm having second thoughts about that poor girl's final act and your involvement in it. Have you already been poking around, dear? Because it looks like you've pissed somebody off. Why else would they be keeping an eye on your house?'

Pissed off. Even with being poked by a feeling of unease, Maya marveled at Uma's usage of slang, which she'd been picking up regularly.

'I was at the scene, Ma. There were a lot of people there.

Who knows who might have seen me? Other than you, I've only talked to four people about Sylvie – Veen, Justin, Atticus and Hank. I can't imagine any of them staking out my house. And Atticus, too, is being watched, or so he says.'

'Who's Atticus?'

Maya gave a summation of her meetings with Atticus. That included details about him being attacked by goons and facts about his guru.

'The guru – I must say I find him interesting,' Uma said and went back to her chores.

Maya scooped up her cellphone from a side table, called Atticus and asked for an appointment with the guru.

'No visitors, that's still the guru's order,' Atticus said. 'And he doesn't want a bodyguard. He's getting on in years and mostly stays indoors, except to do prayer walks or visit relatives. But I've talked him into giving his part-time assistant, Samuel, a full-time position. Samuel is a judo expert. He'll accompany the guru on his errands whenever he can.'

'Good move,' Maya replied.

After disconnecting, Maya checked the time and approached Uma in the kitchen. 'I'll pop out for a while to check out a lead. Call me right away if you see or hear anything suspicious, will you?'

Uma nodded. She drew her eyebrows together and her eyes darted about in concern. That look would stay with Maya.

SEVEN

At a few minutes to 1 p.m., Maya entered Spices & Sweets, where the walls were painted a candle-glow yellow. She paused and inhaled a multitude of fragrances: incense, rosewater and sandalwood, with chili and turmeric battling for attention in the background. Much like in an Indian bazaar, every wall displayed jars, paper bags and plastic packages. A glass display case lined up next to the counter was loaded with confections in white, maroon, yellow and orange, all laid out in trays. Arranged on the floor were café-style tables and chairs for those who wished to nibble while in the shop.

At this hour, the store was empty. The only sound came from a television fixed high up on one wall, blaring out a Bollywood musical. Jazzed by the tune, Maya stood for a moment and tapped her foot. On the screen, a coterie of khaki-uniformed policemen, in the process of arresting a crook, improbably broke into an energetic bhangra dance routine while wielding their guns.

'Afternoon.' A woman's strangled voice came from behind the cash register. Maya turned. Aged about forty-five, dressed in a multicolored cotton dress, she had a nest of curly hair and a restless gaze. Her face had the sheen of someone far better educated than this job demanded. She swept a hand toward the display case, saying, 'If you have any questions or want a sample . . .'

'My name is Maya.' Bending down, she pointed to a tray containing rich, plump, spongy, white rounds of *raj bhog*. *Once in a while, they won't kill you.* 'I'll have my usual order of a pound.'

'I'm Jeet, the owner.' A brisk but cultivated voice, a wan smile, a no-nonsense manner – an all-work, little play type of person. She reached into the display case, scooped out a few *raj bhog* pieces with a spatula, laid them into a square white bakery box, weighed it and placed it on the counter, saying, 'Did you come in the day before yesterday? We closed early so we're giving fifty percent off to those customers who didn't get their orders filled.'

Maya shook her head and produced a credit card. 'Any particular reason why you had to close early?'

'Haven't you heard? We lost our most valued sweet-maker, Anna Kamala. I feel so miserable, I didn't make it to work yesterday. Wouldn't have come today, either, except one employee called in sick and another is on vacation.'

'I know all about how you lost your employee.' Maya paused, feeling the creeps. The incident had happened so quickly, like the sudden snap of a cruel whip, two self-immolations well-choreographed and perfectly executed, as though part of a larger plan. Once again, Maya was put on edge. 'My best friend's sister, Sylvie, was also involved in that protest. She died with Anna. Did you know Sylvie?'

Jeet shook her head. A pen resting on the counter clattered to her side of the floor. She didn't pick it up.

Maya dug a business card from her purse and handed it to Jeet. 'Hate to disturb you so soon after the tragedy, but if you have a minute to talk . . .'

Jeet's brown eyes held Maya with distrust. 'Two law enforcement officers have already been here. They gave me such a grilling, made me sick in my stomach. And now a P.I.? I always thought a P.I. would be a big, muscular man who carried a gun. You look like a grad student. Who do you work for?'

Never mind how I look. Chin up, Maya stood straight and made herself appear taller. 'That's confidential.'

Jeet looked toward the door. 'What's the point? My most valuable employee is dead. You poking your nose into it isn't going to change a thing.'

'Sylvie was like a sister to me. She died too. Her family is heartbroken. It'd mean so much to them if I—'

Jeet thought a moment longer. Something must have clicked; her eyes rounded and softened. She guided Maya to a table, saying, 'Fine. Have a seat.'

The flat box in hand, Maya drew up a chair. 'Even though I've come here a few times, I don't believe I ever met Anna. Do you have a picture of her?'

Jeet grabbed a remote, turned the television set off and receded into the back room, her necklace and bracelets clicking as she hurried away.

Maya checked the surroundings for a pointer to get in with the retailer. A collection of framed photographs depicting bountiful farmers' markets and a large, black-and-white poster flyer on malaria decorated the walls.

Jeet returned with a nine-by-twelve-inches group photo. Four women and one man stood in a semicircle, frozen in time. 'Your staff?' Maya asked, glancing up at Jeet.

'Yes.' Jeet dragged a chair across from Maya, reached over and pointed to a smiling young Asian woman standing at the center of the group. 'This was taken before the Diwali holiday last year.'

Anna, a petite woman, wore a black skirt, white blouse and a radiant smile, the smile of someone who lived a simple but rich life. Her eyes held a special light in a face surrounded by a mid-length bob of thick, straight black hair, complete with bangs, what looked like a pricy salon job.

'She was the sweetest person you ever met.' Jeet took a shaky breath. 'Unassuming and kind, got along well with my other employees. Took her job seriously and was always on time, which is not the case with every person I hire. Willing to work overtime, unless she had an appointment for a haircut.'

Haircut: Maya noted that. 'By the way, did you get a text from Anna?'

'Text? No. My assistant broke the news to me.' Jeet dabbed her eyes with a tissue. 'I was paralyzed, couldn't speak or do anything for a while. It was like losing a close relative. Later, when the police called, we were all bewildered. None of us had the will to take care of the shop, so we closed. One gentleman, our regular customer and a strict vegetarian, left an irate message on the phone. He'd missed his cashew squares made by his favorite sweet-maker, his "protein for the day."'

Maya breathed in the dry, dense air that had surrounded Anna as she'd toiled in the shop's kitchen. The mystery she'd left behind was equally dense. Maya kept a questioning gaze on Anna's photo.

'Her parents were Tibetan and she was raised here in Seattle but she could produce our delicacies,' Jeet said. 'She's the one who kept my business going. She thickened the milk more patiently than I ever could, added the right splash of rosewater and shaped the *mawa* into perfect rounds. At the end of the day, she always remembered to pack the broken pieces for the food bank. Her kitchen duty was her service to the people. But that wasn't enough. She went beyond. Yesterday, the whole universe got to see her love of her roots in action.'

'So you've noticed her devotion for Tibet?'

'Oh, yes. Although she'd never been there, she had the hope of visiting, maybe even living there someday. The Potala Palace in Lhasa had a special attraction for her. She'd seen a photograph of it shot by the late photographer Galen Rowell at an art exhibition and been smitten.'

'Could her death have been prevented?' Saying so, Maya watched Jeet carefully.

Her face ablaze, Jeet looked away. 'Yes – I mean, no. I don't know. I don't know everything. She was an employee, not a relative. And there were times when . . .' Unconsciously, Jeet covered her mouth with a hand. Seeing a pair of customers who had just blown in, she looked relieved, excused herself and rose. 'I've got to go now. Thanks for coming by.'

And there were times when . . . Maya read guilt in Jeet's gestures and in her leaving this crucial sentence unfinished. Yet she couldn't keep the retailer away from her operation.

'I'll be back.' She thanked Jeet, bid her goodbye and walked out, smelling the sweet scents and perturbed.

EIGHT

Two young, white-robed women, one a malaria scientist, the other a sweet-shop worker, stood next to each other. They knelt down willingly, a yellow blaze swirling around each, the smell of flaming muscle tissue settling over the area. In a matter of minutes, they were gone, only their burned flesh and memories were left.

Had they taken any mood-altering drugs? Maya wondered.

Might Sylvie's boyfriend have any clues?

Maya would at least like to get acquainted with him.

The next morning at about ten, still picturing the fiery deaths, the evil chanting ringing in her head and wondering about the role, if any, of narcotics, Maya phoned Atticus.

After exchanging niceties, she said, 'What can you tell me about Sylvie's boyfriend?'

'Oh, Ivan.' Atticus' voice was grim. 'Sylvie once invited me to join the two of them for dinner. I didn't much care for him, and I can't tell you why – chemistry, you might call it

– but I could see Sylvie had fallen for him. First serious boyfriend. She was glowing.'

'How can I meet him?'

'I thought I saw the dude walking around Green Lake the other day when I was standing on my balcony. He's a junior scientist, pumps iron at a health club by the lake during his lunch hour. Quite the body builder. But . . . I don't mean to sound like a father, but . . . I'd stay away from him, if I were you.'

At around noon, the sun's rays battering her face, Maya read the neon signboard above the entrance of a fitness club near Green Lake.

Meet Market
Pool, Weights, Massage, Group Workouts

In a happier time, Maya would have smiled at the 'Meet' Market joke, but not now. Somehow she'd have to get into the club and strike up a conversation with Ivan. Given that she was seeing him as a friend of Veen and not as a P.I., she could at least offer him her support.

The floor-to-ceiling windows gave a view of toned bodies in skimpy outfits pedaling away on various machines. A flyer offering a free trial membership was pasted on the front door.

Maya entered, introduced herself to the young receptionist and explained her purpose in visiting, mainly her relationship to Sylvie. After a moment's silence, the receptionist glanced at the wall clock. 'Ivan is still swimming – he should finish shortly. By the way, we're having a membership special. Two weeks of free unlimited access, daytime only. Do you care to—?'

'Maybe another time. Please, I'd like to speak with Ivan. Now.'

She followed the receptionist down a long corridor flanked by locker rooms on either side, the air sharp with a sweaty odor. They took a right turn and came to a rectangular lap pool smelling strongly of chlorine.

In the water, a lone handsome man swam laps. 'That's Ivan,' the receptionist said amidst splashing sounds before she drifted away.

Ivan squinted at Maya and continued swimming – his arms carving the water – to her end of the pool. When he reached the edge, he boosted himself out of the water and stood on the platform. Chest heaving, his muscular body dripping, skin glistening, he stepped toward a large plastic basket and grabbed a plush white towel. He wiped it over his face and hair and wrapped it around his body. A blue athletic bag sat next to the basket.

'Hello.' He looked her up and down, obviously wondering why a fully dressed woman stood there watching him getting out of the pool. His lips curved into the beginning of a smile.

'Maya Mallick. You're Ivan Dunn?'

'That's me.' He snagged another fresh towel, dried off a plastic chair, motioned Maya toward it and smiled warmly. 'Are you from the club's social team? Somebody has been asking me to join them.' He spoke with flair; words seemed to churn and dissolve in his mouth like a coveted morsel of food.

'Yes, the social team, but I also want to get to know you personally.'

Ivan didn't seem to notice her exaggerated reply, busy occupying the opposite chair and dabbing his face with a corner of the towel.

She capitalized on the opportunity to steal another good look at him, what Uma might call, 'taking the measure of the man.' Attractive in an all-American way, Ivan had a head of shiny red hair, smooth complexion, glowing cheeks and sloping shoulders. She placed him in his mid-thirties. He had a presence, a liveliness about him; one would pick him out in a crowd. His eye color changed from pale blue to dove-gray in the wavering light near the pool. She didn't detect grief in those eyes.

'I'm not that good a swimmer and won't be much good for your swim team.' He stretched out his legs and glanced down at his diaphragm, strong and flat like a board. 'I only try to stay fit. My brother is a swim champ. He's won several international fifty-meter freestyle events. Now he coaches all over the world, owns several homes in different continents.'

OK, sibling rivalry. Unfair comparisons made by parents during childhood, a sense of being an outcast in the family, forever compensating while growing up. 'But you seem to work out a lot,' Maya said.

'I do and I walk the lake, but I need to watch my diet. You know, burgers, fries, donuts and ice cream – they're everywhere.' Hands resting on his knees, Ivan finally peered at her with interest, gave a little laugh, and asked, 'What's this about?'

'I'm a pal of Sylvie's sister, Veen.'

'Oh,' Ivan mumbled, lowering his chin.

'If there's anything I can do to help . . .'

'This has been the worst week of my life – I'm trying to get over it, although there are days when I can't get up from bed. Today I was late for work.'

And yet Ivan seemed to be coping well, a little too well: he was getting into work, swimming at his lunch hour and smiling at strange women. 'Still working at the lab?'

Ivan's eyes had turned gray. 'Yes. I could have taken time off but judged it best to keep myself occupied. My boss has given me the flexibility to come and go as I please.'

He lifted the towel and began rubbing his head vigorously, mumbling about needing a haircut. Maya pictured Sylvie standing by his side. Yes, they made a lovely couple. Although he didn't have a similar spark of brilliance in his gaze, it was clear to Maya that Sylvie would have been attracted to his easy-going manner, charm and muscle-chested sensuality.

'Did you know Sylvie for a long time?'

'Well, we spent a most pleasant eight months together.' Ivan lowered the towel from his hair. 'People called me lucky, like I'd won a prize. She was a senior scientist, the goddess of vaccines, and pretty. We'd have dinner after work and end up at her place.'

'When did you last see her?'

Ivan rose, picked up the athletic bag sitting next to the towel basket and pulled out a protein bar, which appeared to be chocolate-flavored from the color of its wrapper. He lowered himself to the chair again while unwrapping the bar and began munching without bothering to answer her.

Maya kept her hands motionless in her lap. 'Will you be going to the memorial service?'

Ivan shook his head, his forehead scrunched in a frown,

and became lost in his thoughts. When halfway through the bar, he asked, 'Excuse my poor memory – what did you say your name was? Did I even ask?'

'Maya Mallick.'

'You're not from the club, are you?'

Maya blushed; smiled at him.

He seemed amused. 'Are you Indian?'

Taking it as a sign that they'd established a rapport, she nodded.

He turned to her earnestly. 'You single?'

'Why is that important?'

'Please don't be offended. It's a habit I got from my mother. She says, "We Russians like to know a little about a person before talking about serious matters."'

Yet another Russian link. 'Excuse my question, but were you as much in the dark about the intended suicide as Sylvie's family and I were?'

'Oh, yes.' Then, after a long pause, 'Sylvie was shy, sensitive and secretive – the effect of being adopted, I think. She didn't talk much about her cares, although family issues were in her mind constantly. She didn't believe her adopted family really loved her. She felt she was simply a showpiece for them, except for her mother.'

A shocked reaction went through Maya. She arranged herself differently in the chair. 'Well, she had you in her life. Where were you when it happened?'

'I know all this is important to you – you're loyal to your friend – but it's difficult for me . . . You understand, I hope.' Ivan's voice was gentle – he didn't seem offended. He stood and picked up his athletic bag. 'It was nice of you to stop by, Maya. I have to go back to the lab now. I just stopped here for a while to clear my head but I'm not being paid to swim. Or to stand around talking to beautiful women.'

Maya stood and gave him a small, sympathetic smile. His compliment, she assessed, was not so much a pick-up line as the result of his natural charm. 'Besides swimming, do you also walk the trails of the lake?'

'Yes, several times a week. I know every single duck that lives there.'

He'd started for the locker room doorway and she walked along beside him, saying, 'I love seeing the ducks as well. I also like to check out the flowers.'

'I respect people who take an interest in growing things.' He stopped and turned toward her. 'And Sylvie's friends are my friends. Maybe I'll run into you on the trails one of these days. You can teach me about the plants that make their life around the lake.'

'How about Friday?'

'Yes, why not? About this time? Shall we meet just north of the Aqua Theater?'

Maya glanced down at her watch. It was 1 p.m. She nodded and smiled, bid him goodbye, walked back to the entrance, thanking the receptionist as she passed the counter, and went out the door. Out on the sidewalk, she called Hank and left a message: 'How would you like a free, two-week gym membership?'

She paused for an instant to collect her thoughts about Ivan. Despite the rapport, this Adonis had left her with at least one grave, unanswered question: what role did he play, if any, in Sylvie's suicide?

Justin's voice leapt to her mind: *Where there are questions, there are usually leads.*

NINE

'Any breakthroughs?' Simi Sen asked from the other end the following day when Maya called to discuss the case with her.

'I suspect the sweet-shop owner is hiding things from me, although her background is clean. I've shadowed her on a number of occasions and learned her patterns. Nothing much has turned up.' Maya proceeded with a longer explanation. From private databases, the Internet, former employees and members of the Asian-Indian community, she'd gathered enough on Jeet. She had no criminal records of any sort. Due to job dissatisfaction, she'd walked away from a career in chemical engineering and started an Asian-Indian *mithai* shop in Seattle. Although the Asian-Indian community in the Puget Sound area numbered in the thousands, few such sweet shops existed. Despite it not being a high-profit operation, Jeet had been able to make a go of it. A childless, divorced woman, she resided alone in a one-bedroom apartment and rarely attended community festivities, the Diwali celebration being the only exception. Former employees and current customers, interviewed secretly by Maya, gave Jeet high marks for her gentleness and generosity. 'Home, sweet shop, bank and grocery shopping seems to be her life,' Maya said in conclusion to Sen.

'Sounds like you've reached a dead end?' Sen said.

'Yes, I'll have to go back to square one and pursue a different path, although I'll certainly do a follow-up with Jeet. She has a malaria poster in her shop, I noticed, which is rather unusual.'

They chatted for a few more minutes. After clicking off, Maya considered the malaria angle once again, her memories coming to the surface. A year or so ago, she had gotten together with Sylvie at one of Veen's parties. Standing in the kitchen, they'd sipped wine and traded views on the subject of global health, Sylvie's primary concern as a scientist. Thin as a bamboo stalk, stylishly smart in a black-and-white pantsuit and French salon haircut, her face lightly made up, Sylvie had made clear what she stood for, starting with: 'Everyone should be able to go to the doctor, regardless of how much they can pay.' Maya had merely listened and made approving noises, until the conversation drifted to the topic of controlling malaria. Then she'd had plenty to add.

As a child in Kolkata, Maya was warned by her mother: if a mosquito infected with the malaria parasite feasted on your blood, it could transfer the disease to you by injecting a parasite from its own body into your bloodstream. So Maya would slap those bloodsucking creatures into submission in the daytime before they had a chance to bite her. At night, to ward them off, her mother would drape a gauzy, insecticide-treated net around the bed, which would form a tent over Maya's hot, sticky body. 'I hated crouching under the nets,' she'd said to Sylvie. 'But I managed to avoid infection so was ultimately thankful for that low-tech solution. My mother hasn't had such luck.'

Sylvie had regarded her intently, so Maya had continued on about Uma having been bitten by mosquitoes while traveling in the countryside in India. The symptoms had begun to appear upon her return to Kolkata. Maya, by then living in Seattle, had learned about it from a phone conversation: the high fever that would come and go, causing Uma to be down for days with muscle aches, sweating, nausea and hallucinations, the disease weakening her. Sylvie had recommended a highly respected specialist, Dr Palas, who practiced medicine in an exclusive clinic in Kolkata. Sylvie, a professional acquaintance of Dr Palas, had been well familiar with his work. Her recommendation yielded results. Although Dr Palas accepted few patients, Uma had got an appointment with him. She'd begun her treatment and over time developed immunity.

Seven months ago, Maya and Sylvie were together, again clutching wine glasses at Veen's place. Maya had thanked Sylvie and said, 'My mother's symptoms do come back but they're no longer severe.'

'Glad to be of help,' Sylvie had replied. 'It's a worldwide issue. Millions get infected every year. You know we could get rid of the bed-net and manage malaria if new low-cost vaccines were in place, and that's what I'm concentrating on.'

How easily the scientific name of the parasite, *plasmodium falciparum*, had rolled out of Sylvie's mouth, although she'd insisted that creating a fully effective commercial vaccine to control the disease was no easy job. Instead of using weakened parasites to trigger an immune response, as had been done for other infectious diseases, Sylvie had been scrambling for a lab-synthesized monoclonal antibody that would bind to the malaria parasite and alert the body's immune system, which would then target the parasite for destruction. Sylvie had spoken about this game-changing new technology excitedly, her unrouged cheeks flushing as she hinted at having made a breakthrough.

'So a commercial vaccine is in the pipeline?' Maya had asked.

Sylvie, busy pouring more wine, had ceased discussing the

subject. Maya hadn't pushed her. She'd respected Sylvie's need for privacy in this matter. Instead, changing the subject, she'd asked, 'Where did you get that haircut done?'

'Salon Martin, unisex, on the Broadway. Check it out.'

Maya had intended but never managed to visit that salon.

Less than an hour later, Maya again sat at a table at Spices & Sweets. A large brown package resting near her elbow contained two boxes of *raj bhogs* and a pricy jar of premium cardamom. While she waited for Jeet, who was finishing a phone call, Maya fixed her gaze on the sizeable, black-bordered flyer on the opposite wall.

Written in a gigantic font were three words: War on Malaria.

A photographic image below the words depicted a long black mosquito. Its mouth resembling a straw, it hovered over the smooth, bare arm of a woman, ready to suck her blood. The image made such a vivid impression that Maya rubbed her arm.

'So you're interested in malaria?' Maya asked Jeet, who had pulled up a chair.

'Not me, really. Anna brought that poster.'

Jeet got up again because a gust of wind coming through the open door had knocked the napkins off their stand on a table. Maya wondered if her action was to avoid the subject or cover her emotion. A sudden chill enveloped Maya as she sat alone.

When Jeet returned and joined her, Maya asked about Anna's hobbies.

'Oh, she liked to volunteer for causes.'

'Such as?'

Jeet expelled a sigh. 'There's no malaria in Seattle or Tibet that I know of, but Anna volunteered to be a participant in a malaria challenge trial project. Such a selfless person.'

Malaria participant – the thought gave Maya a pause, a shove and a warning. 'I can't imagine why anyone would get involved in a high-risk trial.'

Jeet remained silent.

'She trusted you. Didn't she confide in you?'

'Well, yes, Anna did explain her reasoning to me,' Jeet said. 'It was eerie.'

'Could you perhaps share it with me?'

'What does it have to do with anything? She gave her life for Tibet. Isn't that enough for you? I, for one, would like to hold on to only the sweetest memories of her.' She paused. 'And why have you been stalking me, if I may ask?'

'In my line of work, I have to stalk people sometimes . . . Sorry if I made you uncomfortable. Getting back to Anna's death . . . I was present and I have many questions. Please share any recollections you have of Anna.'

'You're so persistent, young lady.'

'This is a serious situation. I have to be. Please—'

'OK. Quite by chance, Anna had come across an ad in the paper asking for voluntary participation in a disease trial program. She visited their website and was satisfied enough to contact the volunteer coordinator. He talked her into being an early malaria vaccine candidate and enrolled her. Can you imagine sitting in a cubbyhole and offering up your arm to be bitten by mosquitoes? Hundreds of them? How gross.'

'You see, my mother had malaria and she has horror stories to tell,' said Maya. 'I'd worry about the trial being unsuccessful and me winding up with one or more different strains of malaria.'

'That was precisely my concern. I . . . I told Anna if she ever contracted the darn disease she wouldn't be able to get rid of it. She might even lose her permit as a food service worker. She smiled and said that the risk was low and that this was a small sacrifice to pay when you consider how many children it could save worldwide. "I won't even feel it," she said. According to her, clinical trial programs were generally safe and she didn't mind signing a waiver.' Jeet shifted her position. 'Still, the whole idea of her healthy body being infected with a parasite made me feel creepy, so creepy that I did something I'm not proud of, something I don't usually do.'

'What was that?'

Jeet glanced out the window, stayed quiet.

'If I knew my friend was involved and risking her life for a volunteer project,' Maya said, 'I might not be proud of the things I did to protect her, either.'

'You keep trying, but I can't bear to . . .'

'You were one of the few people who knew Anna. What you reveal can only help bring justice to the case.'

'This is how it went. When Anna told me about her plan to be a vaccine candidate, I wasn't feeling so generous but didn't show it. We were standing right here, as a matter of fact. After she went back to the kitchen, I got my cellphone out and called the volunteer coordinator. I raised hell for putting my employee's health in danger. We had a shouting match for which, I'm sure, he would hate me for the rest of his life. He called me malaria naive. Said I was acting like a controlling mother, which I had no right to do, Anna being an adult.' Jeet paused. 'I gave Anna the time off. Amazingly enough, a few weeks later, she returned to work, rosy-cheeked and robust. It came as a relief when she told me proudly and confidentially she'd passed the trial. No chills, shakes or flu-like fever – she had no symptoms of the disease. Even though the doctors had detected no malaria parasites in her red blood cells, they kept monitoring her for a while.'

'Did she look different over time?'

'She did, but the symptoms were of a different sort than I'd expected and had a different cause.' Jeet hesitated. 'Anna swore me to secrecy.'

'Anna is dead. And the circumstances of her death are murky. The police could make the assumption that Anna committed suicide due to job stress and hold you responsible. What will you do?'

'Not true, not true – it was something else altogether.'

'I might be able to help you, but only if you tell me the real story.'

Jeet kept her gaze low. She obviously needed time to settle.

'If you'd rather wait for another time . . .'

Jeet raised her head. 'It was weird, it was scary, like Anna was under the influence of something or somebody. Distracted, smiling big and forgetting things, losing interest in her job, dressing better than usual, even putting make-up on.'

'Maybe she'd met someone?' Saying so, Maya went back to the time when she'd first met Justin: those days of romantic madness, when she was wildly happy, hearing music when none existed and glued to her cellphone.

'Is that any of my business?' Jeet said.

'Yes. You cared about her, didn't you?'

'She couldn't wait to get out the door when her shift ended. Eventually, she confided in me that she was hanging out with a foreign man, one with a temporary visa and soulful eyes. She could look into those eyes forever, she said. Other than that, she kept her relationship a secret. Why? I don't have the foggiest. Then, over time, she began to seem grumpy, not quite herself, and the quality of her work started to slip. That charming guy might have been taking advantage of her.'

'What? Was he providing her with any "designer" drugs?'

'He could have, although I have no idea what kind.'

'And did he eventually . . .?'

'Yes, I think he did drop her. Toward the end, she seemed hungover a lot, started swearing, stopped talking and looked nervous as hell. She lost weight. Back home in Madurai, if this was happening with my sister I'd have thrown cold water on her face and said, "Wake up, girl. Seriously! Wake up!"'

Anna's death wasn't natural, Maya reflected, only made to appear so. What would make a confection-maker the target of a violent crime? 'I, for one, find it hard to believe that two young American women my age—'

'I share your feelings. You're Indian. You must know the word *prana.*'

'Certainly, *prana* is the life energy.'

'Yes, good. *Prana* is life force and I believe it's strong in everyone. No matter how difficult life is, if a woman tries to take her own life, her *prana* will put a stop to it, unless . . .' Jeet's voice trailed off and she looked blankly at the wall.

'What else did you notice in Anna?'

Jeet gave Maya a 'get out of my face' look. Maya sat patiently, even drew the chair closer to Jeet's in an attempt to establish more trust.

'On her last day,' Jeet said, 'Anna dropped a spice jar and spilled my most expensive cardamom powder. She stood there like a zombie, didn't try to clean up the mess, didn't even apologize. I suspected she'd broken up with that guy and was taking it hard. I was so angry. I told her that I couldn't afford such expensive mistakes. "One more time and . . ."'

'You were getting ready to fire her, weren't you?'

Jeet put her face in her hands. When she raised her head, tears spilled from her eyes. 'Yes. I feel terrible for having been so harsh to her. I regret not having asked her more about what was going on. She didn't kill herself because of that. Still, it tears me apart that I didn't help her. You see, we don't poke our noses into the personal lives of our employees.'

Maya read guilt and regret in Jeet's face and allowed her a few moments to recover. 'I don't suppose Anna had any close relatives nearby?'

'None that I know of. Didn't have many friends, either. A loner, she was.'

'No friends?'

'Wait. She often mentioned that malaria-nut, that volunteer coordinator, who's also a Tibetan-American, who put her life at risk, who wanted to "help eradicate malaria from the planet." Such pretenses. They'd have coffee together. That weirdo is, in my view, formidable. Pink hair, you know? Why would a man my age go pink?'

Maya reached into her purse for a pen and piece of paper. 'How do I get in touch with him?'

'You should've been a lawyer. Would've made more money. Promise not to mention where you got it from?'

'Promise.'

'Cal Chodron, bless his *prana*, works part time at Rent Me, an apartment rental agency on Aurora Avenue. You can probably walk into his office and speak with him. But be careful. He'll charm you, make you listen to his rubbish pitch and try to get you to sign up as a malaria volunteer. And if he offers tea, refuse it. Who knows what he'll put in it? I do sound like a mother, don't I? Poor Anna. That vaccine trial might have nothing to do with her death but, after our talk, I'm beginning to wonder.'

'Has Cal Chodron threatened you in any way?'

'Well . . .' Jeet struggled to get the words out. 'I don't know. It probably wasn't him – he doesn't visit this shop – but a few weeks ago someone left a handwritten note on the counter. It said, *Mind your own stupid business, you old crow*.'

'Do you still have the note?'

'No.'

'Are you sure?'

Jeet's attention was drawn to the front door. A woman, who had glided in, now searched the room. Jeet waved at her. 'There she is, an applicant for the kitchen worker position. I have to interview her – we're pitifully short-handed. A couple more days and my display case will be empty. End of supply, the death of my retail operation.'

Maya glanced at Anna's potential replacement: skin-and-bones, frizzy-haired, a tattooed arm and a slutty look. She got out of her chair.

'One more question, Jeet. Where did Anna get her hair cut?'

'I'm not her mother.'

'Could it have been a fancy salon?'

'I suppose. It was her only extravagance, her "snip tour."'

Maya rose. 'May we talk another time?'

Jeet shook her head, teary-eyed. 'Make *raj bhog* runs as often as you like, but I can't help you out any more. You're one hungry girl. I've already given you more than enough ammo. I have to get my business going. A competitor will eat me up if I don't.'

Maya thanked Jeet, adding, 'We'll keep Anna in our hearts, won't we?'

Outside, she shook out her shoulders, dug out her cellphone and left a message for Detective Justin, aching to speak with him.

TEN

Her hands smeared with fresh cheese, fragrant sweet syrup simmering over the stove, the buzz of the retail shop drifting through the door, Anna Kamala bent over a bowl on the kitchen counter, intent on preparing the next batch of *raj bhogs*.

That image swirling in her head, the same afternoon at around 5 p.m., Maya cruised down Aurora Avenue, a seedy stretch of state highway notorious for drugs, crime, failed businesses and streetwalkers. Through feeble sunlight, she parked on a side street and walked two blocks down the avenue, past shoulder-to-shoulder buildings housing small retail operations. The wind howled over the dusty tops of trees. She squinted at the numbers and checked the storefronts, glancing back every now and then to see if she was being followed. Sandwiched between a dilapidated motel and an X-rated video rental shop, her destination stood across the street from a gun dealership.

The signboard above the door declared: *Rent Me. Apartment and Storage Rental Services.*

Inside, a short, stocky man of East-Asian origin was perched behind a rectangular steel desk. Aged about forty, he tapped intently on a computer keyboard. The wood-grained desk nameplate read Cal Chodron. Maya would have known who he was even if the nameplate wasn't there. His spiky, fuchsia-pink hair gave his identity away.

Natural light flooded the small, square, tall-windowed room. A map of the city, highlighting the neighborhoods served by the agency, lined the back wall. The desk held several personal effects, including two wood-framed photographs sitting side by side. The first displayed Cal with a Caucasian woman and three beaming young boys, one with similarly pink hair. The second was that of a grave, elderly man who resembled Cal: same eyes, cheekbones and nose. To the left of the photos stood a glass of water. To the right squatted a small clay figurine of a sitting Buddha; it held the inscription: *What would Buddha do?*

Cal looked up at Maya, swiveled his chair to face her and offered a smile. 'Pardon me, I didn't hear you come in. Looking for a rental?' He gestured toward a chair.

Maya shook her head, plucked a business card from her wallet and slid it across his desk. 'Maya Mallick. Sylvie's sister is my best friend.' At Cal's nod, she added, 'I've heard about Anna from a mutual acquaintance. I came here to talk.'

A tremor passed over Cal's body. His smile grew grim. 'According to my family's belief about dying, which goes back to ancient Tibetan traditions, we don't observe grief by talking about it.' Cal's voice was choked with emotion. 'Only by fully experiencing grief can we let it go.'

Maya nodded. 'I certainly respect your tradition. I happened to have been there when Sylvie and Anna died . . . it was beyond belief . . . I can't forget what I saw.'

Cal stared at the family photo on his desk and sighed. 'I tell my children what my Tibetan grandmother impressed on me. "Let events run their own course. Don't constantly try to channel them to rivulets of your liking."'

Maya sighed. How well had *she* been able to accept reality? Justin flared to her mind and along with that came a twinge of torment. He used to call her the 'Mistress of Trying Too Hard.' It dawned on her now that Justin hadn't returned her last phone call.

Cal scrutinized her business card. Maya noticed the neatness all around him. It befit a traditional, duty-bound man, hardwired to do the right thing.

Cal raised his eyes, a tightness about him. 'You're a private detective?' Then, at Maya's nod, 'Why did you come to see *me*?'

Maya got her pen and notebook out of her purse. 'I understand you were the malaria volunteer coordinator who recently worked with Anna.'

'The question most people ask me is how I got so pink. But you're asking me about the malaria trial. Who told you about it?'

'A friend of Anna.'

Suspicion stirred on Cal's face; he lowered his eyes to the desk. 'I'm not at liberty to talk about my activities at the malaria clinic.'

'You were friends with Anna. No doubt you're mourning her loss. The circumstances surrounding her death – let's say they're murky. I bet you have an interest in figuring out—'

Cal sighed, then glanced through the window. 'OK, Ms Mallick. At this late hour, I don't expect anyone to show up for a rental. How can I help you?'

'Please, call me Maya. And please tell me how a malaria trial is conducted.'

Cal's gaze was skeptical. 'What makes you ask about it?'

'My conversations with Sylvie Burton about her malaria research.'

'Why should I talk to a perfect stranger about the trial?'

'The trial is a common element between the two women. I wonder if it has anything to do with their untimely deaths.'

'Do you have any idea how many untimely deaths there are because of malaria fever?'

Maya had heard the grim statistics from Sylvie, the mosquito expert, but to keep Cal talking she shook her head.

Cal turned to his desktop, clicked his mouse and positioned the machine so Maya would have a full view of a world map. Cal traced the malaria-endemic areas of the African continent and the Indian subcontinent successively, his fingers moving in a knowledgeable fashion. 'These continents are ravaged by that godawful disease. Something like five hundred million are infected every year. The pity of it is mostly kids die from it, especially kids in Africa. India and Bangladesh haven't been spared, either.'

Maya noted the deep sorrow in his voice. 'Anyone in your family?'

Cal glanced at the photograph of the elderly man on his desk. 'Yes, my father, brave soul, who escaped from Tibet – what a story he had to tell about that. Settled in Northern India but contracted malaria within six months. He didn't make it.'

'I'm sorry.'

Cal's voice shook as he went on: 'I was only six then but I'll never forget his suffering. Shortly thereafter, my mother had a chance to immigrate to this country. I was raised on the East Coast.'

This gave Maya a chance to offer a brief recap of her mother contracting malaria in India. How Uma was able to manage the disease, but only after much suffering and prolonged treatment. As she spoke, Maya looked steadily at Cal.

Cal got up, crossed over to a small refrigerator in the back of the room, pulled out two bottles of water and handed one to Maya. 'My association with malaria didn't end with my father's death. After graduating from college, I moved to Seattle to look for a job. Guess what I found? The city had a malaria center, one of the largest in the world. I got hired as a clerk in that center and worked there for a few years. When I married and needed a better income to support my family, I quit and got into the real estate business but still spent my spare hours at the center. I worked first as a volunteer and eventually took over as the coordinator, a part-time position for which I now get paid a stipend. I recruit participants for the malaria challenge trial. Anna's boss, that sweet-shop lady, accused me of brainwashing her but that's hogwash. There's no pressure, none. It's entirely up to an individual whether to join or not.'

A wave of discomfort passed over Maya. 'How do you recruit participants? How'd you recruit Anna?'

A screeching sound came from beyond the windows. Maya turned a concerned gaze toward the sound only to see a bearded, unkempt man, his ample body clad in rags, with a reddish-yellow cast to his eyes, pressing his face on the window. A cigarette on his lips, a hood covering his head, he scratched on the glass with discolored, overgrown nails.

'Oh, that's Arthur, our street poet.' Cal smiled at the window. 'He's a regular. He's opened my eyes to issues and even beauty I didn't know existed. Every so often I serve him a cup of coffee and we sit and talk.'

Arthur waved at both Cal and Maya, then drifted away.

Maya met Cal's eyes.

'Where were we?' Cal asked.

'You were telling me about your recruitment process.'

Cal sat back. 'Our website has a call for volunteers, and yes, we currently need them. We generally get a few responses every week. So many people in Seattle are dedicated to one cause or another. They find us through our website or the ad we put in the daily and they email us. I look for healthy adults and ask them to come for an in-person visit. I explain that the vaccine will not harm them. Very few actually sign up.'

'I'd assumed they would try the vaccine on animals first.'

'Animal trials were, indeed, the first phase.' Cal grew animated. 'That phase was successfully completed; now we're on to experimental human trials, which have to have sufficient safety controls or else the FDA won't allow them. They monitor our efforts closely.'

'What about Anna?'

'When I met with her for a screening appointment, we talked for quite a while.' Now Cal gave his pitch detailing his malaria eradication campaign, presumably the same one he'd given to Anna: how important it was for a low-cost cure for malaria to reach the market, how crucial it was to test the reactions to this vaccine on a small control group, maybe even a single individual first, and what a valuable contribution a participant made to society. Besides, they'd be reimbursed for their participation and any health-care expenses should they succumb to the disease. 'I impressed upon Anna that she might miss a few weeks' work but she'd be serving millions by joining. You should've seen the glow on her face – she was such a giving person. "How amazing it'll be to be part of this," she told me. She immediately signed up to participate in our human malaria challenge trial – my sole recruit. Within days, she was administered the experimental vaccine.'

'What was the next step?'

Cal frowned. 'Well, all the public needs to know is this: the human trial involves deliberately exposing a vaccinated subject to bites of malaria-carrying mosquitoes. The vaccine prevents the disease.'

Maya leaned in.

'The process is confidential.' Cal lowered his voice. 'I'll describe it only if you sign up first.'

'I appreciate the offer, but . . . look, two young women have died under suspicious circumstances. They're linked by your malaria trial.'

Cal held his breath; he seemed shaken. 'Are you—?'

'No, I'm not trying to scare you but the police could very well be interested. By now they've checked Sylvie's background as a scientist. How long will it be before they want to know more about the vaccine she'd come up with?'

'Not too much escapes you, does it?' As Cal plunged into the topic in the sure voice of authority with an occasional quiver, Maya saw the process before her mind's eye. Anna had been vaccinated three times – prime dose and two booster doses. The vaccine was nothing but a malaria-specific protein or antigen. Minimally clothed, Anna would have lain down in the close, dark quarters of a cubbyhole called an insectary, confident that her vaccinated body, with the help of her immune system, had generated antibodies against the parasite.

Anna would have heard the hum in the air, anticipated one or more bites from a cloud of mosquitoes infected with *plasmodium falciparum*, the dreaded malaria parasite, and before long have felt a prick on her exposed arm. That would have been followed by itchiness, swelling, a warm sensation. Rather than be scared, Anna would have nurtured a feeling of pride in herself.

When Cal stopped speaking, Maya said, 'I suppose Anna would have been treated right away if she became infected?'

'Of course. The nurse drew blood from Anna on a regular basis.'

'Pardon my ignorance. How does that go?' Meeting silence, she said, 'It's a routine procedure, right? No harm in disclosing it? In any case, I'll never reveal to anyone where—'

'I have to give you an explanation? OK.' Cal now laid out the process. Maya could almost see a needle puncturing Anna's arm, crimson fluid filling a syringe. The blood sample was transferred from a syringe to a tube marked with Anna's identification and the date of collection and sent to the lab technician, who then prepared the results of the specimen test. The doctor at the clinic studied Anna's test results, monitored them closely for immune reactions and checked her liver functions, of course. Everyone was ecstatic when Anna passed all the initial safety tests. 'She didn't develop malaria. In fact, she had no trace of the disease in her body.'

While Cal gulped down water, Maya silently went over the sequence of events. Sylvie had worked in an infectious diseases lab for decades and developed a potential remedy for malaria. Elsewhere at a malaria clinic, completely separate from the lab, arrangements were made to trial that antimalarial drug. Cal had sent out a call on the clinic's website for fit, healthy individuals, who had never been infected by the disease, to participate in the trial. Anna had responded to the call and joined, eventually passing the test and proving the effectiveness of Sylvie's vaccine.

'Did Sylvie and Anna meet over the trial?' Maya asked.

Face flushed, voice raised, Cal replied, 'No, that's impossible.'

Maya flinched, surprised by Cal's reaction. 'Are there privacy issues?'

'You'd better believe it! Scientific and ethical standards as well. Our clinical trial is in no way related to the lab research. The scientist – Sylvie, in this case – working on the vaccine in the research institute is kept in the dark about who the trial participants are and whether anyone has successfully gone through the initial safety test. This is so the scientist has no influence over the results. We do our best to maintain a high degree of impartiality and separation. In fact, we insist on it.'

'Well, then, Sylvie and Anna met somewhere else. Anna must have told Sylvie about her participation in the study, the fact that she'd passed the trial without developing malaria.'

'No!' Cal's voice rose again. 'Again, you're making assumptions! Anna had signed a consent form saying that she would not reveal the trial results to anyone, except her immediate family and possibly her employer.'

Maya sat firmly in her chair. 'Makes me wonder if anyone outside Anna's immediate work and family environment was interested in the trial results, someone who might have wanted the two women dead?'

'Do you read much science fiction?'

Maya shrugged off his comment and took a wild guess. 'Has anyone ever tampered with Anna's blood specimens?'

Cal reflected for a moment. 'No, I mean . . . I'm not sure. Actually, we didn't worry too much when . . .'

'Yes, Cal, I'm all ears.'

'Oh, no, I don't know what I was saying.'

'Please, Cal, what else can you tell me about the specimens?'

'Well, a tube of blood specimen after the vaccine had been administered to Anna got lost and never reached the lab technician. He had several others specimens to work with and we forgot all about it.'

'Goodness me. Looking at the bigger picture, I'm now puzzling over the link between the events, such as the suicide taking place not long after the trial. There's also the issue of a lost specimen.'

'If you're blaming the clinic for Anna's death, you're wrong, dead wrong, and you're a troublemaker.' Cal's face reddened;

his pink hair looked pinker. 'We're not responsible in any way. We'll bring a defamation case against anyone who—'

'Please, I'm not assigning blame to your clinic by any means. I'm simply trying to draw lines through the dots. I'm also trying to bring closure to a grieving family.'

Cal, steepled fingers beneath a small chin, blinked, regained control and went quiet. In his reflective posture, Maya detected the same doubt as hers. He, a loyal worker, simply tried to protect the clinic's reputation, worried that its confidentiality had somehow been compromised. *A blood sample got misplaced and never reached the lab.*

'Is the trial over?'

'Only Phase One-A, with Anna as the sole participant.' A forthcoming note was evident in Cal's voice, as though he, too, sought resolution in this case. 'The results of this phase inform additional research, which then leads to Phase One-B and beyond.'

'But you still don't see a possible link?'

'Between the suicides and the vaccine trial? For the last time, no, no, no!'

Maya rose. Hearing a sharp screech behind her, she peered out the window, saw a blue sedan flowing past but caught only the letters AMH on the license plate. She memorized the letters, glanced at the statue of Buddha and then at Cal.

Cal got up from his chair as well. 'I didn't mean to be curt with you. I teach my sons not to lose their temper like I tend to do. Do you know what my middle son suggested? "Dad, get pink hair – everything will look different." He's that age when you know everything. So I went pink. And still . . .'

'Could we talk another time? We might be able to help each other, even though we'd have to kick up waves doing so.'

Cal nodded, came around the table and shook Maya's hand, as though confirming they'd established a working relationship. Maya expressed her gratitude and walked out. A fact Cal had supplied remained stuck in her mind. *A blood sample got misplaced and never reached the lab.*

Who was responsible for the safe-keeping of the blood samples? She should have asked Cal. The late afternoon sun in her eyes, she saw a giant knot of a problem before her which would be painful to untangle but which she must do. Would Cal help her? She couldn't be sure. Did she trust him? She couldn't be sure of that, either.

As Maya rushed toward her car, a suspicion sliced through her: she might be under surveillance. She checked every movement on the block; didn't see a soul. Then she spotted Arthur, the street poet, standing at a corner and smoking a joint, saying, 'Screw you,' to another figure further away. A grocery cart overflowing with Arthur's belongings was parked nearby. He turned, saw Maya and gave her a sly smile.

'How're you doing?' she asked, feeling unsettled. Wrong question, perhaps.

'Never better. A dead rat on the sidewalk, a schoolboy getting stabbed on the block ahead and two restaurant-goers shooting each other over a parking space not far from here.' Without waiting for her reply, Arthur picked up a snack package from the cart, removed the joint from his lips and popped a few potato chips into his mouth.

She wouldn't be able to engage Arthur in a long chat, that much was certain. She waved, turned and heard him say, 'Hope to see you again soon, miss.'

As she jogged the block and climbed into her car, Maya sensed the invisible presence of a pair of eyes on her back. They weren't Arthur's.

ELEVEN

That Friday, at 1 p.m., Maya arrived at the trails of Green Lake, at the spot where Ivan had said he'd meet her, and waited. It distressed her as the minutes ticked by. She saw a mother pushing a stroller, a skateboarder going backwards, a leash-free puppy galloping and barking and a jogger weaving through a knot of pedestrians.

As she took a few steps along the periphery of the lake, a rare variety of a gray-barked black walnut tree came to view. She gave it a look of admiration. Beyond the tree, next to a jungle of wild roses, she spotted Ivan. Though she'd met him only once, she recognized the fine features and a physique the envy of professional athletes. His mass of red hair looked trimmed and had golden highlights; he'd made a visit to a salon. Maya stepped toward him.

'Oh, Maya.' He gave her a warm look, pecked her on both cheeks. 'Have you been well?'

'Thanks for meeting me again,' she said, still startled by his effusive greeting style. They started walking, exchanging pleasantries for a few minutes. Unable to wait any longer, she said, 'I want to talk about Sylvie, why she killed herself.'

Eyes on a stand of vigorous white-trunk birch, Ivan burst out, 'My mother goes wild over birch. She hugs them because they heal. I used to tell Sylvie that instead of meditating she should be outdoors, hugging trees.'

'I've never been able to meditate for a long period. I prefer hugging trees, too. But Sylvie—'

'Well, she got into meditation to destress from her job but it made her more introspective. Who knows what sorts of stuff they feed your mind? Let me warn you. Don't ever get into a weird cult like the one—'

'A weird cult?'

Ivan's gaze skittered over ducks paddling in unison and gliding in his direction.

'You must have a lot bottled up inside you.' Maya gave him a look of sympathy. 'Would it at all help to talk? About her guru, I mean?'

'That scumbag – how else can I say it? He's an assassin.'

Passing by the wading pool, half-listening to children shrieking, Maya said, 'You mean she'd still be alive if it weren't for him?'

Silently, Ivan viewed an approaching jogger taking his dog for a spin.

Maya persisted. 'What did you notice that made you—?'

'To have to sit in the lotus pose for three excruciatingly long hours? Chant words you can't pronounce? Don't you see? They try to break a person down, make them do what they'd like them to do.'

'And her guru . . .?'

'Someone who downloads instructions from heaven? Give me a break. I told the cops to arrest Padmaraja. He's the criminal who instigated the whole thing but they haven't locked him up yet.'

Maya was still waiting for an appointment with the guru. In order to formulate her next question, she mentally changed her focus onto the sad case of Anna. The über sweet-maker, another Tibetan-American, had fallen in with shady characters. Anna's employer, Jeet, had noticed behavioral changes in her. Did a similar transformation occur in Sylvie?

'Sylvie's family might have missed signs of coercion,' she said to Ivan, 'but I don't imagine you did.'

'Correct. About six weeks before her death, Sylvie had a private audience with that crafty man. She came back changed, like a switch had been flipped. He must have talked her into killing herself.'

'Really? What changes did you notice?'

'She went inside herself. Family issues were also on her mind. She told me how much she loved her mother but despised her sister, how she didn't want to see her ever again. She called her a monster.'

Maya almost took a pace back. Veen would go to pieces if she heard this. Maya would have to keep it under wraps as best as she could. 'Veen didn't get the last text message from Sylvie. Maybe you . . . did you?'

Ivan shook his head.

For a moment, Maya saw a white-robed Sylvie stepping toward her death: the blaze, the lilies, the sounds of chanting, the stench and her last cry.

Ivan, peering into the branches of trees, swallowed hard. 'Quite honestly, we'd split up and were no longer in touch. I was sound asleep in my apartment when she . . . That morning, I went out for coffee. By then, the news was everywhere.'

'I don't mean to pry into your private life, but how long had you been separated?'

'Oh, weeks. Happened gradually. She got weird after meeting with the guru. She'd always been clingy. Made a big deal if I even looked at another woman.'

'What about Tibet? Neither Veen nor I have the slightest

notion how Sylvie's interest in Tibet began, how it might have pushed her over the edge.'

Ivan turned away, either to gaze at a canoe floating by or to keep her from noticing his expression. 'It was a surprise for me, too. Suddenly it was only Tibet, Tibet, Tibet. She was born there but left before she was two. How much could she remember?'

Maya watched a squirrel hurriedly cross the trail. 'Her allegiance to Tibet—'

'Oh, yes. Tibet, if you ask me, is a lost cause.' Ivan spoke more rapidly now, as though the explanation were bottled up inside him. 'China will never hand it back to the Tibetans. What is there on that plateau anyway besides yaks, prayer flags, Buddha statues and steep mountains?'

Maya brushed past a bamboo grove, stopped for a moment and picked up a fallen bamboo leaf. As she rose, she noticed Ivan staring at her. Did he suspect she didn't trust his words, especially his attempt to downplay the significance of the Tibetan movement for self-rule?

'OK,' she said. 'So Sylvie was idealistic. Could it be that she might have felt a genuine attraction for her ancestral land?'

'She liked to hyphenate.' His voice was emphatic. 'Isn't that the current fashion? Tibetan-American sounds grand, but what did it buy her?'

A teenager rollerbladed past. Maya moved to the side, her leg brushing against Ivan's, and the tingling sensation gave her a feeling of quick embarrassment. 'I imagine you guys had discussed the Tibet issue.'

'It's really too painful to go back to our last few weeks together. It wasn't fun anymore. We argued. Hell, it was like seeing a train wreck before your eyes. You know what I mean?'

'How did you cope?'

'I started seeing other women, of course.'

Colder air blew in; summer would soon draw to a close. Maya shoved her hands in the slash pockets of her fleece vest. 'I can only imagine how you must feel about the loss, even if you weren't together at the end.'

Ivan, staring off in the distance, didn't seem to hear her. Or maybe he didn't want to express more of his feelings. Or he was hiding something.

A dry twig fell from a tree and struck Maya's forehead. 'I'll peel off here.' She pointed to a path that led to the parking lot. 'When will you be back here next?'

'Next Monday at about the same time. Hope you'll join me. And do stay away from that meditation group.' He held her gaze and spoke in a grim tone. 'You're the type they prey on – young, lovely, unattached.'

'I'd make a lousy member of that group.'

'I can see you're different from her.'

He left an unsaid 'but' hanging and shook hands with her, his grip strong enough to put her on edge.

TWELVE

The next morning, Maya entered the back room of her office.

'Good morning,' Hank said, typing away at his desk. He paused and turned his chair to fully face Maya. 'Thanks for turning me on to *rosgullas* at Jeet's shop. Weird stuff, even better than *raj bhog* – they're now a daily habit of mine. I shared a piece with my critique group buddy who writes purple prose. He put it this way, "Sweet, tender rounds, like a poetic phrase cloaked in fragrant flowing syrup."'

Maya claimed a chair. 'Wait till you taste my mother's.'

'I'm waiting. I must tell you, though, I feel for Jeet. The lady's scared. Somebody left a dead rat at her front door. That has never happened before and she thinks it has a meaning. Who could hold a grudge against a sweet-shop lady who feeds you samples and gives you a discount whenever she can?'

Oh my God. 'It has to do with Anna – that'd be my guess. Jeet was one of the few people who knew her well. Someone's trying to scare Jeet so she'll keep her mouth shut.'

'Talk about getting weirded out.' Hank recapped his efforts on the Sylvie case so far. He hadn't been able to access Sylvie's email, Facebook or credit records, all due to a lack of authorization. His calls to Sylvie's lab had gone unanswered. He'd even disguised his voice and assumed a new identity before telephoning the meditation studio, but the woman at the other end had replied she was only an answering service and couldn't elaborate. 'And I thought cranking out short fiction was punishing work.'

'Stay with it.' Maya rose, turning toward the front office. 'Something's got to break.'

'Perfect, boss. And thanks for getting me in the gym.' Hank smiled brightly. 'Ivan and I are now chums. I'll have more scoop for you soon.'

The same evening, at 7 p.m., Maya and Uma attended the candlelight vigil in memory of Sylvie and Anna. Under a grove of red oak trees, Veen and her family, friends, community activists and Tibet-sympathizers assembled on the northern shore of Green Lake. Harsh blue light from the street lamp accentuated their faces.

Absent was the prayer group that had surrounded Sylvie and Anna during their self-immolation. A surprise, if indeed they were in cahoots with the two women. Maya recalled the single familiar face among them – a ruddy-skinned, mustachioed man, someone she'd occasionally seen in the neighborhood. In the last several days, taking long walks through streets near her home, Maya had tried to track him down, to no avail. Her eyes now searched for Ivan. He wasn't present, either.

The mourners floated wood-frame white paper lanterns on the lake surface. Candles tucked inside them made each lantern gleam like a teardrop in flames. Heads bowed, holding visions of peace, the crowd maintained several moments of silence. That was followed by a few short speeches.

Standing there and listening, Maya was reminded of an in-depth article she'd browsed on the Internet that very morning, a follow-up story about the death of Sylvie and Anna. Evelyn Manus, a social scientist, had made the following observation: 'Denial, remorse and soul-searching are some of the stages of grieving that often lead to final acceptance.' To that list Maya could add one more item: finding the real story underneath the calamity. She pictured Sylvie. A velvety-black curtain of hair framing her face, Sylvie urged Maya in that direction, which made her investigation that much more important.

Once the speeches ended, Veen, seemingly ill at ease, scooped Maya into an embrace and said in a desperate whisper, 'See you tomorrow at four p.m., like our usual.' With a hurried goodbye, she vanished.

Veen's mother, Angie-Auntie, pulled Maya aside. The robust woman, divorced for decades, usually maintained the poise that came from her years as a college professor and a public intellectual but not today. Eyes crimson and sunken deep in their sockets, her hair unkempt, she pointed to a wreath-style gold chain at her neck and said in a sad, low voice, 'Tuesday would have been Sylvie's birthday. During my recent visit to Delhi, I bought this chain for her. She loved gold, you know.'

Silence gnawed at Maya. The genuine gold bangle bracelet on Sylvie's wrist the day she'd died flashed in her mind.

'I feel horrible for Veen,' Angie-Auntie continued. 'I wish I knew what to do for her.' At Maya's troubled glance, she added, 'Yesterday, she wrote a long, loving note to Sylvie then tore it into pieces. She hardly eats. Anyhow, keep an eye on your friend, will you, dear? You're her anchor.'

An anchor – steady, unshakable, grounded. If only Maya could describe herself that way. She also wondered if Angie-Auntie was trying to make a point about her daughter being implicated in Sylvie's death, if only unconsciously. Veen was not her favorite offspring, by any means.

That night, in her dream, Maya slept in a satin bed covered by a warm, creamy blanket. Someone hovered over her bed, as though trying to inhale her fragrance. She could hear his short, fast and evil-smelling breath, which blocked out all other night sounds.

Who is he? How did he get in? What does he want?

An arm snaked around her throat, tightened, then tightened some more, its touch slippery.

Maya didn't know she was screaming until Uma's voice from outside the door registered. 'Are you all right?'

Maya sat up in darkness, shaking. 'Yes, Ma, sorry to wake you. It was only a bad dream.'

She stayed awake for a long time, reflecting how much the two deaths – from the first-hand observation and countless replaying in her mind – were embedded in her psyche now. She'd have no rest until she could cut through the fog of enigma that surrounded the event.

Still mulling over that dream the next morning, Maya dragged a chair up to the breakfast table where her mother arranged platters. A spicy aroma drifted into the air. Uma looked fresh and pulled together in her light yellow sari bordered with vermilion.

Maya mumbled a 'good morning' and served herself from the platter of Indian comfort food: *poori aloo*, a combination of freshly prepared flatbread and a potato sauté. She gave Uma an appreciative glance.

Uma nodded knowingly. 'Go ahead and fill up, my dear. Our *poori aloo* also empowers you. You go out, look the world in the eye and say, "Bring it on," or whatever the current expression is. No insipid, squishy croissants for me, thank you. My stomach turns at the thought.' She pointed at the third platter containing spongy, white rounds of luscious *raj bhog* drenched in sugar syrup. 'I found these in the fridge. Tried one – heavenly. Who made them?'

Maya squirmed in her seat; Anna's touch might still be in those concoctions. She poured out to Uma about her visit to the sweet shop and the things of interest she'd gathered about Anna. She glossed over the part about the sweet-maker's dalliance with a supposedly bad character, so as not to wipe the gentle expression from Uma's face.

Uma cocked her head to one side. 'My God! Both Sylvie and Anna were of Tibetan origin and involved with malaria prevention?'

'You keep up with malariology, do you?'

'Oh, yes. I read all the tidbits I can get my hands on. Remember Doctor Palas, my malaria physician in Kolkata? Bless him. He recently made a visit to a malaria center in Holland. After he returned, I pumped him for all the tidbits I could get. Once the fever has made you feel like you're on fire, you can't help but be vigilant.'

'What did you find out?'

'The money angle, of course. Any research institute that comes up with a low-cost commercial malaria vaccine can hope to benefit from it. Pharmas will do anything to get hold of such a formula. They could mass market it and make a killing. There's also a do-good angle. Doctor Palas hopes that a scientist with benevolent intentions will try to make such a vaccine a low-cost solution available to all.'

'Well,' Maya said, standing, 'thank you for the lovely breakfast. Now I have to go run some errands.'

'Keep out of trouble, my dear child.' Affection shaded by fear filled Uma's eyes. 'I can do a few searches from home and not arouse any attention but you're out there, stepping on toes. Evil people might try to stop you, like they stopped Atticus.'

'No worries, Ma, I pay close attention to what's going on around me. I'm not like Atticus. I don't drive to the grocery store at midnight. Besides, don't you see the danger Atticus and his guru are in? It goes beyond that. Atticus talks about his "Sylvie connection" that got him into a predicament he'd rather not have. Veen, her family, you and I all have that in common now. Those evil men out there could strike again unless I—'

'You sound like your father.'

Maya noticed Uma's misty eyes and allowed her a few moments. Even after so many decades, Uma had a difficult time talking about her late husband, a police detective in India who had met an untimely death at the hands of an assassin. He'd been stalked for weeks prior to his murder, in what would remain an open case.

'Do I, really?'

'You slip in too many questions or you imply them,' Uma said. 'Lie low, dear. Wrong questions scattered on wrong ears sprout like poisonous weeds.'

A warning came to Maya's head and ramped up her pulse. 'Have you seen that blue sedan lately?'

'Yes. It passed by here yesterday.'

Maya stood stock-still for a moment. Somehow, she must get the full license plate number. Uma's worried visage haunted her as she went about her day. She called Uma several times to make sure she was all right, then swung down to Veen's apartment in a four-story green complex in Fremont. She pressed the doorbell. It was a few minutes before four p.m.

Veen emerged, closed the door quickly behind her and drew Maya into a long hug, her eyes sparkling, if only for an instant. After they left the building and climbed into Maya's car, Veen spoke in a desperate, low voice, her face worked up in frustration. 'I'm going insane, living with loonies. Mom has practically gone on a hunger strike. I'm both worried and pissed off. She already has heart trouble and now this? My youngest brother, Ben, flew in from New York, along with his wife and children, and they're all still here. I'm grateful to have a full house but there are times when I fucking wish I was alone. It's a treat to be able to get back to our sipping sessions.'

In the warm enclosure of the vehicle, keeping in mind Angie-Auntie's warning, Maya gave her best friend a close look. Her appearance had changed dramatically. Forever on a diet, Veen had been trying to lose the thickness around her waist without achieving any noticeable success. A week since Sylvie's death, her face was gaunt, her cheeks pale and waistline slimmer.

'They're taking it hard.' Veen fiddled with the cuff of her fresh white blouse, loose around her body and missing a button. 'Either being totally silent or bitching at me and blaming me. Why didn't I see it coming? What did I do to her?'

Maya sensed her melancholy and gave her a warm look.

'You know, I was never my mother's favorite,' Veen continued. 'I didn't go into law like she'd hoped. I swear too much, I'm overweight, I don't have a boyfriend – she can't show me off. It wouldn't surprise me a bit if she stopped all contact soon.'

Maya pictured Uma: a beaming face, her way of showing her acceptance of people was with an eager voice of welcome. To Maya, Uma's approval signature was as important as the air she breathed. She couldn't imagine ever losing that, of ever being thrown out of a warm nest. How dark Veen's days must be. And yet, the questions Veen's family had raised regarding Sylvie stuck in Maya's mind.

She met Veen's eyes. 'Do you mind my asking why you and Sylvie didn't get on?'

Veen sighed, became lost in reverie for an instant. 'I don't want to talk about it, ever. I do, however, owe you an apology for the way I spoke to you the other day. I love you, Maya. You're the best. But I'd just gotten the news and wasn't in my right mind. It seemed to me that you were needlessly digging into the incident.'

Maya waved a hand to erase Veen's concerns, saying, 'I accept your apology,' but inside she was rattled. What *did* Veen do to Sylvie, if anything at all? She considered revealing to Veen what she'd found out so far from her visits with Jeet and Cal Chodron. Then she anxiously wondered how Veen would react to her exploits. Veen, unaware of Maya's contract with Atticus to serve as a private investigator, might consider them intrusive, and that could affect their friendship. Maya would have to tread cautiously. She couldn't bear the prospect of losing such a dear friend. The irony hit Maya: she was pursuing this matter at least partly because of Veen and yet couldn't be straight with her.

'Would you like to wander up to Revenge, get your blood sugar up?' Maya asked.

'Oh, yes. They have the best fucking bread pudding in town. Just wish the bowl was bigger.'

'Do you know their secret?'

Veen winked at Maya. 'Not arsenic, I hope.'

'No, brioche,' Maya replied, noting Veen's odd humor.

Maya eased into the flow of traffic. Within minutes, she pulled up to the curb in front of the bakery, elated to find an empty spot to park in. She turned the ignition off.

Veen squinted at a pedestrian through the passenger window. 'Holy shit.'

Maya peered out through the windshield to see a familiar male figure on the sunlit sidewalk; she fell back on her seat.

Detective Justin, lanky and informal in denim jeans and a blue sweatshirt, walked toward them on the sidewalk. Maya snapped her attention away from her former lover. For an instant, her insides did a dance as she imagined what his reaction might be upon bumping into the two of them. It had happened once before, at the same haunt, in the earlier days of their courtship. *Maya!* he'd exclaimed, hurrying over to her, his eyes softening. *What a pleasant surprise*. He'd said a warm hello to Veen, joined them for tea and bread pudding, and the three of them had spent the afternoon in lively conversation. But this time, on second thought, she had reservations about engaging with him. It wasn't only because of her last encounter with him at his house, but also the way he'd left her so many months ago.

'Oh, it's Justin,' Maya said casually.

A shadow crossed Veen's face. 'Look – he's with somebody.'

Maya had only noticed handsome Justin. *You mustn't use tunnel vision when you're casing*, Justin used to say. Now her gaze locked onto his companion: a young Eurasian woman, no more than twenty and flat-out pretty, even though her hair was uncombed and she appeared to be helpless, troubled and needy.

'Oh, she could be a colleague at the police station.' It didn't escape Maya's attention that Justin was keenly aware of his companion. Even from inside the car, Maya could see how he drunk in her words as she giggled at his side and swung her arms. Although the bulge in his pocket indicated he was carrying a gun, his detective eyes weren't scoping out the place, and this a man whose philosophy had always been: *Always know where you're at*. Instead, he clasped her hand, smiled with delight and, after jerking the bakery door open, placed his hand on the small of her back.

A heavy black curtain dropped before Maya; it darkened her senses. She fought the urge to start her car and dash off to another café. She was about to suggest this when Veen hopped out of the car, saying, 'I'm curious. Come. Let's be detectives ourselves.'

Reluctantly, not wanting the strong-willed, confident Veen to see how shaken she was, Maya followed her friend. They swung the door of the bakery slightly ajar and watched Justin lead his companion to a table on the right. He sat opposite her, leaned in and spoke. She planted a small kiss on his lips. He leaned toward her solicitously.

Maya drew in a breath; a stabbing pain in her heart choked her.

Her forehead settling into a frown, a note of apology in her voice, Veen whispered intently, 'Shall we go someplace else?'

'Sure.'

They walked back to the car. Pulling out onto the main road, Maya gave herself a pep talk. *Nothing has been lost, Maya. He's now only a ghost in your life. You're doing fine without him, just fine.* As she drove through thick traffic, Maya silently argued with herself. Why shouldn't Justin date other women? He was young, still under forty and handsome, was he not? He had a winning personality, had he not? She struggled through a few turbulent 'yes, but' moments until a scene from the past surfaced in her mind.

They'd been seeing each other for about two years then. On that evening, he'd come back to her after work, making excuses about being so late, a different air about him. There had been many other troubling signs. On that three-quarter-moon night she couldn't take it any longer; the ache inside had made her feel like she was about to burst. Her assertiveness winning out, she'd sat him down in her living room to have a heart-to-heart. 'We need to talk.'

He'd looked up at her for a moment, as though he'd been expecting this, and given her a wordless nod. The frustrations she'd kept bottled inside poured out, all the neglect, all the 'why's,' the accumulation of sadness congested in her chest. As though swept up in a wave of power, she sat boldly, her back straight.

Head down, glassy-eyed, he'd listened without denying, arguing or confessing that he was cheating on her. In the end, he'd stood up and shot out the door, not listening to her call from behind and stealing all the light from the room.

Veen broke her trance. 'What the hell is Justin doing with that broad? She's cute but too young for him to fancy her. And did you notice how she walked? She's probably a hooker. He dumped you for someone like that?'

Oh, Veen, do you always have to say it like it is? Still, something nagged at Maya's spirit. She called up the scene in the bakery to double-check her own impressions, hating herself for being so judgmental. Justin's companion . . . Although animated in his company and kissy-faced, she appeared to be what some might call a lost soul. Beautiful and dangerous. Veen was right. It grated on Maya that Justin would shower his loser of a date with so much care and attention. Just now Maya had detected a different side to Justin. It was as though he'd made a commitment to her, something he'd been unable to do with Maya.

'He could be faking the relationship,' Maya said, knowing that was unlikely. 'She might mean nothing to him.' If Justin was undercover, he would stay clear of places where he could bump into people who might recognize him. Still, she ventured, 'She could be an informant or a cousin?'

'Informant? Backseat of the police car type of informant? Cousin? Pardon my bluntness, Maya, but you could see for yourself he wasn't treating her like his little sister.'

Maya concentrated on the river of traffic around them, waves of cars merging and separating, reckless, speedy and uncaring, while raindrops struck the road like a thousand little slaps on the face. 'Where to?' she finally asked.

'Well, I thought a cup of tea would make me feel whole.' Veen watched Maya's face. 'Now I'd like to get fucking high. Dang, my back hurts. Shall we hit the happy hour someplace before it gets any crazier?'

'I don't see why not.' After this downer, a drink, a dim room and the sound of boozy laughter sounded like a spa visit. Maya sailed into the traffic.

THIRTEEN

A day later, at about 9:45 a.m., Maya was weaving through the streets of the bustling Lake City neighborhood, a few errands in mind, when she got a call from Hank. It had to be about Ivan. In the days that had passed since the deaths, she'd spent time on Ivan's trail. He seemed to frequent Betty's Breakfast on Northeast 45th Street, a tip she'd passed on to Hank. Noting the urgency in Hank's voice, she pulled over to the curb.

'Ivan and his best bud showed themselves at Betty's this morning, as expected,' Hank said. 'I eavesdropped on their chit-chat. Kinda cool. I sort of got that Ivan had heard something terrible is going to happen today at ten o'clock at the intersection of Bryant Lane and Woodview Place. The dudes spoke a mixture of English and Russian. I didn't get everything but Ivan mentioned that intersection more than once.'

Maya's shoulders shook. She studied her watch. She had fifteen minutes. 'That's where the meditation center is located. I'm not too far from it – I'll head over there pronto.'

'I could be wrong – you don't have to rush like that. I'm new at this and just in case it's risky to—'

She'd brave it out. 'No, no, I can't take a chance on this.'

'Call me if you need any help – OK?'

Maya made a U-turn, drove, found a space and parked two blocks from the meditation center. She'd checked out the place once before: a single-story, flat-roof building painted white.

Annexed to the north end of the building was a small square parking lot, empty of vehicles. On the sidewalk bordering the lot, a crowd of about ten people had gathered. A young Caucasian woman stood alone on a mat at the center of the lot.

Heart beating faster, Maya watched her. The dark-haired, dark-eyed, late-thirties woman wore a white robe; a matching scarf embroidered with a lily design partially covered her head.

Recent events swam before Maya's eyes.

Oh my God! Oh my God! Not again.

Maya stepped aside, rummaged through her purse to retrieve her cellphone and dialed 911. She kept herself calm as she recited the address to the dispatch, explained the situation and insisted that help be sent without delay.

Voice barely audible, the woman, still standing on the mat, delivered a speech. 'I'm here to protest against the unbearable situation in Tibet . . .'

The crowd listened to her in rapt attention. In between conveying to the dispatcher, once again, the urgency of the situation, Maya kept an eye on the woman.

'Tibet, my love . . . Sylvie and Anna, your fiery passion burns in my soul.'

A petrol canister, partly hidden under a towel, sat next to the woman.

Jaw stiffening, gritting her teeth, terminating the call with the dispatch, Maya made her way to the front row. *There's still time.*

The woman bent down.

Tiny black dots danced before Maya's vision. 'Please, don't!' she shouted as she raced to the woman. 'Please.'

A man disengaged from the crowd as if to join her. But it was too late.

The woman had already poured liquid from the canister over her head and her clothing. She held what resembled a matchbox in her other hand.

'Sylvie and Anna, my sisters, I join you,' she uttered. A small scraping sound, a flickering light and fire leapt out hungrily.

A fitful breeze picked up.

The flame swirling about her, screaming from the pain, the woman collapsed on the mat.

The crowd gasped. A passing car honked. Maya had seen this before, not long ago, when Sylvie and Anna died so tragically. This time, Maya wouldn't be helpless. She took her cotton jacket off. She sprinted forward, dodging the crowd and, ignoring all the warnings, threw her jacket over the burning woman. She watched the jacket smother the flames. *How long before the firemen arrive?*

Grayish smoke rose, even as the air heated up, striking Maya's face and suffocating her. She couldn't move.

The wailing of a siren pierced the air and startled Maya. She took a few steps back. A fire truck, followed by an emergency medical van, pulled up to the curb. Two firemen jumped out and quickly doused the fire with their extinguishers.

After checking the woman's vital signs, they gently lifted her onto a stretcher, then into the van.

'Will she be all right?' Maya asked a fireman, wiping off her sweaty temples with a hand.

'Let's hope so,' he mumbled, without looking at her.

Two hours later, Maya sat with Hank in the back room of her office. With the memories of the morning's tragedy still so excruciating, she'd double-locked the front door, cancelled a meeting with a vendor who'd offered her a special deal with surveillance video cameras and neglected to return a call from Uma.

'Hey, you look shaky,' Hank said. 'Next time, I'll come with you to where it's happening.'

'No, you stay here or tail Ivan.' Hank, who had offered her half of his caprese sandwich, tossed the plastic wrapper into the waste can. He plowed through the food, but Maya could barely pick up her portion of the sandwich or stir her tea.

'Thanks for sharing,' she said.

Hank's slender fingers picked up the remnant of a piece of flatbread. 'I'm a wordsmith and wordsmiths are always ravenous.'

Maya mentally logged a note to invite Hank for dinner at a future date. 'Let's check the news, shall we?'

They browsed the latest headlines on her iPad.

THIRD PUBLIC SUICIDE ATTEMPT
ROCKS SEATTLE

According to a police spokesman, the latest self-immolator has been identified as Tara Martin, age thirty-six, the former owner of a beauty parlor, Salon Martin. She's being treated for severe burns at Harborview Medical Center, where her condition is reported to be critical. Investigators found a suicide note in her apartment, which stated it was her own decision to end her life. Martin, who lived alone, suffered from bipolar disorder. In the opinion of her sister, Daniella Martin, Tara had made previous attempts. 'She felt terrible and wanted to escape the pain. She couldn't function. Even sold her hair-dressing salon, which had loyal customers. She didn't have anything to live for.'

The police spokesman declined to couple this incident with the recent fiery deaths of Sylvie Burton and Anna Kamala, although some of the public remain suspicious.

Maya shrank against her chair. 'Sylvie got her hair cut at Salon Martin. My guess is that Tara Martin, the original owner of that salon, chose the meditation center as her site in Sylvie's memory. Much as I wanted to, I couldn't stop Tara. Severe burns can be fatal.'

'But you called nine-one-one.'

'Still, it tears me apart, this cluster of suicides. Let's concentrate on Ivan. How did he know about the incident ahead of time? Might he also have been a client at Salon Martin? Did Tara tip him off, perhaps inadvertently?'

'What will you do?' Hank asked.

'I'll go visit that salon in a day or so when things have calmed down a bit. Now tell me about Ivan's personal pal. What's he like?'

'Couldn't get a good look at him without being obvious. I think I've seen him once before near the gym, meeting Ivan. I parked myself at a nearby table at Betty's, with my back to them, and buried myself in my tablet. Only once did I turn around. I got that he's of South-Asian origin, most likely from India, Bangladesh or Sri Lanka. I had many friends in college from that part of the world and can spot them. Ivan's bud spoke both English and Russian fluently. How did he learn Russian? I'm jealous. I'm no good at languages. Anyway, he's smart, hunky and acts like he owns the world. Has a stylish "do" – you should see it: a shiny pomp, the job of a blow-dryer and gels. He checked out the women. Paid the bill.'

'Did he wear sunglasses?' Maya asked.

'No.'

'Name?'

'Didn't get that, either.'

Maya asked Hank to track down Padmaraja, Tara Martin and Ivan Dunn online and even search court filings.

'Will do,' Hank said. 'Ivan is still giving me pointers on swimming at the gym. There I'm known as Henry. The lessons are so exhausting that at night I'm swept away by slumber like driftwood on the shore.'

Maya laughed, then rose from her chair. 'How's your latest short story coming along?'

'My shitty first draft – it's a real struggle.' Hank's face clouded. 'When I workshopped it in my class last week, the comments I got were it needed a beginning hook. Should I have a *hara-kiri* in my first sentence? It's a relationship story with a hot Japanese babe as the protagonist and change agent.'

'Well, I'd stay away from an actual homicide. What if you

had something like . . . If looks could strangle, he would have already been lying in his coffin?'

'Mind if I use that sentence? It's the next level. Thanks, Maya.'

FOURTEEN

The same day at four o'clock sharp, Maya answered the buzzer, feeling rather frazzled after the morning's incident. Atticus stood, stiff and gloomy, dressed in a cotton shirt and khakis but without his crutches. Maya wondered if he'd gotten the terrible news. Why else wouldn't this gorgeous day put a smile on the dour man's face? He'd confessed the other day he'd be ecstatic to get rid of the crutches. He'd sounded interested and delighted over the phone to receive an invitation to tea at her house. And he'd also said, in a gushing manner, how he couldn't wait to meet Maya's mother since they hailed from the same state in India.

Maya welcomed him and steered him to the side yard. Fenced on three sides, it was furnished with a marble-topped picnic table and a set of vintage chairs. The space buzzed with pink and gold-tinted perennials, although a strong wind earlier had caused most of the petals to drop. 'My mother should be along shortly.'

Atticus settled himself across from Maya. 'This morning, the doctor examined me, announced I'd healed well and removed the cast. I'd have waltzed, except I don't dance. To be able to walk on my own two feet, without those damn crutches . . . I only wish my apartment hadn't been burgled.'

'What? What happened?'

'I got home and got a shock when I found the door unlocked. The intruders went through my stuff but didn't take my computer, the sitar or my cash. I'd have thought it was my goddamn neighbors' kids, except they smashed my guru's photograph on the wall, as though they had a grudge against him. It's like they smashed my chest.'

Maya pondered for a moment. 'Whoever broke in could

possibly have planted a monitoring device in your apartment. Have you checked?'

'Goodness gracious. How do I find it?'

'I'll have Hank run you through the bug detector procedure. And I'll personally follow up with you.'

The back door creaked. Maya's gaze drifted over to Uma. Carrying a tray, she had popped out of the house and was approaching them. Maya made the introductions.

Atticus folded his hands and bowed slightly. 'My great pleasure to meet you, Mrs Mallick.'

Uma, dignified in her voluminous white sari, uttered a greeting, folded herself into a chair across from Atticus and began pouring *chai*. Hand steady, her opal ring glinting in the sunlight, Uma asked about his family in India. The smile of warm reception she wore suggested she would like nothing better than to hear about the past and present of this new acquaintance. Maya excused herself, went back inside, called Hank and returned, only to find Uma and Atticus chatting like relatives. They did so over honey-colored *chai* and a stack of syrupy, pretzel-shaped, orange *jalebis*. Atticus, now warmed to Uma's motherly gestures, addressed her as *Mashima*, aunt-mother.

'So, I suppose this isn't one of your meditation days?' Maya asked, leading the discussion in the direction she wanted.

Atticus picked up the floral-patterned throw pillow on the empty chair beside him and patted it. 'No sitting this week. Our guru has cancelled all the sessions for the first time.'

'Does it have anything to do with another self-immolation in our fair city?' Maya asked and checked Atticus' reactions.

The light in Atticus' eyes grew dimmer; his voice had an edge of fright. 'You already heard about it?'

'Actually, I was there.' She spilled the story, once again feeling the horror and the fear. 'Strange – it happened on the parking lot of your meditation center.'

'You're asking why did she pick that site? I have no idea. Goddamned timing. I wanted to rush over there but stopped myself. What would be the point? The police would have cordoned off the place and my presence would have aroused suspicion.'

'Are you involved in this in any way, Atticus?'

'Absolutely not. Neither is our guru.'

Uma sat rigid, then rose. 'Excuse me a minute. I'll check the latest developments.' She moseyed off toward the back door, quite the tablet addict these days.

Maya kept her eyes steady on Atticus. 'Does Tara Martin, by any chance, belong to your meditation group?'

'Thank the heavens, she doesn't. I called our administrative staff. They checked their records. No one has ever heard of her.' Atticus picked up his teacup but didn't sip from it. 'No meditation contact. Like Sylvie's death, which had no association to our center.'

'Not everyone is so sure. I've had a couple of visits with Ivan Dunn.' As Maya spoke, she heard Ivan's cold, hard, accusatory tone, saw the rigidity of his face. 'He told me of his complaint to the authorities that the guru is the guilty party and should be investigated in connection to Sylvie's death.'

'Let me get this straight.' Atticus' eyes flared up and it looked as though he might drop the teacup. 'Ivan, the hoodlum, tried to pin something on our beloved master? How dare he? Our guru is as pure as you can get and still live in the material world.'

'Look, after a few incidents like this, spread only a couple of weeks apart—'

'You're not sold, I can see that, but it's the truth.'

'Ivan had the opportunity to observe Sylvie's behavior, if not in her last days, at least in the weeks before. To my knowledge, more than anyone else, he'd been around Sylvie during that period. The sad picture he painted of her—'

'You trust that pretty boy? He's seen with all kinds of women.'

She didn't trust Ivan but decided to play the devil's advocate to find out as much about him as possible. 'If you have any proof about the pretty boy's untrustworthiness in other matters, I'll be all ears.'

'His mother is Russian, for God's sake, and he speaks the language. He could very well be mates with the bastards who beat me up. Those guys looked like bodybuilders, too, and spoke with a Russian accent.'

Again, she'd take the opposing viewpoint. 'I happened to have looked up the Russian population on the Internet after meeting Ivan. Ten thousand of them live here in Seattle. It's indeed very possible that there's no relation between Ivan and your assailants.'

'So you've also fallen for that bad boy?'

'No. What else can you tell me?'

Atticus tipped himself back. 'That good-for-nothing guy wasn't worthy of Sylvie. She went downhill after she met him. It was hard to watch. Sylvie, usually the quietest person, always in control, started to get moody, then began to drink heavily. At first, I assumed it was job stress. I asked her. She said no – her work was going fine. She even confided in me about the breakthrough she'd made with her malaria research after years of hard work. No vaccine currently exists but she'd come up with a low-cost one, if the trials were successful. That was as much as she'd reveal to me.'

Since she worked for Atticus, Maya would reveal a bit more. 'At least one trial *was* successful. I've heard that Anna Kamala, a trial participant, didn't catch the disease.'

'Truly?' Atticus said. 'A successful trial would have been a major career boost for Sylvie. As a scientist responsible for the vaccine, she wasn't allowed to be part of the trial. She could only be told of the final result. So job stress is only a milder possibility. What's left? Relationship. And that sure as hell makes Ivan, the pretty boy, of interest.'

'I'd still like to have a private audience with your guru, if you could kindly arrange that. In view of this new tragedy, it's extremely urgent—'

Uma had walked back to the yard. She interrupted Maya and said to Atticus, 'Especially since your guru is in the hot seat.'

'He sure is,' Atticus said. 'Yesterday, when driving to a relative's house, a rare time when he was alone, he had the impression a man was on his tail, keeping an eye on his movements.'

'Police surveillance, perhaps?' Maya said. 'Or someone else who has a stake in this matter? So . . . when can I see him?'

'That's absurd, Maya. I can't ask the guru to bend his schedule.'

'Please,' Maya continued, 'I might be in a position to help the guru.' Fleetingly, Maya envisioned Detective Justin and his woman companion inside Revenge, wrapped in a cocoon of cozy intimacy. She wavered between phoning Justin to offer him new evidence and never speaking to him again.

'I'll see what I can do,' Atticus said.

'Are there protocols I should follow when I visit the guru?' Maya asked.

'Oh, yes. Wear white, cover your hair with a white scarf and bring an offering of fresh flowers, if you would.'

'What flower is his favorite?' Uma asked.

'White lilies.'

Maya was on edge as she pictured the delicate lily garland around Sylvie's neck and the lily-printed scarf on Tara Martin's head. She held her tongue and looked toward the flower patch to her right, her gaze caught by the pure, distinctive, vase-shaped blooms of white calla lilies.

Atticus got up from his chair, offered Uma his gratitude for the tea, then turned to Maya. 'More points of protocol for when you meet with the guru. Listen, be respectful and please don't probe.'

Easily done, except for the probing part, with another young life lost in the flames.

FIFTEEN

The next morning, at 8 a.m., Maya walked into Betty's, a cozy, informal café with light green textured walls, a tiled floor and high noise level. A whiff of freshly baked cinnamon rolls emanated from the pastry case. In the past few days, she'd stopped by here on several occasions during the hours when she knew Ivan would be at work. Her aim had been to check out his Russian-speaking friend, who also apparently patronized this place.

Maya got a cup of oolong from the counter and looked around for an empty table; there were none. Aware that communal seating was encouraged, she looked for unoccupied chairs. She spotted several at a corner table for four, where a man sat alone, his laptop and a journal open before him.

Tanned and handsome, he fit the description Hank had provided. He must be Ivan's friend. Finally.

'Mind if I sit here?' she asked.

He looked up, taking in as much about her as he possibly could, and gave her the grace of a nod. The even-featured mid-thirties man, with a honey-maple complexion, had probing eyes conveying confidence. Those eyes even had a little mischief thrown in for balance.

She put on a charming smile and took the farthest chair. 'How can you concentrate with so much noise around?'

'Oh, I'm used to it.' Voice smooth and confident, he had an aristocratic air about him. 'I come from a large, extended family. Never had a quiet moment growing up. Noise actually concentrates my mind.'

She moistened her mouth with a tiny sip from her cup and glanced at the journal next to him. 'Looks rather scientific.'

'You got it. I work in a scientific field. Hope that doesn't turn you off.'

She laughed. 'Not at all. I find it rather fascinating. This is my clumsy way of asking, but are you suggesting that science, at least the public perception of it, could use an injection of human feelings?'

'Well put.' His animated eyes fully on her, he smiled: teeth like white petals, cheeks high and radiant. 'Science is not divorced from human emotions. I, for example, am at my best when surrounded by beauty and light.'

She blushed, smiled awkwardly and admitted to herself that she found him intriguing.

'I haven't seen you here before,' he said. 'Are you visiting?'

'No, I'm a Seattleite.'

'I'm from Moscow. Isn't it amazing the extraordinary coincidences that bring two people together?'

'So you think our meeting is not a random event?'

'Quite the opposite, speaking hypothetically, of course.' His cellphone trilled. His expression changed to one of concern. 'Pardon me. This is an important call. I have to take it.' He sprang to his feet and hastened toward the back entrance.

Frustration surfed through her. She could have used a bit more chit-chat to get a fix on him but best not to linger; she didn't want to reveal her identity. Quick on her feet, she exited the restaurant and breathed deeply only when she'd driven several blocks. She now had somewhat of a picture of Ivan's charming co-conspirator; a feeling of unease shook her.

Around 10:30 a.m., she arrived at her next destination, Salon Martin. On this, her first visit, she needed to poke around a bit. The high-end, unisex beauty salon boasted a long, narrow room. Minimalist, with stark white walls and a wood-laminated floor, it had an orange-accented color theme. A row of styling stations, separated by huge planters, stood empty. The faint sound of a solo jazz drummer provided energetic background music.

Maya stepped in, walked past a couch and greeted Cindy King, the owner who stood at the reception desk. A stocky, forty-something woman, gentle-eyed but seemingly dispirited, Cindy led Maya to the shampooing station in the back. As warm water flowed through her hair and a herbal fragrance permeated the air, Maya, now in a reclining position, refreshed the facts in her mind. Cindy, an employee, had bought this salon from Tara Martin, the original owner who suffered from mental illness. An image of Tara, who had set herself alight and died yesterday, as reported by the media, flickered in Maya's mind.

Fifteen minutes later, Maya sat in an orange leather chair in the main room, her body covered by a black nylon cape, hair damp, soft and shiny in the large mirror affixed to the wall. At Cindy's question, she indicated her preference for an understated, chin-length bob, no color change and no bangs. Cindy sectioned her hair. Wrapping each section in a big roller, she pulled out a pair of scissors and held them at a forty-five-degree angle over Maya's head.

'We begin our "snip tour"!' Maya said.

Amid the snipping sound of the scissors, Cindy made a cut across a section. 'One of my clients used to say that. Anna Kamala. Did you know her?'

Maya gave a nod.

'What a sweetheart she was. I simply don't get it. How in the world?' Cindy sounded as though she spoke through a tightened throat. 'I bought this shop, thinking . . . I don't know what I was thinking. Now I am simply going insane. Some mornings I can't even get up.'

Yes, three suicides, connected to this salon. Maya sighed. 'Did you style Sylvie's hair, too?'

'Who are you?' Cindy stepped back and examined Maya's face. 'Why are you asking all these questions? And I really must be nuts, or else why am I answering you?'

'I'm a private investigator. My job requires talking and feeling my way into situations. I'm digging into the deaths.'

'Oh my God, a P.I.? Do you carry a gun? I don't allow guns here. And shouldn't I exercise my Miranda rights and not speak with you without lawyering up first? You have to leave. Right now. No charge.'

'Hey, I can't go out like this with wet hair. And no, I don't carry a gun. Look, you have nothing to hide and, believe me, I'm on your side. My investigation can only throw light on why Tara chose that particular path. Don't you want to understand her motivation? Aren't you curious about why Tara's customers are cancelling their appointments? Wouldn't you like to see your new business take off? Calm down and finish the cut.'

'I'm sorry.' Cindy resumed cutting, her eyes round in sadness. 'I'm under a lot of stress. I'm taking medication for depression. Sometimes I think I'm going to faint. You're right – I'd like to be able to make a go of this new business. I want Tara's clients to come back.'

'Was Sylvie a client of this shop?'

'Yes, Tara did her hair. I met her at our Christmas party.' Cindy picked up a spray bottle of water to further wet Maya's tresses. 'A lovely young woman – Sylvie had ace hair. Every year Tara threw a Christmas party here for our clients. A hustler, she was. They all came. We'd drink punch, eat truffles and yak all evening.'

'Did Sylvie and Anna become acquainted here?'

'Yes, hon, quite often they'd make pedicure appointments together. Gave them a chance to catch up. They were different, though. Sylvie dressed like a million bucks and was more confident. Anna was shyer, less upfront, less talkative. But you couldn't miss the sisterly chumminess they had between them.'

That confirmed Maya's suspicion: Sylvie and Anna had formed a bond at this beauty parlor, a place where both came to unwind, perhaps at first ignorant of each other's involvement in the malaria trial. She kept listening.

'Tara jokingly called this salon her Not-So-Lonely Hearts Club.' Cindy, smiling, gripped her shears tightly. 'I called it Styling Plus.'

Yet another point of interest, this being a unisex salon. 'Did Ivan Dunn ever get his hair cut here?'

'Oh, quite regularly. He was Tara's buddy and confidant.' Cindy stopped working and looked Maya full in the face. 'You've met Ivan?'

Glancing at Cindy's face, Maya saw a flicker of her interest in the man. Ivan was, after all, a 'looker.' 'No, I knew him only as Sylvie's partner. Does he, by any chance, still patronize this place?'

'He did have a cut recently. Acted a bit cagey. Would hardly say a word. It's not like I had designs on him. I got a splitting headache when he left.'

'Are any of Ivan's friends also customers of yours?'

'No, but they might have been Tara's.'

As Cindy did the blowout and final styling, she spoke more about her health concerns. Frequent headaches, lack of appetite, insomnia and a feeling of desperation.

Maya suggested the name of her physician, Dr Moore, and urged Cindy to make an appointment with him.

At Cindy's request, Maya checked her final do in the mirror. Her face had more definition now and her hair was bouncier. And she'd received some valuable feedback. She paid with her credit card, wished Cindy well and promised to return.

Yet for the rest of the day, as she went about her business, she couldn't forget Cindy's distressed face.

SIXTEEN

How did the media react to the latest attempted self-immolation? The next morning, in her office, Maya opened a related article on her iPad.

Hank swung into the office, greeted her and put his coffee cup down on her desk. 'What are you up to?'

'Reading blogs, posts and editorials on the topic of political suicides.' She elaborated: an op-ed piece had disclosed that, to date, there had been more than one hundred political suicides in Tibet. The world media played it up for a while and Tibet-sympathizers mourned, but then it was back to business as usual.

'Are you saying these suicides are symptoms?'

'Yes, they're symptoms, not causes, of extreme public dissatisfaction. The same goes for self-harm, which is a topic of interest here, too.' Maya pointed to a piece and they browsed it together. Gavin Kerr, a suicidologist, stated that over 30,000 Americans commit suicide each year. More than three times as many people try but do not succeed. Reasons for such attempts? Pet theories abound: desperation, isolation, lack of joy, life gone out of whack, possibly even societal breakdown.

Maya stopped reading and thought out loud. 'Generalities aside, I still wonder why Sylvie and Anna pursued that path. And what made Tara Martin follow their example. Not for the first time, I wonder about a third party being involved.'

'I'm a bit stymied myself.' Hank proceeded to lay out the details of his legwork. The Facebook accounts of both women had been removed, leaving hardly any clues as to their social lives. The rapidity with which this had occurred had left him profoundly suspicious. Also, he'd called various members of the meditation center but received no new dope. And when he tried to make an appointment for Maya at the research lab where Sylvie worked, they wouldn't consent, for security reasons.

Hank moved his cup closer to him; his eyes became wistful. 'When Sophie and I met for tea yesterday, I talked to her about this. She's a psych major. She said, "Now you're acting less like a me-me-me-and-my-short-stories kid, less thirsty, and more like a grown-up. You're binge-watching less, too." She seriously thinks this job has been the best thing for me. Do you think I'm adulting?'

A sensitive, intelligent face, tender eyes and an eager expression of a millennial. How Maya wished Hank and Sophie would get back together. She examined Hank's face with mock seriousness. 'Yeah, I think you are.'

Hank rose and went to his desk at the back office. Maya reviewed her notes on the case and called her boss in Kolkata, who worked late in the evening.

'Yes, Maya, tell me,' Simi Sen said.

'They might seem unrelated but this is what we have in our hands.' Maya ran through the salient points: two fiery deaths and now a copycat third; Atticus' friendship with Sylvie, which, according to him, led to his brush with gangsters; an unobtrusive single woman named Anna, her voluntary role in the malaria trial and her suspicious romantic relationship with an unknown party; how Sylvie's research had led to a secretive malaria trial conducted by Cal and participated by Anna.

'Are you saying Sylvie and/or her malaria vaccine is a potential link to all these?'

'Precisely.'

'It's like peeling an onion,' Sen said. 'You cry sometimes.' She wished Maya a restful weekend.

On this bright Sunday morning, Maya finished her bowl of oatmeal and got up from her breakfast nook. With Uma attending a traditional Indian wedding ceremony in Redmond, she was free to spend the day as she pleased. As she stood in front of her dressing table and combed her hair, she thought of Justin. On Sunday mornings he usually lounged on his lawn, sunning himself, and leisurely browsed the newspaper. She had an absurd urge to see him, to hear more about the coroner's report. Surely he'd be more relaxed and they might actually have a productive conversation.

She got into her car and started driving. She was still half a block from Justin's house when she noticed a blonde getting into a Chevy Impala parked ahead. Even from a distance, Maya recognized Justin's new companion. Only days ago, she'd spied her accompanying Justin to Revenge. Hands intertwined, they'd acted like an intimate couple. Now Maya watched her from the back. The blonde took a minute to settle herself, then pulled away from the curb, leaving a parking space for Maya. But no, Maya would not take that space.

She'd had a change of heart. On impulse, she decided to follow the woman, allowing a car between them. Her pulse raced with the excitement of the chase. The blonde did a few rights and lefts, then headed north and eventually arrived at the fenced parking lot of a school building. On this Sunday, the open-air spot had been converted to a flea market bustling with bargain hunters.

The blonde pulled into the last available space on the street. Maya drove around for a few minutes until she found parking on a side street, then walked to the flea market, only to have lost sight of her target. Well, she told herself, she'd keep looking.

She meandered through the narrow aisles and idled before a messy antiques stall to lose herself for a few minutes and check out the merchandize. Her hobby of collecting antique teacups had helped her heal after the heartbreak caused by her split with Justin. For weeks afterwards she'd scour estate sales, thrift shops and antiques stores, spending hours scrutinizing a cup from different angles under different lighting conditions. She would check the size of a teapot, which must have the capacity to hold enough tea for her guests – four to six, usually.

Now she checked a chipped cream-and-sugar set in a purple violet bouquet pattern; a somewhat discolored gold-plated tea service with missing pieces and an overly modern Japanese red cast-iron teapot. None of these suited her.

Her eyes searched for Justin's new girlfriend as she resumed her walk. She passed a series of food hawkers who offered popcorn, pretzels, frozen yogurt and oversized chocolate chip cookies. Beyond these vendors stood a gazebo where a band played a lively folk tune. She people-watched for a moment, smelling both salt and sugar, her attention caught by an ice-cream-happy mob that were hustling about a stall.

Finally she spotted the blonde, lingering to the right of the stall, and walked toward her. Up close the long-limbed, young Eurasian woman had slanted eyes and golden skin. Her ancestry covered a lot of geography, of that much Maya was sure. Dressed in ill-fitted sweats, her long hair uncombed, she stared at nothing in particular. Belatedly, Maya noticed the baby in her arms.

The boy, about five months old, wearing a blue body suit and red booties, waved his arm at Maya. She took the opportunity to sidle up to the mother, smiled and said above the overlapping chatter of shoppers, 'What a cute baby!'

The blonde tilted her head and smiled. Her face softening, she nuzzled him. 'My first time – so nice, this market.' Obviously foreign-born and not quite at ease, she seemed to struggle to get the words and sentiment out in English.

Maya looked around. Her gaze floated to the smiling boy with kicking legs and her insides went still. He, with the sweetest of faces, was a replica of Justin – the same impenetrable blue eyes and cheekbones, and a nose that didn't vie for attention. Even the smile matched that of Justin when he was pleasantly astonished. 'What's his name?'

The woman fixed her proud eyes on her child. 'Justin, Junior. My son like outside. So we come out.'

The name lashed at Maya. Justin, supposedly a bachelor, had a son? Maya did the math. The boy must have been born when she and Justin were still seeing each other. And the boy's mother, this woman standing in front of Maya – what sort of an involvement did she have with Justin? Although Justin moved in a different social circle, he still hung around with two guys who had approached Maya, when she worked as a nutritionist, for advice on weight-loss. Neither had mentioned him getting hitched.

Had her relationship with Justin been a complete lie? Had Maya been only a sideshow? Her eyes scanned the surroundings. No trace of the man yet. Would he soon appear? *How could you do this to me?* Maya wanted to scream.

The blonde studied her. Maya recovered and introduced herself by her last name, Mallick, then regretted it. What happened to her P.I. instincts? What if the woman mentioned her to Justin and described her? Mallick: five foot four, dark hair and dark eyes, dressed in the same white tunic and black pants she'd worn a hundred times with Justin. What if the woman had already heard Maya's name?

'My name is Jennifer,' the woman said hesitantly.

An adopted name, Maya could tell; a name that was a mask or a robe, a substitute, not a flesh-and-bone, blood-and-guts type of identification. A different person resided in the inner recesses of her mind – a person born and brought up elsewhere, whose name at birth was not Jennifer.

Plump-cheeked, with a thatch of blond hair, the boy again smiled at Maya. 'Such a sweet smile,' she said. 'His father must dote on him.'

What a silly thing to say. How revealing it might be to someone who wasn't as clueless as this Jennifer. Then again, was she so clueless? On a closer look, her eyes appeared to be full of guile. Maya mentally pointed a finger at Jennifer, a woman who did whatever it took to get what she hungered for, using beauty, sex and charmingly poor English. Except a wedding band, that is. She wore only a jade ring on her middle finger and somehow that helped Maya cope better.

'His daddy like to play with him.' Turning to the boy, her voice buttery-soft, Jennifer said, 'Dada come soon, take us to park.'

The boy stared at Maya for a long beat and grunted. 'He like you,' Jennifer said.

Emotions tore through Maya. One minute, she adored Justin Jr and couldn't take her eyes off him; the next minute she couldn't bear to look at him. The boy, displaying an expression of tenderness and kicking his legs, reminded her that a child much like him could have been hers. How Maya would have liked to hold her own baby to her breast, place the pillow of her cheek against his satin hair and smell the milky sweetness of his skin. She glanced at Jennifer. However down-and-out in appearance, she was younger, taller, prettier and luckier than Maya, and she had this lovable child by Justin. Maya hadn't known she was fighting in a battle all along – one she had lost.

She shuffled her feet. She shouldn't linger just in case Justin showed up. She wouldn't be able to look him in the eye. Yet she couldn't help but risk one last question to Jennifer. 'Oh, there are so many great parks in Seattle.'

'We like Golden Gardens.'

How many times had Maya accompanied Justin to that park, joining bonfire parties, grilling tofu, watching beach volleyball and listening to the surf, mindless of the itch of the sand in her shoes?

Maya jerked back. 'Enjoy the afternoon.'

Her eyes focusing on an invisible, buzzing insect, Jennifer took a step back. 'Not another mosquito.'

The word mosquito coming out of Jennifer's mouth sounded significant, but she stopped herself. A flurry of thoughts raced through Maya's head. Had her jealousy about Justin's new lover gotten out of hand? Or could there be something more sinister about Jennifer drawing her attention?

Before turning away, Maya gazed at Justin Jr one last time. His attention had shifted to a man walking with two muscular, gray-and-white Irish wolfhounds, each weighing at least a hundred pounds. Justin Jr looked down, stretched an arm out toward the creatures and let loose a happy, gurgling sound.

Maya spun around and walked away toward her car.

SEVENTEEN

'Justin called while you were in the shower,' Uma said the next morning at breakfast. She placed a platter of stuffed parathas on the table. Her gold bracelet shone against her olive skin, smooth but for a network of blue veins on her slender wrist. 'He's got the coroner's inquest. The coroner had already spoken to Veen. Knowing of your interest, Justin wanted you to hear the report, too. You can call him.'

'Be right back.' Maya stepped into the living room. A brief call to Justin brought her the news. The women were alive before the fire started. No suspected homicides. The two deaths have been called suicides from the burns.

After hanging up, Maya reclaimed her chair and served herself a *paratha* and condiments. 'I worry, really worry, Ma, that this report will give the police an excuse to close the case.'

'Well, my guess is Justin will go along with the findings of the coroner unless it's proven to him that there's more about those two "suicides." He'll, as they say, follow the party line.'

Although he'd been kind enough to make a phone call with

the coroner's conclusions, yesterday's scene at the flea market still ate away at Maya – the discovery of Justin's current lover and son. She slammed her fork down and took Uma through the sequence of events, while a sense of unease about Jennifer fluttered inside her.

Astonishment flooded Uma's face; she wound her shawl tighter around her shoulder. 'My God – Justin has a son? Well, since we don't know the full story yet, we mustn't jump to conclusions. I don't approve of him because of what he did to you. But who knows what situation he was put into due to circumstances?'

'Ma—'

'It's a gut feeling, that's all.' Uma's voice grew stronger. 'Given what you're going through, I don't blame you. But do try to feel the pressure *he's* under.'

'What pressure of his are we talking about?'

Before Maya could begin the next sentence, her cellphone vibrated from a side table. She rose, stumbled and snatched it, wondering, with a surging heart, if it might be a call from Justin. Instead, the caller ID indicated a restricted number and she caught Atticus saying a pleasant hello at the other end. She uttered a greeting.

'You don't know how lucky you are, Miss Maya.' Atticus sounded as though he was a proud messenger declaring the results of a lottery. 'Our guru has squeezed in half an hour for you at ten. He doesn't usually receive those who don't follow his discipline but it fascinated him that you were a nutritionist. He's into herbal medicine.'

'Thank you. Did you tell him that I'm working for you?'

'Not exactly.'

'You keep secrets from your guru?'

'Well, no, not usually, but in this case . . .' He paused and added, 'I must warn you – our guru is frank. You might find it hard to accept what he says.'

'Let me first hear him out. Then I'll decide if I can accept his views or not.'

'Our guru also has X-ray vision. He can take pessimism and convert it into spiritual energy. No one knows how he accomplishes that.'

Some guru. An X-ray machine. A transformer. A black box.

Atticus rattled on about the master: he spent much of his day taking solitary walks in the neighborhood and afterward praying in his house. The latest fire death in front of the meditation center had upset him considerably. He'd been praying for longer hours and receiving fewer visitors. 'Be aware also that the police might be watching all the comings and goings from his house,' Atticus added, giving her the guru's address. 'Only a guess on my part.'

Maya thanked Atticus profusely and disconnected the call. Seeing a text from Hank, she called him right away.

'OK, Maya, here it is.' Hank summarized his findings on the guru: a Tibetan, Padmaraja had been reincarnated a zillion times. In this life, he did academic studies in London, then went to India, where he studied yoga and a secular form of meditation and spirituality at the feet of a renowned master named Atman. In due time, he was entrusted with the responsibility of carrying on Atman's teachings. Following Atman's death, he roamed the globe and lectured on the benefits of gentle living, pure thinking and a consistent spiritual practice. He finally settled in Seattle, where he now had a studio: Padmaraja Meditation Center. Rather than make his teachings accessible to the general public, Padmaraja preferred the ancient Indian way of taking in a few promising students and devoting special attention to each.

'His students literally give him high marks as a spiritual master,' Hank said in conclusion. 'But his neighbors consider him quiet and secretive, maybe even a suspicious character.'

'Any parallel to your writing world?'

'Oh, yes. A scene can't be about what it appears to be about. You have to, like, dig deeper to get at what's really going on. Talk about a challenge! I go nuts trying to even figure out a character on a page, much less in real life.'

'How's it going with Sophie?'

'She's a chill girl, a puzzler to me. Hasn't returned my call offering to take her out to chow, like, in forty-eight hours. I'm going nuts, Maya.'

'I'll advocate the practice of patience, even though I don't always exercise it myself.'

'Whatever you say, boss.'

Maya hung up her cellphone and turned to Uma. 'Getting back to the guru – how might one approach a god-man?'

Uma smiled from her heart. 'Be respectful, speak little, don't ask direct questions and take a pack of paper tissues with you.'

'I'm OK with the first three, but what are the tissues for?'

'Oh, you might find yourself tearing up. That happened to me when I was introduced to a renowned mystic from Kerala whose title was Babaji. As you know, I'm not religious, nor am I the tear-shedding type. A friend who was a devotee of him had invited me to come along. I was curious and told myself to be open-minded. It was a group session, with fifty or so people crowding the room. There he was, Babaji, settled on a throne, and I could see the golden aura around him. After he gave a brief talk, we lined up in front of his throne. Each of us, in turn, was asked to step forward and face him. My turn came. I greeted him with folded hands. He blessed me by extending a hand and touching my head. Although I was in my forties then, my knees got wobbly. I stood staring at Babaji, feeling like a lost little girl, tears falling down the sides of my nose, no tissue in my purse. Babaji handed me one.'

'Mind you, Ma, I'm investigating the guru, not going for his blessings. My mission is to figure out whether he and his meditation program were behind Sylvie's suicide. You're telling me he'll reduce me to tears? That'd be perfect, just perfect.'

'I think this is the right time for you to visit Padmaraja, see if he's any good, whether for Sylvie's sake or your own. You're coming unglued, dear.'

Maya's chin dropped. How right her mother was. She was so frazzled that she had a sense of being broken into pieces.

'And remember to pick some lilies from the garden, like Atticus suggested.'

White lilies. Sylvie. Self-immolation. And now the guru?

After excusing herself, Maya retreated to her bedroom, dug through her closet, swapped her workday skirt and blazer for an eyelet white dress and wrapped a white scarf around her head. Satisfied that she'd met the guru's standards of propriety, she slipped out the back door and stepped into the yard under a sky cloaked with heavy black clouds. Her patch of white lilies emitted a sweet perfume. She snipped a few blossoms – some fully open, others still in the budding stage. For a brief moment, holding the lily bouquet, she allowed the wind to caress her face. Now breathing like a whole person, she somehow felt better about things.

EIGHTEEN

At ten minutes to ten, Maya reached Linden Avenue and turned onto the gravelly driveway of Guru Padmaraja's private residence. She must see the holy man with her own eyes and make an assessment. The two-story standard stucco, a well-maintained property set back from the street and serenely detached from the adjoining buildings, appeared solemn under a gray-purple cloud cover. The sun's harsh rays, peeking through the clouds, gave a brilliant sheen to the triangular roof.

After parking her car, Maya ventured up the brick-paved pathway across the front lawn, her instincts whispering that someone had set a tail on her. At the entrance, she stood for a moment and scanned her surroundings but, upon seeing no one, pressed the door button.

Finally, a young, wiry and expressionless man, dressed in a checked shirt and denim trousers, answered her summons. Although his bowed head initially suggested humility, he lifted his chin and appraised Maya with his coffee-tinted eyes.

'Maya Mallick. I'm here to see Guru Padmaraja.'

'Samuel.' He waved her inside and led her down a carpeted hallway.

She paused inside the doorway. Now in a watchful state, she studied the living room, struck by its simplicity and unique decor. Laid with a bluish-purple carpet, it was dominated by a raised platform illuminated by a row of candles. The platform housed a low chair, a small bowl of water and a box of tissues; shedding tears was expected.

Arranged in a semicircle around the platform was a series of low stools. The back wall, paneled in oak, was spottily drenched in daylight from an open window. Wearing a loose maroon attire, the guru emerged from a side door. Although he had to be approaching eighty, there was a bloom of color on his face as well as an overflow of vitality. Displaying grace, a warm expression and an erect bearing, he bowed gently and took the chair on the platform.

Samuel prostrated himself before the guru and touched the floor with his forehead, as though his master was a god to be worshipped. At first, Maya recoiled. She'd come here only to question the man but she mustn't offend him – how well she understood that from her childhood in Kolkata. She lowered herself and touched the floor with her head, just as Samuel had done, then rose slowly.

Samuel introduced Maya to the guru, who murmured a Sanskrit mantra and swept a hand over her head in a reassuring manner. As she extended her hand and presented the flower bouquet to him, he bent forward in a humble gesture, accepted the bouquet and his eyes took on a shine. Maya seized this opportunity to observe him more closely. Soft gray hair, as sparse as summer clouds, framed his forehead; an aura of thoughtfulness encircled him.

Samuel left the room, only to return in a second with a crystal vase filled with water. He arranged Maya's lilies in the vase and placed it on a nearby table.

The guru dipped his fingers in the bowl of water and sprinkled drops of it onto Maya's head. Then he invited her to sit. Maya's stool was so low, she could touch the floor with her hands. She felt like a lowly servant before a great king.

As Samuel took a similar stool to rest on behind her, the guru spoke in a deep voice. 'You've worked as a nutritionist. Have you ever recommended any healing plants to your clients?'

'Oh, yes, quite often.' Maya felt flattered to talk about a topic familiar to her. 'I grow some myself. Yarrow to help heal bruises, feverfew to lessen fever and stinging nettles to alleviate joint pain.'

A pleasant smile played on the guru's lips. 'You grow healing plants; I heal people. Our ways are different but we try to seek the same result.'

Speak little. Uma's voice echoed in Maya's head. Yet, given that she only had half an hour, she had to plunge into the topic of her choice. 'I suppose that is why Sylvie came to see you several weeks prior to her death.'

'Yes.' The face was cool and unperturbed. 'And I suspect you have reasons for wanting to see me, too?'

The guru's utterance cut through Maya. Although she'd come to enquire about Sylvie, if she dared to admit it, she needed healing herself to get over the agony of her severed relationship with Justin. The guru, with his keen eyes and grandfatherly presence, had set loose that issue and accompanying bleak emotions inside her. The pressure of tears behind her eyelids, she took a deep breath and tried to speak, but couldn't formulate any words. She hadn't expected to feel so humbled, to lose all control, to become once again like a child.

The perfume of the pungent incense clogged the air. The guru looked away, as though to give Maya a few moments to recover.

She steadied her feelings and spoke calmly. 'I'd like to ask what, if anything, you'd noticed about Sylvie that might have struck you as unusual before she stopped coming for meditation.'

The guru closed his eyes and went silent for a moment, as though collecting solace from within. Half a minute later, he spoke in a quiet, unwavering tone. 'You see, Maya, we live in the shadows of life. Only a thin line separates us from the light of death. You cross that line when you wish to do so. I could see in Sylvie's facial expression that she had already stepped to the other side.'

'Do you know why she made that decision? Her family can't accept that she could have wished to die. To their knowledge, her life was going superbly. It'll help me a great deal to hear—'

'The truth?' the guru said in a genial tone. 'You must understand, the words exchanged between a teacher and his disciple are private.'

Maya leaned forward, her heart thumping faster in the urgency she felt. 'As you might expect, Sylvie's family is grief-stricken. They're innocent people whose lives have been turned upside down by her death. They also feel terribly guilty for having failed her in some way. If I could appeal to your sense of compassion . . .'

Samuel cleared his throat a little forcibly. 'I'd like to answer our guest, master.'

Maya turned to face Samuel.

'Let me go back a little further.' Samuel's eyes were cool. 'Sylvie joined our group two or so years ago of her own volition, due to a friend's recommendation. She began attending our sessions and became a regular. She visited us here a number of times, whenever she wished to talk about her life issues in private. Then one day she left us – that was her decision, too.' His tone turned condescending. 'We're not a political organization. We don't discuss China or Tibet. Neither are we a religion, and we don't provide psychiatric assistance. We simply sit and meditate for personal growth and world peace. Our meditation practice and those suicides are not linked.'

Why should I believe you? Maya looked back up at the guru again. 'Please think back to the stories of trouble Sylvie might have taken to you. Given that you're from Tibet, I'd imagine, Sylvie would have expressed her feelings of distress about the condition of her motherland.'

'I mourn the loss of Sylvie.' The guru's voice was drenched with sadness. 'And I see what you're going through, but we rarely discussed our country of origin.'

'Does your discipline advocate taking one's own life, even for a just cause?'

The angry voice of Samuel came from behind. 'Take care how you speak to our master.'

Eyes moist, the guru replied, 'No, we don't advocate any such thing.'

Maya twitched in her seat, a stool without any support for her back. Would Samuel try to throw her out if she asked more probing questions? She drew in a deep breath and decided to take the risk.

'You said you didn't discuss Tibet with Sylvie. Please think again. Her zeal . . . well, that seemed to have come out of the blue. It surprised Ivan as well. How would you explain her sudden advocacy for her old country?'

A slight ripple became evident underneath the guru's calm voice. 'The issue of Tibet wasn't foremost in Sylvie's mind, if it was in her mind at all.'

'But . . . but . . . at the immolation she must have been thinking of you. She carried lilies.'

The guru sat with his palms open, showing no sign of tension or duplicity, only signaling his willingness for more discussion. Still, Maya had a hard time swallowing the answers he and his assistant had supplied so far.

'What you've been led to believe is wrong.' Now Samuel joined in the conversation. 'We didn't know about the self-immolation until after it had happened. Why did she carry lilies? Beats me.'

Although his words lashed at her back, Maya again ignored Samuel and asked the guru, 'Are you suggesting there were complications in Sylvie's life that nobody but you were aware of?'

'Yes. I might have been the only one privy to them. As you know, secrets are like jewels. You must protect them.'

A gentle breeze blew in through the window. Several candle flames fluttered; one died. Samuel got to his feet, knelt before the platform, pulled a matchbox from his pocket and relit the candle, which flared with double intensity. Only then did Samuel reclaim his stool, his expression one of agitation.

'Sylvie's dead,' Maya plunged on. 'Could you share her secrets with me?'

The guru shut his eyes. Instantly, his eyelids relaxed, two domes bathed in a gentle light, and he became still. Was he channeling Sylvie and asking for her permission? Where did he have to transport himself to for that? Maya, never having witnessed any channeling firsthand, wondered if it was a tool for manipulation or some sort of con artistry.

Her gaze descended on Samuel. He, too, had his eyes shut, seemingly in a trance-like state. Both faces looked smooth and blissful, whereas she experienced turmoil within.

The guru snapped his eyes open and said in a warm, level

voice, 'You're still here, Maya, as I thought you might be. You still want your answer, stubborn girl. OK, here it is. Sylvie came to visit me every now and then. One of the last times she came because . . . brace yourself . . . she'd strangled her beloved kitten with her bare hands.'

Maya's eyebrows rose; her throat closed in on her. She could so easily imagine pet-loving Sylvie curled up in a chair. She could see the kitten, Augustine, flowing from a corner, purring and rubbing her head against Sylvie's legs, then jumping up to the cushion of her lap. Sylvie would hold her and stroke her, she would never . . . could never . . . Maya tried to imagine Sylvie's slender arm stiffening as she reached for Augustine's neck . . . *Impossible.*

Maya shook her head. 'Sylvie was a cat person; she bonded with all cats.'

The guru's expression became keen. 'Much as she was a cat lover, she felt like doing it. That's how she put it. It was in her mind constantly. A monster standing before her and ordering, "*Do it, do it, do it, do it now.*" She had to obey it. Although she hid the evidence from everyone, insisting the kitten had been killed by a hit-and-run driver, she found she couldn't lie to herself. Day and night, it tore away at her insides. She couldn't eat, sleep or do her lab work. Before long she dropped out of the meditation classes. We didn't see her for a while. She came back once or twice. She looked worse.'

'Sylvie had meditated regularly for a long period. One would expect such a practice to get her back to—'

'No doubt the effect of meditation spills over and makes us happier, calmer and wiser overall, but the practice alone can't save us from our shadow selves or memories of acts we've committed in the past, dear girl. We're still individuals responsible for our actions. There's no avoiding karma, no escaping the consequences of our thoughts, actions or beliefs, whether or not we meditate.' The guru paused, as though for emphasis. 'The poor girl had become dangerously delusional. She actually believed she'd be able to bring her cat back to life. She came to see me because she couldn't. The cat was dead.'

'Sylvie, the scientist, filled her time doing research to benefit people everywhere. I mean, how many people care about malaria when we hardly come across any cases locally? It's not easy for me to imagine that an angel like her could harbor such sick impulses. Or that she'd be able to continue to conduct herself professionally in a scientific environment.'

'Let me explain the chain reaction, cause and effect, if I may, that drives our lives.' Words cascaded out of the guru's mouth. 'An impulse can originate simply as a fleeting thought in your head, an image planted by you or someone else, or a shadow you can't get rid of. The power of association in your mind magnetizes similar elements to it, a copy-and-paste job, you might call it, and soon you've given in to a small bad habit. You think nothing of it. Then, over time, that small bad habit fuels far worse ones. You begin to contemplate the unthinkable. Are you with me so far?'

Maya nodded, adjusted her position on the stool and gestured for the guru to elaborate.

'Pardon me, Maya. I'm sorry to have to break through what you hold precious. Sylvie, the young, beautiful, star scientist, with the world at her feet, fooled her loved ones.' The guru's voice dropped slightly but still rang with conviction. 'I believe this dark side of Sylvie was brought about partly by substance abuse.'

For an instant, Maya looked without seeing. She recalled her conversation with Jeet about Anna's possible flirtation with drugs. She couldn't imagine Sylvie smoking pot or drinking excessively. 'Our Sylvie?'

'Yes. She was incoherent. Being smart, she could see right away that she was on a downward spiral. She paid me a visit because she reasoned I had special powers to "cure" her.'

Maya had a sinking feeling, perhaps just what Sylvie had experienced, of sliding down and down and not reaching any solid surface. With effort, she rose above it. 'And did you have any such power?'

'No. Besides, in our practice, we respect the choices an individual makes. Although I counseled her, I could see that she would handle the matter as she saw fit.'

Why couldn't you have sent her to a doctor or the emergency room, or asked her to speak with her family? Why did you stay so passive? Maya's eyes roved the room. It was furnished simply, every object in its place, which indicated how much the guru loved a sense of order. Sylvie came to see him, a storm bulldozing the perfection of that arrangement. No wonder he couldn't help her find a way out of the trap she'd fallen into.

That understanding, however beneficial, couldn't cool the anxiety inside Maya, a brute emotion trying to rise and assert itself. Sylvie must have felt this way too and far worse. Poor Sylvie, without any help, without a lifeline.

'Sylvie came from a respectable family. Her mother is a college professor and her sister, Veen, is an architect. They all adored her. They'd have helped her, if she'd only asked.'

The guru smiled slightly. 'Be aware that when a woman is in love, her lover often becomes the most important influence in her life. She might decide to take her counseling from him, not her family, not her friends. She might decide to live according to the rules he sets. Perhaps I wouldn't be remiss if I said a woman's fate, in certain instances, is determined by the man she loves.'

Maya bristled. 'I'm much too independent, and I thought Sylvie was too.' She paused. 'Are you blaming Ivan?'

'Well, a rejection from him, on top of her guilt for killing the cat, might have been the last straw.'

Maya opened her mouth and turned, only to find Samuel shooting an angry glance at her, as if signaling that her questions were a sign of disrespect to the guru. Although a pang of awkwardness followed and she was all wound up, Maya jumped in to make her point. 'Unfortunately, Ivan seems to see the matter differently. He's considering criminal prosecution.'

'But truth can never be erased.'

A glance at the guru and the genial expression on his face infuriated her. She wished he didn't take Ivan's threats of bringing up the matter to the police so coolly. Nothing seemed to knock him off-balance. Still, she'd hoped he'd show more surprise and sorrow about Sylvie's death.

'But please consider all the evidence.' The rumble of a bus disturbed the air and drowned out the rest of Maya's remark.

'Ivan speculates that there might be an affiliation between your meditation group and Sylvie's death. He says he's already talked to the police.'

'How well do you know this Ivan?' the guru asked when the bus had passed.

Something in the guru's voice, a faint warning, caused Maya to lean back. 'Oh, he's a new acquaintance.'

'I would suggest you stay away from him and his associates.' The guru's eyes conveyed a silent but clear message of caution. 'He is – how do you say it? – very bad news.'

Maya stared at the triangle of sudden afternoon light illuminating – almost burning – a corner of the room. 'Ivan, on the other hand, talks of his suspicion of the meditation practice you teach.'

Maya heard the harsh noise of a stool scraping. Samuel stood up in one abrupt motion and pointed a finger at her. 'Enough – you must leave immediately.'

'Please, I didn't mean any disrespect.'

'It's all right, Samuel.' The guru extended his hand in a calming gesture. 'Please take your seat and go into meditation.'

'I can't meditate when this woman is present.'

'How many times have you been told you mustn't let any outside influence disturb your sitting?'

Samuel dropped down to his seat and shut his eyes, although his lips remained tight and his eyelids showed movement.

'Time for my mid-morning prayer walk.' The guru turned to Samuel and said, 'Since you have errands to run, I'll go alone.'

'I apologize for taking so much of your time,' Maya said. 'Shouldn't someone accompany you?'

'Thanks for your concern, but I'll be fine.'

'Perhaps we'll continue this conversation another time?'

'If you so wish. You came to talk about Sylvie but that's not all you had in mind. You're in a spot of trouble yourself, are you not?'

Maya was taken aback. She hung her head.

'It has to do with a man who had once a claim on your heart. Am I correct?'

Yes, another fairy tale gone wrong. 'I'm trying to cast him out of my mind.'

'You're frustrated and confused by his actions. Believe me, in time, there'll be a satisfactory solution for everyone concerned.'

Maya dabbed at her eyes and looked up at him, surprised that he'd figured this out. If only everything was that simple, that natural, that predictable. If only every herb in her garden flourished.

'I must go now.' The guru folded his hands at his heart center and examined the white flowers in the vase. 'May the purity of the flowers touch your heart. May you carry nothing but affection within you. May you merge with the flow of universal peace.'

Maya stood, absorbing as much of the guru's quiet strength as she could, and drew herself to her full height.

Samuel opened his eyes and got to his feet.

'Show her the letter,' the guru said to Samuel, rose and slipped out of the room through an interior door.

Samuel led Maya to the front entrance, saying, 'Please wait,' and disappeared into a small office. He returned and handed her an envelope. 'This is from Sylvie, received on the day she died.'

Maya checked the postal stamp; the date was accurate. Inside, handwritten on a fancy notecard, was a succinct, two-paragraph message from Sylvie thanking the guru for all he'd done for her. Maya recognized the loopy, angled-to-the-left, elegant penmanship as being unmistakably Sylvie's.

By the time you receive this . . .

Maya diverted her gaze for an instant.

In case there are attempts to blame you, I want everyone to know that my decision is mine alone. You didn't coerce me or make the arrangements. You were unaware of the date and time. In all these years, you've given me nothing but love. And now I must leave you lovingly.

Silver

Slowly, Maya returned the letter to Samuel. A deep, achy sadness welled up inside her.

'Do you now see it?' Samuel asked in a bitter tone. 'Our guru isn't so concerned about himself, but I trust this letter will put an end to your rude inquisitiveness.'

'No, I don't see it all.' She paused for a moment and, with a dismissive wave of her hand, stepped outside.

Glass beads of rain shocked her cheeks but also awakened her. As she walked toward her car, her head spun with the motherlode of information received in this visit. It was quite a list: Sylvie getting addicted to recreational drugs, losing control, murdering her cat and taking her own life, Ivan being implicated somehow in her tragic end. But there were several missing links in all this.

Maya started her car. Despite the guru's warning, she'd have to approach the handsome, chivalrous, 'very bad news' Ivan.

NINETEEN

After her visit with the guru, Maya drove home, her shoulders slumped from the gravity of the encounter. She exited her car, wondering if the guru had divulged all the secrets about Sylvie or if any crucial fact was still missing. If, in fact, his safety was in doubt.

In the front yard, she drank in her white lilies. They each looked like a star when viewed from the front and she was reminded of Sylvie.

She entered the house, stood in the doorframe of her living room and looked toward the window. Eyes shut, Uma lounged in a chair, one hand drawn across her chest and pressing on the opposite shoulder. A book and an iPad rested on an end table.

How unusual for Uma not to fill every spare moment either leafing through a novel, huddling over her iPad to surf the Internet or preparing yet another delicacy in the kitchen. Something was up.

Maya cleared her throat. Uma stirred and lifted her gaze; her eyelids were heavy. In the purplish afternoon light coming through the window, her usually serene face was wrinkled with concern.

'Oh, you're back.' Voice tight, Uma continued to massage her shoulder.

Maya dropped down on a chair and crossed her legs. 'Is everything all right?'

'Well, no. I . . . I'm a bit on edge. I don't want you to be concerned, but . . . someone hit me . . . hit my back with a rock. It scared the crap out of me. Kind of medieval, don't you think?'

'What?' Maya jumped up and stared at a small, reddish bump on Uma's shoulder. *What if the rock had hit Uma's head? How much more serious would that have been? It could have claimed her life.* Steaming inside, Maya squeaked out a deeply concerned, 'Who did this, where and when?'

'I wish I'd seen his face. After my walk I went to get groceries from the corner market, came home, put down the bags on the porch and unlocked the door. Man oh man, something hit me hard on the shoulder. I felt a shot of pain and blacked out for an instant. When my vision cleared, I spotted the rock lying behind me on the porch and saw a cyclist racing down the road. He had on a blue nylon jacket. Not sure it was him, but he was moving fast and no one else was around.'

'I'll take you to the doctor right away, but let me call the police first. This is assault and battery.'

'Oh, no, we don't need the police, nor do we need a doctor visit.' An edge of fear was evident in Uma's voice. 'I'm fine. A little swelling is about all I've suffered.'

'You should see a doctor.' Maya pulled her cellphone out, called her primary-care physician, Dr Moore, and left a message about scheduling an emergency visit with Uma. She turned to her mother. 'That coward – he didn't confront you, he was probably waiting in an alley, watching your comings and goings. You know what? That rock was meant for me.'

Uma looked panicked. 'For you?'

'Yes, hurting you would hurt me and the guy knew that,' Maya said firmly, looking into Uma's eyes. 'You're paying for me. I'm so sorry, Ma.'

Still standing, Maya tried to feel the comforting touch of the rug under her feet; it wasn't there. She couldn't put her finger on whom she might have spoken to recently who could have become angry enough to start throwing rocks, but maybe she should back off on her investigation, if only to protect her mother.

'Don't be sorry, my dear, and don't blame yourself. You're obviously in somebody's way. You won't let them cover Sylvie's ashes with lies. You're doing what you're compelled to do.'

Maya tuned into the raging vehicle noises outside the window to drown out the dreadful feelings twisting through her. 'If you want to catch the next flight back to Kolkata, I'd understand. I know your gentleman friend Neel would like that.'

'What are you talking about? You're my only child, precious to me. I can't leave you here like this, with an investigation still open. We *are* investigating this case, aren't we? And we share the fate together. Yes, we do. I want to see you succeed.'

'What about Neel?'

'He'll have to be patient. Next time he might want to come with me.'

'Your safety is foremost in my mind, Ma.'

'Do you think I'll be able to rest in Kolkata, even for a millisecond, knowing you're here alone, being pursued by evil men? That's scary, and we don't see the full picture quite yet.' Uma bestowed a smile, her eyes crinkling in a new light. 'Going back to my Gestalt days . . . oh, it sounds so overused now but the whole is really greater than the sum of its parts.'

Maya reminded herself of the concept she'd repeatedly heard from Uma: how we anticipate the whole, even when parts are missing. Our brains fill in the missing data and before long a solution emerges.

'OK, partner,' Maya said. 'It'll be so but, from now on, let's watch our step. Whoever did this will try a different tactic the next time.'

'I've phoned Atticus and he's on his way.'

'You phoned that oddball?' Even though irked, Maya kept her tone genial. 'We don't have the foggiest what his involvement was in Sylvie's death or whose side he's on. Even though I'm working for him, I have my doubts.'

'I'm not finished checking him out yet but I expect he'll turn out to be OK.'

Hearing a rap on the door, Maya leapt to her feet, looked through the peephole and yanked the door open to let Atticus in.

He muttered a hello to Maya and flew into the room, his face reflecting his concern. '*Mashima!* How are you?'

'Much better.' Uma, with a fond expression on her face, gestured for him to sit. She reiterated the incident, concluding with: 'Didn't mean to disturb you in the middle of a workday, but I'm so worried about Maya. She's in and out of the house all day long. Who knows who might be stalking her?'

Atticus' face was troubled. 'The freaking truth is both of you now have a Sylvie connection.'

'Yes, there appears to have been much more to Sylvie than any of us had an inkling about.' Maya watched Atticus' face; she tried to gauge his reactions. 'We didn't talk about this in great detail earlier. When did you last see Sylvie?'

'Sylvie disappeared from the meditation scene about six or eight weeks before her death,' Atticus said, his eyes downcast. 'No calls, no emails – maybe she didn't want us to see her. I'd certainly have tried to talk some sense into her head if I'd known any of this was going on but never got the opportunity.'

'What do you mean you didn't get the opportunity?'

She was still formulating more questions in her mind when Uma said to her, 'Going back to the suicide scene . . . you saw that prayer group . . .'

Her clever mother. 'Oh, yes, Ma.' Maya turned to Atticus. 'The chanters – you saw them, right? All those people wearing white, pretending to be devotees of some sort? Seemed to me they were well prepared for what happened. At the time, I'd assumed they were supporters of Sylvie and Anna.'

Atticus put on an innocent expression. 'I didn't see or hear them.'

Really? Maya gave him a searching look. 'And did you also not hear the sunglasses dude saying *nyet* to you? You stopped me from pushing forward. Look, if you want me to investigate this case . . .'

'*Nyet*? What is *nyet*? What are you talking about? I only stopped you because I didn't want you to interfere with Sylvie's wish to step into the next world. Her text indicated so.'

'That's outrageous, letting someone—'

Uma's stare was hot with annoyance. She was only pretending to go along with Atticus; that much was clear to Maya. Uma wanted to draw Atticus out and maintain a flow of conversation despite his lying. Although they were co-conspirators in this, she couldn't follow Uma's lead; impatience stopped her.

'Let me repeat,' Maya said to Atticus. 'I heard Sunglasses Man yell out to you in Russian.'

Atticus wore a remote expression. 'Might that be a figment of your imagination, Maya? And that prayer group around Sylvie and Anna? They were all friends, I'd guess. It sounds like you're not thinking things through, like you're developing theories prematurely. Is this how a P.I. should work?'

Disgust pricked Maya's cheeks. She couldn't offer any tangible proof of her theory but she had facts to back her up: the prayer group wouldn't allow her to get closer to Sylvie. And Atticus stood by and let it all happen. 'As far as I know, neither Sylvie nor Anna had a large social circle. If they did, those people would have showed up at the memorial. Sylvie was quiet and hung out with a few friends, Ivan being the closest to her.'

Atticus' face flared in anger. 'That jerk. He's been seen with my ex-wife recently.'

'Since she's your ex, why do you care?'

'It still hurts,' Atticus replied hotly. 'He's a bad influence. A friend of mine recently saw him with another woman. She's part-Russian, used to be a drug addict and now sleeps with a cop. Ivan's choice of friends concerns me, especially if he's starting something with my ex.'

Maya had stopped listening. Ex-druggie? Jennifer? Justin's companion and mother of his son, now seeing Ivan?

Atticus checked his watch and erupted from his chair. 'Gotta go. I'm expecting a client. He's probably already waiting in the lobby of my building, about to text me.'

Both Maya and Uma were startled by their guest's sudden movement. But Uma, elegant as always, turned a graceful head toward Atticus. 'Shall we continue this discussion at another time over *chai*?'

'Most certainly, *Mashima*,' Atticus said. 'Meantime, I'll drive by here periodically to check—'

'You don't need to patrol our street,' Maya said firmly. 'We can take care of ourselves.'

'We mustn't refuse Atticus' help, Maya,' Uma said gently, a warning note evident in her voice. Uma despised rudeness – oh, how well Maya understood that – especially when her own daughter exhibited it.

Atticus bade them goodbye and slipped out onto the porch. After closing the door behind him, Maya returned to the living room; she felt drained. 'He's lying, Ma, lying by omission.'

'He's not a complete liar, only in spots. He's a work-in-progress. His mouth is shut in fear. He knows Justin is a cop so he's even more tight-lipped.'

'A cop who also hangs out with an ex-druggie, like Ivan, apparently.' Maya chewed her lower lip. 'I have to wonder if Atticus' wife has any relevance here other than her being the next in line in what has been a long string of lovers for Ivan. The guys who were following Atticus probably still are, and now his wife is mixed up with Ivan. This is just one big mysterious mess.'

'It's a *khichuri*.' Uma was referring to her favorite rice-and-lentil dish, taken to perfection with a jumble of other ingredients.

'Atticus is making a serious mistake by hiding the identity of the guilty parties,' Maya said. 'We have to somehow get him to spill out the dark truth.'

A notion glinted in Uma's eyes. 'I'll help you. We'll have him cough up the details, one samosa at a time. How'd that be?'

Maya gave Uma a thankful glance. 'We have to be quick, Ma. Sooner or later, whoever is behind this will get Atticus or us, unless of course they get locked up, which is what I intend.'

A faint sound of rustling leaves came from the front yard. Maya rushed over to the window, only to see a squirrel digging through fallen leaves on a flower bed. Tiny, tender strawberries, deployed as ground cover on an adjacent bed and blooming for the second time in the season, peeked out from under their deep green foliage.

Yet Maya could feel a vine of fear creeping along her back. She drew the curtains and returned to her seat, swallowing an ominous feeling of imminent crisis. She speculated that the guru knew more than he had let on. Both he and Ivan had their roles and Atticus was hiding crucial facts. Winsome

Jennifer only added to this puzzle. But it was the attack on Uma that caused Maya the most anguish.

I'll find out what there is to find out, even if it kills me.

TWENTY

Several days rolled by. Although it was six p.m., sunlight streamed through the treetops at the Washington Park Arboretum like shining needles of gold. In the sticky-hot atmosphere hectic with bees, insects, flowers and squirrels, surrounded by a grove of rhododendron, Maya laid out a rose-printed cloth on a picnic table. As she raised her head, she felt someone watching her from behind the grove. An elderly woman with a bulky body and a narrow gaze hurried away, leaving a ripple of unease behind her. Maya stood up; she saw only a receding figure. She reclaimed her seat.

Veen, with her back toward the grove, hadn't noticed or pretended not to. She looked better than the last time they were together. Her eyes were shinier, her face smoother, her vibrant self somehow peeking through. A gauzy, navy V-neck tunic created a slimming effect around her bulky chest. She'd drawn her dark hair back into a neat ponytail. Lips tinted a glossy pink, she'd rouged her cheeks to match. That pink shade took Maya a few months back to when Veen had appeared especially well-groomed. She often dressed in indigos and magentas and accessorized with gold jewelry. Never the perfume type, she would wear a bold gardenia fragrance. She was often self-absorbed. Her creamy skin had had the glow of sex, or that was how Maya saw it. Veen didn't care for the men in her office. 'Too wimpy and not good in the sack.' So who had it been? Maya didn't get to see Veen much in those days; her evenings were often filled. It hurt the worst when Veen didn't confide in her. But that was Veen. She could cut someone with her bluntness as well as her silences.

A *taiko* drum boomed in the distance. 'Hey, I forgot all about it until now.' Veen pushed away a curl that fell over her eyes.

'That strange phone call I got, supposedly from one of Sylvie's classmates at the meditation center – Lola is her name. She blabbered for a while about the tragedy, what a big loss it was, et cetera, asked how I was taking it, then questioned me about the guru. What guru? I know nothing about him or his center.'

Maya hid her shock, noted the stiffness of Veen's posture and her unblinking gaze. 'Did you check to see if Lola was really from—?'

'No, why? Wouldn't that be a bit melodramatic? The guru's probably fake. What are you thinking?'

'Did you at least get Lola's number?'

'No. The caller ID indicated an unknown number. She had a faint accent and an aggressive manner, kept me talking even when I wanted to get off the phone.'

'Why didn't you tell me this sooner?'

Veen's voice cracked. 'Shit – it slipped my mind.'

I don't believe it. However, Maya tried to answer the question herself. Veen had no idea of Maya's involvement in the case, the fact that this scoop could be important in her investigation. Or it could be that Veen was lying.

'Hey, what do you have for us to eat?' Veen asked jovially.

'Plenty. Mom insisted on feeding us well.' Maya unloaded the contents of her basket: a stack of fresh chapatis, spicy roasted eggplant, green beans coated with a sweet brownish sauce and a tall carton of coconut water. While doing so, she brooded about her mother. Several days had passed since Uma had been struck by that thrown rock. Not a clue existed as to who had done it. The injury turned out to be minor but Uma's blood pressure went way up, which had got Maya concerned. Using a digital blood pressure monitor, as suggested by Dr Moore, she kept track of Uma's blood pressure on a regular basis. Whereas Uma had managed to erase that horrible incident from her mind and prepared this elaborate outdoor meal for them, Maya still stewed over that assault.

As Veen served herself, Maya looked all around to see if any mysterious, heavyset women lurked nearby. She saw no one. That in itself concerned her, squeezed the oxygen out of the air. Her instinct suggested someone was hiding somewhere and watching them.

They finished their meal. 'How about a walk in the Japanese garden?' Maya asked, ready to talk with Veen about a topic of her own. She wanted to put aside those damaging thoughts about her best friend and get away from any surveillance.

'Yes, sure.' Veen winked. 'I need some Zen.'

The sunset had turned the sky a delicate mauve, the evening still young and frivolous around them. With Maya leading, they strolled down a narrow walkway and crossed over to the miniature garden, a green vista opening before them. She recalled how many times, especially during the last three or so months of their relationship, she and Justin had shared the twenty-minute stroll through these pathways. As a police detective, he needed to destress; he'd quite possibly been punched, knocked down or pepper-sprayed during his hours of duty. And so they'd take off after dinner, drive up here and walk hand-in-hand. Feet floating over a carpet of pebbles, chest filled with fresh air, Maya would point out a patch of velvety moss, a pale pink bud that peeked from underneath the leaves or a tree sculpted so expertly as to resemble an installed art piece. Clouds, if there were any, wore a silver mantle.

'You know,' Maya now said to Veen, a flutter in her throat, 'it's an odd coincidence but I met Justin's companion and infant son quite by chance.'

'What?' Her eyes round, Veen gripped Maya's elbow, giving it a shake. 'His *companion*? You mean the chick he was with the other day? And his *child*? You never told me he had a child. In the name of Ma Kali, spit it!'

Maya hesitated, feeling wounded and ashamed, as if she herself had not been woman enough to keep Justin's love. But Veen, wide-eyed, was waiting.

'Oh, I happened to go to the flea market, where I noticed Justin's new girlfriend.' Maya took a deep breath and gave Veen the account of having 'accidentally' met two of the most important people in Justin's life. Her cheeks burned again as she admitted that she'd posed as a stranger in order to chat with Jennifer, and how she'd been charmed by the plump-cheeked Justin Jr. She left the mosquito part out.

'So,' Veen said when Maya had finished, 'our detective

prince has either started a legitimate family in secret or has an adorable illegitimate child.' Veen let go of Maya's arm and looked out over the pond. 'Goodness me,' she finally said, gazing back at Maya. 'There's got to be more to this story.'

They stood on the bridge and watched the koi fish flap their tails, their amber, orange and blue bodies churning the water as bubbles rose to the surface. 'I'm afraid that Justin is being duped by that woman.' Although she tried to keep her voice casual, Maya could tell it was laced with caution. 'I'd like to find out a bit more about her.'

Veen turned to her quickly, her eyes knowing. 'More than that, isn't it? I mean, why else would you pretend you didn't recognize her? Why would you approach her at all if you weren't curious? Come on, Maya, be honest. You want full disclosure – why Justin dropped you, why he took up with that woman, why he's keeping his son a secret, why they don't seem to be living together, the whole mess. I'd be dying of curiosity. I'd get a headache. Then I'd have to go to the store and get three scoops of gelato.'

'Look,' Maya said, 'how could I possibly find any of that out? It isn't like I can start stalking Jennifer and then ask her all about it. She thinks I'm just some woman who bumped into her at a fair, who thought her baby was cute. She couldn't be dumb enough to answer questions from a stranger about Justin's private life.' She paused. 'I've been pondering this and an idea has cropped up. Hope you don't think it's ridiculous or laughable. I'm thinking of retaining your friend, Annette. I think I can trust her. And my guess is she'd be up for the job.'

'That she would be. She's a Martha Stewart-type of organized woman. Although retired from SPD, she has a long roster of useful contacts. Her friends surely have all sorts of databases at their fingertips. But . . . you surprise me . . . to hire someone to spy on a former lover – that's not at all like you.'

Maya nodded, head down. *It's not him, it's his new girlfriend, who somehow raises suspicion.* She couldn't tell Veen of the case Atticus had assigned her. Confidentiality issues. Yes, even with your best friend.

She began walking again with a constricted throat. Veen followed her.

'Everyone does background checks on their partners, especially if they sense something isn't quite right,' Maya said after a while, keeping her tone companionable, encouraging. She reminded Veen that, in the cyber era, you don't really have to stalk a person the way chain-smoking private eyes did in old detective novels. Now you let the computer do the trailing for you, discreetly, in the privacy of your own home, with your cat purring next to you. 'Tell Annette I'll pay her full fee in advance.'

'OK, then,' Veen replied enthusiastically. 'I helped Annette move three hundred pounds of books when she rented a dig in Issaquah last winter, so she owes me. All I have to do is ask her and she'll shovel into the dirt.'

It was easy for Veen to get excited about invading Justin's privacy – *she* hadn't loved him. Maya had done that and, on second thought, it was difficult to consider entering his life again as a snoop. She berated herself for stooping so low. 'One concern. What if Justin finds out?'

'Aw. If I were you, I'd be done with being too nice, too much of a doormat. He probably *will* find out. But who gives a fuck about what he thinks?'

Looking down at the stony path as they strolled along it, Maya felt annoyance. Veen wouldn't care how Justin felt about anything.

'Have you wondered what else Justin has hidden from you?' Veen said, her voice firm. 'There's a lurid tale here, what you ought to know, what my mother calls, "every frickin' detail."'

Maya motioned toward a bench; the dirty game had suddenly become real to her.

TWENTY-ONE

Two days later, when Maya arrived home in the afternoon, she saw Uma's handwritten note on the coffee table: *See you around 7 p.m., dear.*

The television was on in the living room; the authoritative

voice of an anchorwoman announced the local news. Uma, in her hurry, must have forgotten to turn the set off before she left the house. And she had reasons to be in a hurry. A friend had come by to pick her up. Maya had given her mother the gift of a spa treatment to erase the effect of that menacing, rock-throwing mishap: massage, facial, manicure and pedicure, the whole works. Uma would never spend money on herself and Maya knew she would enjoy the pampering, especially when a buddy of hers was getting the same treatment. Later, Uma would troop to the home of a family friend in Redmond for a soirée. The Chaurasias had planned a reception for a visiting violinist from India. Maya was invited, too, and would meet her mother there.

'According to the police report, an elderly man was struck by a hit-and-run white sedan this evening at the corner of Winona and Aurora Avenue. The unidentified man wore a burgundy robe and a bystander stated he was a local spiritual teacher.' Maya rushed to the television set and turned up the volume. 'Witnesses report seeing the car hit the man as he attempted to cross Aurora. He was taken to the Harborview Medical Center, where his condition is believed to be critical.'

Maya stood watching the screen in horror. A burgundy-robed elderly man? Over on Aurora? Guru Padmaraja? A video was now up on the screen, showing the intersection where the accident occurred. Police vehicles and an ambulance had arrived on the scene.

A ripple of fear ran across the back of Maya's neck. So many things were happening, so many violent things to people involved with Sylvie.

She left a message on the Chaurasias' phone, saying she'd be late for the party, jogged to her car and drove to Harborview, all the while feeling a tightness in her chest. At the front desk, she asked to see the patient, Mr Padmaraja.

'Are you a friend or family?' the receptionist asked.

'Family,' she said untruthfully, feeling terrible but she had no choice. She would get nowhere without a blood tie.

A nurse's aide came forward, took Maya aside and whispered, 'The patient is in ICU. You may go there.'

In the intensive care unit, Maya held her breath as she stepped to the front workstation. The walls were an emotionless white, the floor polished to an unnatural sheen, and the strong smell of cleaning fluid gave off a feeling of sterility. Even the vase of red carnations at the desk provided no feeling of relief.

'I'm here to see Mr Padmaraja, the man who was hit by a car. We're related.'

The receptionist peered over her glasses at Maya, looked down at her computer screen, picked up her phone, punched in a number and waited.

Maya tried not to tap her fingers on the countertop.

A tall, slender nurse appeared and said in a somber voice, 'I'm sorry, miss, but Mr Padmaraja passed away a few minutes ago.'

The words arrested Maya's response. She stood, staring at the woman.

'Would you like to sit down?'

Through her sealed throat, Maya thanked the nurse and turned away.

As she walked to her car, her mind raced and she kept looking over her shoulders. Why hadn't she thought to ask what would happen to the guru's body? And had there been any other visitors at the hospital? If so, who?

In less than half an hour, she reached home and sat alone on the sofa in her living room, hoping the familiar sounds, aromas and objects would help her cope. They didn't.

Her fingers fluttered as she punched Samuel's number into her cellphone. No answer. She stared blankly out the window, uneasiness nibbling at her heart.

The doorbell chimed. She rose and looked through the peephole: Atticus. Wordlessly, she opened the door and studied him for a second as he stood on her porch. His clothes were creased, shoulders contracted. The usual sour expression had morphed into one of dreadful resignation.

She steered him into the living room. 'Ma has gone to a party in Redmond.'

He slumped on the sofa. She took the high-back chair.

He stared at her over the globe-shaped bouquet of purple

hydrangeas placed on the table between them. Then he slapped his forehead, muttering, 'My God . . . My God . . . My worst fears realized. Our beloved guru . . . has departed this world. I called the hospital and . . .'

'I only got back from Harborview five minutes ago,' Maya said softly.

Atticus gaped at her.

Maya conveyed the details of her visit, her voice almost inaudible at times. 'Aurora Avenue,' she said in conclusion. 'There you run into drugs, prostitution, mugging and heavy traffic. You see vandalized businesses. And you meet street people, although they're the least of the problems. Not exactly the kind of sanctuary a meditation master would seek out. Do you suppose the guru wasn't on that street for his prayer walk?'

'Now that I think of it, Samuel did mention an appointment a man had made with the guru. Maybe he'd asked the guru to meet him there and asked for his help, acting like a troubled soul.'

'Could it be he figured the police would really believe some old man stepped onto a busy intersection at dusk and the driver didn't see him until it was too late?' Maya said. 'Then, to avoid dealing with their negligence, the driver drove off? Doesn't it sound plausible, especially in that part of town?'

'It does.' Grief stiffened Atticus' face. 'Damn it. Only later I found out Samuel had to pick up a relative from the airport, so the guru had to go alone. I only wish I'd known about it. I'd have gone with him. Our guru, I hope, will forgive from wherever he is.'

Atticus went mute, his eyes wild with concern and his forehead etched with strain, as though he was about to be sick. Maya, too, felt queasy. She went into the kitchen, gulped some chilled water and fetched him a tall glass of the same.

He held the glass. 'I'm just so overwhelmed, like a five-hundred-pound gorilla is pressing down on me, like I'm coming down with a fever. I've never been more unsettled in my life except . . . when my father died.' He placed the empty glass on the coffee table, nodded to Maya in thanks and stretched out his legs.

'What I find most disturbing . . . I might as well share this with you,' Maya said. 'It's been about three weeks since the two self-immolations. We now have two more deaths: Tara Martin, which I believe was a copycat incident, and the guru.'

Eyes on the floor, Atticus remained quiet, the silence of iron.

'Atticus, I haven't known you a long time but I'm working on this case on your behalf. After meeting with the guru I'd developed respect for him. And now we're faced with this tragedy. Can it get any worse? I suppose you're reluctant to speak out, and I completely understand that, but please . . . I need your cooperation to do what you've assigned me to do. Who knows who'll get hurt next?'

Atticus clenched and unclenched his hands, then raised his eyes and gave her a piercing look. 'OK, it's difficult for me to talk about this but I'll tell you what I've figured out . . . what came as a shock to me, and . . . will be to you, too. Our guru – and I will love and respect him forever – might have been indirectly responsible for Sylvie's death.'

Maya started. 'How so?'

Atticus clutched at the arm of his chair.

'Atticus?' Maya softened the excitement in her voice. 'Please. Why do you think the guru might have been responsible?'

'Indirectly,' Atticus said pointedly.

'OK. Indirectly.'

'During Sylvie's last visit to him, he passed her a video to watch. You might be wondering, what's the big deal?'

'Exactly.'

'Well, the deal is this. It was quite common for the guru to distribute videos and magazine articles to us. He wanted his students to deepen their understanding of spiritual matters but this was different. Sylvie told me during our last phone conversation that she'd received a video from the guru and she would watch it that night. She wouldn't tell me any more about it and for some reason it niggled me. After Sylvie's death, I went to visit the guru and got him into a conversation about that video. He eventually gave me the title.'

'I'd like to know it.'

'*Burn Give Live* is what it's called. The very title gives me goosebumps.'

'*Burn Give Live*,' Maya echoed. 'It's shocking that the guru would give a video with such a title to Sylvie. Did you try to get a copy?'

'Yes. After I got home I logged on to the Internet. The video turned out to be a limited-edition product directly related to Tibet's political and human rights issues, supplied by a small outfit no longer in business. It incites people to engage in political protests to help the cause of Tibet's freedom even to the point of self-immolation. The guru had wanted Sylvie to watch it alone, secretly and multiple times.'

'Alone, secretly and multiple times? That wasn't my impression of the guru.'

'Please don't form a negative impression of him, only look at it from his viewpoint. When Sylvie confided to the guru about her intention to take her own life, at first he tried to talk her out of it. But, ultimately, he couldn't convince her. She wouldn't budge. She sat there, shaking her head, and he understood she was serious. Being practical, the guru quickly devised a plan in his mind that'd help the cause of Tibet. He gave the video to Sylvie. In the weeks that followed, she watched it over and over again and I suspect it made a deep groove in her psyche about the situation of her birthplace.'

Maya sat, disgusted, horrified. A truck roared at a distance, the noise shaking her more than usual. 'I'm disappointed you didn't tell me any of this earlier.' After a pause, she continued, 'Did you try reaching Sylvie during the last few weeks of her life?'

'Yes, of course, frantically. Something didn't sound right with her. I must have tried a dozen times but got no answer. It was close to midnight on a weekend when I gave up and went to the grocery store, where I got beaten up by a gang. You know the rest of my horror story.'

Maya nodded.

'In the following weeks,' Atticus continued, 'being in constant pain and discomfort, having no one to take care of my needs, not to mention the reduction of income and temporary loss of mobility, I forced myself to focus on matters other than Sylvie. Then, one morning, I woke up early and checked my iPhone, only to find Sylvie's text; she'd announced her wish to self-immolate. I was stunned. The message had come a few hours earlier. I barely managed to get myself to the site of her self-immolation. I stayed quiet throughout the ceremony to respect her wishes.'

'You didn't have to stay quiet.' Maya locked eyes with Atticus and leaned forward. 'Not when you were right there and could have helped rescue her. She was young and brilliant, with a lot left to do, with so many malaria sufferers to help, and she had a loving family. You knew something was wrong, yet—'

'You don't understand.' The muscles in Atticus' face twitched. 'Maybe you will when you're a little older.'

Maya shook her head but Atticus wouldn't allow her to interrupt.

'I didn't realize how bad things had become for her,' Atticus resumed. 'I so regret not acting much sooner, for only selfishly thinking about my own well-being. I'm not saying watching the video had everything to do with Sylvie's decision or the method she chose, but it was a factor. There was much in her life I didn't know about and I still don't.'

Maya shifted her position, hardly able to accept Atticus' lack of concern for a woman he'd considered a friend and a spiritual sister. But she guessed his idea of friendship and sisterhood would be vastly different from her own. Still, she needed to better understand Sylvie's behavior, aware at the same time she wouldn't get more information by insulting Atticus.

'I'd like to go back to the time before Sylvie's visit to the guru,' she said, trying to take the venom out of her voice and changing the direction she'd been going with Atticus. 'The time when she first started thinking about ending her life. A key question is what really drove her to that decision in the first place?'

'You got me beat.' Atticus sat back, his gaze at a distant point. 'During that period, she seemed to drag through her days. All I can think of is she'd suffered a tremendous loss.'

Maya rolled the facts around in her mind. Sylvie, a sensitive soul, affected by the littlest things. Like if a moth flew into a flame somewhere far away, she'd sense that and breathe harder. She must have been so stung by an incident that she saw no point in going on living.

The silence between them hung overhead like a sharp blade.

'It seems a bit coincidental that she also changed the method of execution of her suicide,' Maya said, 'suddenly becoming a big advocate of Tibet because that was an acceptable way for her to channel her grief. Being a Tibetan adoptee, and given that she was going to kill herself anyway, she made it a horrific public event to draw attention to the Tibetan demand for freedom. Correct?'

Atticus nodded, a painful admission of sorts.

Maya looked down at her hands. The bracelet. She saw it now, an ornament of solid gold rolling down from Sylvie's blazing arm to the street, eventually hitting the pavement with a thud. Sylvie must have wanted to leave the bracelet for her beloved mother, to pass a secret message to her family about the personal nature of what she was about to do.

'How she must have felt, knowing what she'd go through, and yet she set it up just right,' Maya said. 'The Chinese foreign minister's visit came in handy. She burned herself in front of the minister's residence, making the Tibetan demand more symbolic, more alive, more newsworthy.'

'You got it.'

Maya, feeling sick, went silent for a moment, then spoke again. 'It's painful to have to dig into Sylvie's past and, as of yet, I haven't been able to put every puzzle piece in its place. Such as the role played by Anna, as well as Sylvie's co-conspirator, Sunglasses Man. He stood right behind her, gave her a lit match and a few instructions, then walked away. Who was he and why did he assist her?'

'For the nth plus one time, I didn't see any Sunglasses Man.'

'Are you sure for the nth plus one time?'

Atticus looked anemic, his face and lips turning ashen. Maya rose, retreated to the kitchen and stood by the sink, where she stared at a tender basil plant growing on her windowsill. She prepared a mug of spearmint tea and returned to the living room.

Atticus took a swallow of the tea and sat deeper in the sofa. 'You mustn't start seeing our guru in a poor light because of what I disclosed.'

'Let me be honest with you, Atticus. You're grieving and I respect that. I, too, am grieving the guru's sudden death. Still, it makes me furious that he would exploit Sylvie in that manner. It's despicable. It's a crime.'

'Crime?' Atticus said mockingly. 'You must try to think more selflessly. You obviously don't understand or care about the desperation Tibetans feel. How many more lives will it take? Tibetans constantly ask but never get any answer. They speak about being in the depth of darkness, undergoing a fire torture, with no light or sound, only feeling the intense pain of burning.'

'You're saying the end justifies the means. As if no regard needs to be paid to the individual's rights and wishes. In my humble opinion, the individual matters.'

'We make too much out of an individual, the "I, me, selfie" generation. We forget the larger society.'

'What's society made of if not individual people? Can you harm a person and justify it in the name of the society?' Maya had far more to say but she held it inside so as not to antagonize Atticus. She stared at the bookcase.

Atticus went quiet for a moment, as though interrogating his own beliefs, as though traversing a murky gray zone he'd rather leave behind as quickly as possible. 'We'll have to continue this debate another time.' He pushed himself out of the sofa. 'I have to get in touch with the members of my meditation class, in case they haven't heard.'

Maya walked him to the door.

'I'll call you and *Mashima* if I hear any more,' he said, warmth evident in his voice.

Despite the arguments, she felt less doubtful of him. They'd finally formed a bond; the guru had been the bridge between them. 'Please keep me in the loop,' she said softly.

'Righto.' Atticus sighed. 'Our center might have to close down. End of an era. End of an important phase of my life. Only hope is our guru has found peace. At least he won't have to deal with constant police surveillance.'

Police surveillance. The two words brought Justin to Maya's mind. Yes, the authorities must have been watching the guru since Sylvie's death. Now that he'd died, not from natural causes but from a hit-and-run, perhaps Justin would finally admit that there was more to Sylvie's suicide than he'd believed.

Maya watched Atticus slowly descend the porch steps, then returned to the living room. Gloom had settled over the sitting area. Even the bright red throw pillows on the sofa appeared dull. The guru's death had given her another wake-up call. The negligent driving pointed to the possible involvement of a criminal element.

What should she do next?

Forget the reception. A visit to a cop might be in order. And, in many ways, cops still meant Justin to her, a guardian of the law and protector, an investigator always kind toward the victim's family. As a law enforcement officer involved in the Sylvie case, he would have speculations about the 'accident,' would he not?

In the bedroom, Maya changed into a light blue cardigan, a pair of jeans and low-heeled shoes, and smoothed her hair. She scooped up her cellphone, first punched in the Chaurasias' number and left her regrets, saying she wouldn't make it to the party. Then she punched in Justin's number and got his voicemail. How could she wait under such circumstances? He should be home by now. Or would he be spending the evening with Jennifer?

Maya drew a pink lipstick over her lips, got into her car, drove through the intermittent light rain and rang Justin's bell. The lights were on. It was a miracle of miracles that he was home this early.

The door jerked open. Justin was framed in the doorway, the father of another woman's child. In fact, Maya could hear Justin, Jr's squeal of delight from inside. She could even picture the sweet-breathed, winsome boy beaming at her.

'All right, Maya,' Justin said with a hearty voice that Maya could tell was meant to cover the sounds of the child within. The coolness of his eyes clearly indicated that he wasn't too glad to see her standing on his doorstep. His face had a reddish cast; he might have had a few drinks. 'What is it now?'

Through the half-open door, Maya could hear Jennifer's cloying voice as well. What if Jennifer caught her here? Although flustered, Maya gathered her thoughts and adopted a neutral expression. 'Came to share a bit of news, if you have the time.'

Justin gave her a quizzical look and angled a nervous glance toward the living room. The fact that half his attention was on his so-called family sapped Maya's energy and humiliated her. She stood tongue-tied, a quake inside her, listening to the sound of intensifying rain.

A second later, she gathered her wits and brought him up-to-date on the video, describing how it came to Sylvie through the guru. 'Considering the content, it might have been just the catalyst to push Sylvie to . . .'

Justin made a doubtful face.

'I'm just thinking,' Maya said before Justin could close the door in her face, 'that the video could still be on Sylvie's bookshelf and you might be able to—'

Justin, standing grimly, cut her off. 'Look, Maya, leave the detective work to me, OK? You must have other things in your life to keep you busy besides playing Super Sleuth.'

'The video is, in my opinion, worth watching. I know the apartment was locked up by the police after Sylvie's death. But by now—'

Justin threw a glance over his shoulder. 'Thanks for the tip but we're not suspecting foul play. I've already told you.' His voice was bland, as though speaking to her tired him. 'Not when the two women left a joint suicide note saying they were dying for Tibet's freedom. The signatures are genuine, according to handwriting experts.'

At this news, Maya felt a stab of disappointment, but she still wasn't ready to concede. 'There's more.' She put up her hand when she saw him shift back a pace, as if to close the door. 'You might not have heard this. This evening, at dusk, a hit-and-run driver killed Sylvie's meditation teacher, Padmaraja.'

'I did hear about it, Maya,' Justin said, as though speaking to a child. 'Of course I heard about it – before you did, as a matter of fact. I'm a police detective, Maya. I get all the news long before the general public – which, by the way, is what you are. A member of the general public. Padmaraja was an old man walking on a dark, busy, rainy street. The driver either didn't notice him when he stepped out onto the road all of a sudden or saw him too late. Either way, we have no reason to believe the old man was murdered. Elders have been known to wander into busy intersections; some of them are confused.'

'I don't . . . I don't buy that. I met with the guru only about a week ago. He was alert and articulate.'

'Be that as it may, Maya, the old man stepped out into the street and we're looking for the driver of the car. It's a vehicular homicide and we're on top of it. Still, you coming to my house with wild stories . . .'

Maya felt heat rise into her face, so angry she couldn't speak. His attitude, cutting right to her heart, arrested her breath. 'I'm not the general public, Justin. You don't know this but I'm a private investigator assigned to this case.' Although she didn't mean to overdo it, she now asked him if police specialists had performed the routine procedure and collected all the evidence, such as the transfer of car paint on the clothing of the victim and shards of glass on the street from the broken headlight. Then she heard Justin Jr howling inside the house and stopped speaking. Justin turned toward the sound. He obviously hadn't been listening to her.

'Maya, I'm kind of busy here—'

'I can see that. Sorry to barge in like this.'

Justin gave her an icy stare.

'Honey,' Jennifer called out from the living room in a seductive voice. 'Come inside.'

Maya mumbled a thank you and rushed into the sprinkling rain, glad for the cleansing effect of the drops on her forehead and the fragrance of the moist earth.

She heard Jennifer's voice at the door as the woman asked Justin who he'd been arguing with. Maya didn't mean to, but she turned quickly to catch a glimpse of the woman who had stolen Justin's love from her. The beauty stood beside Justin, her arm around his neck, and watched Maya's retreating back. Maya could only imagine her expression change to one of recognition.

Maya got burned, as her boss, Sen, would have put it.

TWENTY-TWO

It was past ten o'clock, the dark street slick with rain, and Maya was bone-weary. First the guru's death and then that encounter with Justin. This had been a terrible day of sorrow, grief and regrets. She wanted to get home, to her sanctuary, but first she had to temper the turbulence inside her. So she decided to stop by George's, a neighborhood mom-and-pop grocery open till midnight, to pick up a few staples for Uma.

The night was quiet, but for the wind moaning around the fences, when Maya pulled into the store parking lot. She parked her car under the lights closest to the entrance; she was the only one in the lot. Drawing her wallet from her purse, she slipped it into her jeans pocket, deposited the purse on the passenger seat and angled out of her car.

Cool air caressed her face as she walked inside. Devoid of customers, the convenience store appeared deathly silent. George, a hefty, sandy-haired man of sixty, reclined in a chair behind the cash register.

'Hey there, George. How's everything?' Maya smiled at him as she passed the counter.

'Maya, how're you, hon?' A sleepy-voiced George shut his eyes and leaned back again in his chair. 'Wake me up when you're ready to pay.'

The old-fashioned coffee-maker sat at the far end of the counter. Although Maya had no need for a caffeinated drink, she wanted it for company. She poured herself a half-cup. After taking a small sip, she walked past the refrigerated section, chilled by the vapors emanating from the glass cases, and headed toward the rows of shelves to her left. Uma had run out of mustard, which was unthinkable, since the flavor of so many of her dishes depended on it. The shelf situated smack in the middle housed at least five golden-labeled stout jars, each containing different flavors of the yellow-bodied condiment.

Coffee cup in hand, Maya had started checking the brand names when she heard the sound of someone's footsteps approaching.

She gave a glance, saw the chest of a man twice her size and eased closer to the shelf to allow him to pass.

The man planted himself right behind her, a shadow with density. He'd invaded her personal space. Her heart pounded; hair up on the back of her neck, her breath came fast.

A ski mask concealed the intruder's face. His wavy gray hair peeked out of a black cap.

All it takes is a few moments for a criminal to grab you, she heard her self-defense instructor saying.

'George!' she called out. 'Where's the sugar-free mustard?'

No response. Was he asleep?

Boxed in by a wall on one side and the intruder behind her, Maya had an unkind concrete floor beneath her feet. Her fatigue swept away, she again pretended to browse the items, although a fear alert had given her tunnel vision or, worse yet, no vision. The shelves appeared empty.

She flipped around and tried to get a good, close look at the man. She hoped her face looked sufficiently strong and unafraid, which might cause him to back off. The tallish, broad-chested man reeked of alcohol.

Maya's hands balled into fists. 'Step back!' she shouted at the ski mask.

With what felt like a bear's paw, the man grabbed her around the waist. Maya's head bashed into her assailant's chest, or rather into her pendulous breasts.

It was a woman.

Panicky thoughts swirled through her mind. What should she do?

Hurt her, she heard the voice of her self-defense instructor.

She raised her leg and kicked the side of her attacker's knee with her pointy shoe. The woman yelped just as Maya growled, 'Back off, you bitch!'

The woman fell backward into the shelf behind her. A cascade of cans, jars and bottles clattered to the floor. She grabbed the leg of a shelf and got up.

Maya, too, had lost her balance and her coffee cup in the

scuffle. She held on to the edge of a shelf and straightened herself, only now noticing she'd spilled hot coffee over the woman's pants. Taking a look at the attacker, Maya came to a shocking realization: this wasn't just any woman who had attacked her.

She was ancient and drunk, but in good shape.

At the front of the store, chair legs scraped the floor. 'Maya, you OK over there?' George called out.

'Who are you?' Maya asked the woman, shouting in her confusion and alarm. 'What do you want?'

She shrank back as the woman pushed something in her face, a lightweight white object.

Maya expected pain but the object turned out to be only a small white scrap of paper, with a message scribbled on it.

The elderly woman scurried around the shelves and scrambled toward the front of the store.

'What's going on?' George called back to her again, his voice more serious now and closer. 'Maya?'

She glanced at the note. It contained a single sentence scrawled in a foreign language. She pocketed it and shouted, 'Stop her! That woman!'

Maya exploded toward the counter. The woman almost knocked George on his back and pushed past him. The door slammed after her bulky body and she shot out into the darkness.

Maya ran to the door, digging her cellphone from her pocket, and yanked the door open. Listening to the woman's heavy footfall, she trained her cellphone camera on the retreating figure but her subject was too far away and it was too dark. It didn't matter. A blurry picture of a woman's back wouldn't help the police to locate her.

The woman pulled her Subaru out of the parking lot before Maya could get a photo of only three of the digits of her license plate. Breathing hard, Maya scrambled into her Honda and started driving. She kept a close watch on the assailant. The woman took a right turn, ran a red light and the Subaru soon vanished into the pitch-dark shelter of the evening.

Maya pounded the steering wheel. 'Damn it!' She turned around, drove back to the store and parked on the same spot.

George stood in front of his counter. He stared at Maya, reached for her and asked in a panicky voice, 'Are you hurt?'

Maya shook her head. George escorted her to the other side of the counter, lowering her into a chair. He rushed toward the coffee pot, poured a fresh cup, then hurried back and put the coffee into her shaking hand.

'I have to get home, make sure my mother is all right.' Maya took a swallow and put the cup down. Uma would be back from the party by now. She'd sit in the living room, flip the pages of yet another thriller and muse: *What would happen next?* 'But first, I have to call her.'

'Has your mother been unwell?'

Maya replied no. She couldn't explain it all. She opened her cellphone.

Uma answered at the first ring. 'Where are you so late at night? I just finished reading *The Whimsical Strangler*. Scary is no word for it. I jumped out of my chair when the phone rang and my heart—'

'Do not, under any circumstances, open the door if anyone knocks. I'm at the corner store. Be home in a few.'

'Maya, what are you talking about?'

'*Don't* open the door.'

'What's going on?'

Scary to contemplate at this late hour. 'Wish I could explain it all to you, Ma. But I don't get it myself. See you in a few.'

Maya put the phone back into her pocket.

'That's a first,' George said. 'I've been running this store for twenty-five years. But these are hard times. That hoodlum probably just wanted to grab your purse.'

She patted her jeans pocket. 'Except I didn't have one with me and my wallet was here.' She didn't want money, Maya suspected – she had other intentions. She might even have followed her into the store. Obviously an amateur, the woman was ill-prepared for resistance, easily overcome.

Maya pulled the note from her pocket, stared at the unfamiliar handwriting once again and waved it at George. 'She threw this piece of paper at me. Can you make heads or tails out of it?'

George scanned the scribbling. Then, as though a bell rang

in his head, his eyes opened wider. 'Oh, it's Russian. I can't tell you what it says but I recognize the script. My drinking, diabetic grandfather was part Russian.' He turned for the phone. 'But first things first. Let me call nine-one-one.'

'No, George, don't. Not for me.'

Maya took the piece of paper back from George and put it in her jeans pocket, numbed by the coincidence. Sunglasses Man spoke Russian. So did Ivan. She felt cold again, zipped up her jacket and snuggled in its warmth. 'Have you ever seen that woman here?'

'I couldn't see her face because of the mask but her body looked familiar. Pear-shaped. Bosc pear, if I may add. Pardon me, but a man notices. The next time, I'll take a shot of her and call the cops. I'll have my wits about me. I must apologize for being dumbfounded tonight. You might call me old school – I'm not used to thinking of a woman as an attacker.' He paused. 'What did you want to get?'

'Can't remember.' Maya looked over at the riot of cans, jars and boxes scattered on the coffee-stained floor. 'Can I help you clean up?'

'Not to worry,' George replied. 'I'll put things back and the cleaning crew will come soon. Should I follow you home, to make sure—?'

'Not necessary.' Maya thanked George and turned to the door.

Outside, wind fluttered through the parking lot as though trying to make a change in the order of things, disturbing her even more.

TWENTY-THREE

A day later at Revenge, Veen seated next to her, Maya swished the cocoa in her cup, glanced at a stemmed blood-red rose in a cut-glass vase at the center of the square table and smelled the crostini at the next table. She turned to Annette, who'd joined them this afternoon and who had been frequently looking toward the door to check the movement of customers. Her short, strawberry-blonde hair fell smoothly over a small forehead. In her mid-fifties, Annette, Veen's friend from the police force, gave the appearance of being no-nonsense, cautious and dependable, but tough.

'Oh,' Annette said, had a look around and made sure no one was within earshot. 'I do have some news, Maya. Do you want to hear? It's not pretty.'

Maya leaned in closer, a sour taste in her mouth. It'd be silly to pretend she didn't want help filling in some blanks. 'Go ahead.'

'It concerns Jennifer Marlow – not her real name – Justin's current companion. Veen said that you've met her?'

Maya nodded, easily seeing the mysterious Eurasian cradling her small son at the flea market. She took a big swallow of her cocoa and burned her tongue, but an image of the beauty making love to Justin stung her even more.

'Her real name is Sofiya Bilinskii.' Annette had some difficulty getting the name out of her mouth.

'I guessed Jennifer isn't her real name.'

'I doubt you'll have guessed the rest, though.' Annette recited the next set of facts unemotionally, as though reciting a grocery list. 'Father Russian, mother Chinese. Born and bred in Budapest. Migrated to the U.S. in her late teens. Fell in with a bad crowd. Bedded whoever was around. Quite a life, I'd say.' A sly smile appeared on Annette's face. 'At only nineteen, Miss Jennifer was co-habiting with a drug lord in the Georgetown neighborhood, and that's when our story starts.'

Maya felt a little shaky. The sweet cocoa hardly soothed her.

'Federal agents had an eye on that drug lord for some time. After months of watching, they busted him. I mean the agents, assisted by a local narcotics task force, broke into his home with K-9 dogs. They seized guns, cash and pounds of heroin. Our Justin was part of the task force.'

Veen, until now listening quietly, said to Maya, 'I seem to remember you mentioning that bust.'

Maya did mental calculations, her heart picking up its beat, and reached out and gripped Veen's arm. 'Yes, yes, that high-profile manhunt. Justin told me about it afterward – the planning they'd gone through, how they almost lost a couple of their men once they'd gotten inside the drug house. That raid was the largest of its kind in Justin's work history.' She imagined her ex-boyfriend at the scene and the hair-raising rush he'd experienced, which he would relate to her later, concluding with: 'We got the bastard.' That was the night Justin had changed; their relationship had changed.

Annette quietly sipped her cocoa.

Veen watched Maya, eyes wide with anticipation, and said, 'Spit it.'

'It was a Friday night,' Maya said. 'We had plans to go out to dinner and then catch a show.' As Maya spoke, grief building in her chest, she envisioned herself in her best red dress as she explained what had happened that night to Veen and Annette. Red wasn't the most flattering color for her; she'd worn it only to give the evening a feel of excitement. After all, they'd been together for a year then and she'd felt celebratory – hoped he did, too. She'd applied blusher and lipstick, rare for her; she'd expected Justin to propose to her that evening. With pleasant jitters all over her body, she'd circled the living room in her high heels, waiting for the doorbell to ring, the evening rich with promise. An hour had passed. Where was he? Had he been in a car accident? Involved in a shootout? After all, he'd been working narcotics.

Outside, the high wind had rattled the leaves on the trees and rain hammered the roof. Messages left on Justin's cellphone went unanswered. Darkness descended over her window like a mist gone tired. She'd never felt lonelier. The evening crawled to midnight. By half-past twelve, achy, pooped and feeling the fool, she went to bed.

She'd spent a sleepless night, sweating and drinking water, and a miserable morning, too spent to concentrate on any work. Late in the day, he'd called to say he'd been caught up in a drug case. He'd apologized in broken phrases, his voice weak and edged with guilt, and did plenty of throat-clearing in between delivering an avalanche of excuses.

'For a day or so afterward, Justin was exhausted, but he stopped by and talked about the bust.' Maya's voice was soft, faraway. She felt embarrassment from sharing so much with both Veen and Annette, especially since she didn't know

Annette all that well. With a force of will, she overcame an inner resistance and continued, 'Come to think of it, we never celebrated our anniversary, never saw that movie, never went to that restaurant, either, because he got busy after that.'

'Shall I continue?' Annette asked Maya.

'Yes.' Maya's voice grew stronger. 'I want to hear it all.'

'Here's the rest. I'm speaking like a reporter, but let me warn you, it gets worse. I had a hard time with it myself when I heard it. The drug king – the head dog as they called him – a man known as X-311, was booked into the jail. While he waited for his trial, his darling Jennifer was alone but not for long. Can you guess who that calculating bitch enchanted next?'

For a moment, Maya lost her breath. How could Justin have continued to see her and yet carry on with another woman? He'd shattered her trust, never mind the sordid circumstances. How clueless she'd been. How right Veen had been about Justin all along. The fact that Justin was lured by Jennifer's looks also grated on her. Now she asked an invisible Justin: *Were you that shallow and that stupid and I didn't see it?*

Veen, struggling with the weight of the report, gave Maya a reassuring look.

Maya nodded to Annette. *Go ahead. Torture me more.*

Annette smiled sadly. 'The cops continued to do what they usually do in these cases. They investigated further and Jennifer, the sleaze, was also tried in court on charges of drug trafficking conspiracy and sent to jail. She turned the state's evidence and had her sentence shortened.'

'I see where you're going, but please proceed.' Maya's tone was dead, as if she couldn't be hurt any more than she'd already been by this man whom she'd loved and trusted.

'Jennifer was pregnant then. Justin Jr was born in prison.'

Maya took a hard swallow; her eyes felt strained. Although the answer was obvious, she went ahead and asked, 'But how can they be so sure of the paternity when Jennifer had been living with at least one other man?'

'DNA tests, of course.'

'You mean there's no privacy anymore?' Veen said.

'People talk.' Annette turned to Maya. 'If you're uncomfortable, I'll stop.'

Maya gestured with a hand for Annette to continue. She watched a sleepy-eyed pedestrian stroll by.

'Jennifer got out of prison and is now finishing a drug rehab program. With the computer training she got as an inmate, she's doing clerical work somewhere. That woman finds her way around.'

Certainly, Maya was interested in finding out exactly what Jennifer did and where. But she couldn't expect Annette to fish that out.

'Let me get refills.' Maya sprung to her feet, headed for the counter, produced a credit card and asked a server with henna-decorated hands to fill the cups.

'Your card doesn't go through,' the server said curtly.

'But it did yesterday,' Maya answered, baffled. 'Could you please try again?' She didn't have another credit card or cash with her.

It took a few minutes to sort out the card issue, which turned out to be an error on the server's part. Maya returned to the table and dropped to her seat, only then gulping a big breath.

Both Veen and Annette thanked her for the second cup. Annette resumed by saying, 'Justin supports Jennifer and their child. He's a doting father. They're a family, although they live separately.' Annette paused. 'End of story. Or at least, as far as I've gone.'

Her jealousy hadn't helped, Maya now acknowledged to herself, drinking from her cup. It had raised unnecessary red flags in her mind and clouded her judgement. It wasn't the end of the story, as far as she could see.

TWENTY-FOUR

The following day, Maya smelled the cloying odor of an unbathed body as she entered through the door of Cal Chodron's rental office in Aurora Avenue. A deep breath through her mouth and she saw a kindly but gloomy-faced Cal chatting with Arthur. Ah, that was where the stench came from: Arthur, the street poet. Maya tried not to inhale through her nose.

'The homeless don't lie,' she heard Arthur saying. 'We don't have to put up a front.' Face creased, hair wild and stringy, his ample body spilling out of a chair, Arthur looked up from his paper cup and scrutinized her.

'Hello, Maya.' Cal pointed to the other visitor's chair but didn't flash his Buddha smile. Maya extended a greeting and grabbed the chair, her mind focused on what she wished to discuss with Cal and how to bring that up, given Arthur's presence. The foul odor emanating from Arthur's body and clothing in such close quarters overpowered her thoughts.

'It's been one of those weeks.' Cal hunched forward and recited a litany of issues facing him: his son had sprained an ankle, the plumbing in his kitchen was plugged up and his shrew of a mother-in-law had come for a visit.

Arthur turned to Cal. 'Are you going to keep on complaining, old boy? Or are you going to offer coffee to this lovely young lady and ask her what she needs?'

Cal mumbled an apology and asked Maya, 'Cream and sugar?'

'Thanks, but I don't need a cup.'

Cal ignored her reply and disappeared into the back room.

Arthur smiled at Maya, his chapped lips somehow accommodating that wide, mischievous smile. He wore a soiled, once-stylish ivory vest over his white shirt, the colors barely recognizable beneath the grime.

'I'm from Santa Barbara,' Arthur began. 'Ever been there? They dress like a million dollars in that town. A young actor gave me this vest, said he wore it in a movie. Should I have believed him? They all live in a world of fantasy, you know. Still, all was well for me in that fine town, could always bum for a few bucks, until I ran into trouble with the law and got kicked out. I left with a tarp, a sleeping bag, a backpack and this vest.'

'Do you have a place in Seattle?'

'I spend time in a flophouse – a transitional housing facility, they call it. It's full of cockroaches.' He made a zigzag flying motion with his fingers. Then his tone changed to a more serious one. 'Let's talk about you. You have trouble, young lady?'

'What makes you think I have trouble?'

'A pretty young thing like you wouldn't come to a neighborhood like this unless you had a hot potato in your hand. Perhaps a murder that happened in one of the rich neighborhoods? Rich people murder in style, no knives or clubs for them like us dumb, poor folks.' Arthur laughed at his own joke, a gross laugh, his head thrown back and his yellow, rotten teeth in view, hardly realizing how close to the truth he was. Sylvie and Anna had been pushed to their deaths, Maya believed. And yes, she would admit, it wasn't a straightforward crime. Arthur was proving to be intuitive and amusing, despite his hygiene; even so, she remained wary. Cal might have been filling him in on who Maya was and what she wanted. She could hear Cal rummaging around in the back kitchen.

'Well, whatever brings you here,' Arthur said, 'you're on Aurora Avenue. I don't mean to scare you but we have our share of mishaps on these wretched few blocks. Anything can go wrong. I mean anything. You could be mugged or kidnapped. Or a nasty surprise could flare up. Like a gas main breaking in a motel around the corner. An accident? Someone trying to get at a guest? Who knows? A man sleeping in his bed was thrown out of his window by that explosion. Talk about a horrible death. Literally being shredded to pieces.'

Maya started to rise. She wasn't in the mood for this kind of talk. Arthur was a bit loony.

Cal reappeared and placed a steaming cup of coffee in front of her. 'Sit down, please.' He cast a warning glare at Arthur.

Arthur wiggled out of his chair, saying to Cal, 'Atta-boy. Be nice to the ladies – let them take over.' He gave Maya a long look. 'Do you know you look even prettier when you're scared?' He chuckled and headed for the door.

Idiot. Maya was glad to be rid of him.

Cal diverted his eyes from the retreating figure and gave Maya a steady look. 'Don't mind him, he's harmless. He's getting treatment. What brings you here this morning?'

Tense, Maya turned her attention to the window, now freckled with raindrops, to make sure Arthur was out of sight. 'Well, I'm here to ask you about the lost specimen.'

'It's office confidential.'

'You cared about Anna. Wouldn't you like to know why she—'

'OK – the test tube, one of several, contained a blood sample from Anna, drawn after she'd been immunized and then exposed to the malaria parasite. Surprise of surprises, the tube disappeared.'

'Who took it?'

'Someone in our office claimed she'd seen a new hire put a test tube in her pocket but had failed to report it. Just forgot. It was the new hire's job to pack a number of tubes in a larger container and send it to the lab technician for testing. When we checked the technician's reports, we saw that the requisition paper was there but no tube to go along with it, which meant that particular specimen was missing. It was one of Anna's.'

Somewhere a car engine grumbled; it jarred Maya. 'Why would anyone—?'

'I'm stumped.' Cal sighed. 'I'm not up on medical matters. With two jobs, I'm so swamped that . . .'

'I hope you're documenting all that's going on with this new hire. You might need the details for the police, if we ever need to go that far. It's a theft related to someone who committed suicide under questionable circumstances.'

'We're keeping our suspect under observation, rather than fire her or pull her out of the project. We haven't collected enough concrete evidence yet. And yes, it is a matter for the police. My boss Inez is knowledgeable – her father is an ex-police chief.'

The phone jangled. Cal reached for the receiver and put the caller on hold.

'And the name of the new hire?'

'Because we run a confidential trial in our clinic, we're not allowed to name our staff.'

Maya rose, thanked Cal and stole away. She couldn't wait to discuss the matter of the stolen blood samples with her mother. Uma's eyes would sparkle with excitement when told how useful her medical contacts in Kolkata would be in providing technical details so urgently required.

Outside, Maya looked around at the block, empty but for Arthur sitting at the entrance to an alleyway strewn with garbage, a rotten smell pervading. A shopping cart heaped with his possessions rested nearby. Arthur turned his head and gave Maya a sideways glance.

She drew near, walking carefully past the litter of broken beer bottles. 'How goes it?' A casual question, a friendly manner, to get a better feel for the man. Her instinct about him asked her to do so.

He removed the cigarette from his mouth, crunched a potato chip and said in a serious voice, 'I keep an eye on all that goes on in this hood. Watch where you go, young lady.'

'Do you spy for somebody? Am I being targeted? Who is it?'

He shut his eyes, mumbled a few words she couldn't catch. She acknowledged the ripple of fear inside her, said a goodbye and rushed toward her car.

TWENTY-FIVE

The following afternoon, Maya arrived at the Green Lake trails and searched for Ivan. Even at this lazy, midday hour, surrounded by open space, vast sky and the faint hint of wild berries, she found herself unsettled. It had to do with Atticus' warning: *I'd stay away from him if I were you.* She saw a teenage girl with a goat on a leash, a young boy on rollerblades and a tourist snapping photographs with his cellphone, keeping his impatient companion waiting. An occasional warm breeze rolled over the grass in a threatening manner and rustled the leaves on the trees and bushes like it was punishment.

A couple standing under the shade of a row of red oaks argued if solar power was good for homes or not. Maya paused for a moment to eavesdrop. She heard a voice call from behind her, 'Hello. Sorry to be late.'

Something in the way Ivan looked at her gave Maya the creeps. He sidled up to her and smiled; she recomposed her face. He shook her hand, a chilled, firm grip, and the two of them fell into step on the paved three-mile pathway around the lake.

'What have you been up to?' Ivan asked.

'I'm having such an odd week.' She watched his face carefully, withdrew the crumpled piece of paper from her pocket and held it before him. 'A stranger gave it to me. Can you interpret it?'

He held the piece of paper. 'It says something like "back off or you'll be dead." How odd, coming from a stranger. Must be a nutjob.'

A dreadful feeling twisted through Maya. She hid it, took the note back from Ivan and studied his reactions without being obvious. His voice conveyed genuine surprise. Quite likely, he'd had no hand in the attack. Someone was giving her an ultimatum, trying to get her to back off the investigation into Sylvie's death. Who might that be?

Back off or you'll be dead. She'd consider this later. Now she decided to jump into the topic that was of utmost importance to her. 'I wanted to ask you a bit more about Sylvie. You two worked in the same lab. I've asked you this before. Why would a happy person dedicated to her work and successful at it want to forego it all?'

His face coloring, Ivan stopped to pick up a pine cone. 'Good question. What did you say you do for a living?'

The sun blazed overhead. She stared at a red Hawthorne just ahead of them, the largest specimen around, and stretched the truth. Well, just a bit. 'I'm a nutritionist.'

'Not too much money in it, is there?'

'My profession has nothing to do with my inquiries.' A dog paddled out to retrieve a floating Frisbee. She smiled at the dog's antics and turned back to Ivan. 'I'm so concerned about Sylvie's family. They're broken from grief. It'll take them a long time to recover, if they ever do. What can you tell me about Sylvie's research?'

He wore a non-committal expression. 'Well, Sylvie was the star in our lab, the senior scientist who had made a big breakthrough, one which would have ultimately led to a successful vaccine, except . . . she caused her hard drive to fail. Worse yet, she got rid of all her backups. Which would have made the recovery of the data impossible.'

'After all those years of work? Didn't her breakthrough belong to the company?'

Ivan's steps faltered. His tone turned solemn. 'Not necessarily. It's not unusual for a scientist at a small lab like ours to take all her research with her if she decides to leave. And Sylvie would have left because the funding for the malaria study was ending.'

Maya pushed forward. 'Might Sylvie have been afraid the data would be stolen even from her own possession?'

He flinched, as though he'd revealed too much by mistake. 'I couldn't comment on that. I never analyzed any of the data she produced. Like I told you, I'm not high up on the ladder.'

They strolled past a father walking with his son, guiding a dog on a leash, struggling to coordinate both of them. The dog growled at Ivan and he watched the animal carefully as they passed by. 'These trails rock,' Ivan said after a while. 'I found them on my first day here. Didn't know a soul then. Green Lake and the ducks kept me company.'

'Have you been here long?'

'Not that long. Let me back up here. I'm a Michigander, born and raised, went to high school in Turkey and college in England and Moscow. Pretty cosmopolitan, you might say. I've spent a good bit of time in Moscow, where I still have many relatives from my mother's side. My Russian uncle calls me a part-time Muscovite. I worked there for a while. Then I had the Seattle dream and moved back to the States. I've been here for a little more than two years.'

Maya registered an unspoken yearning in Ivan's voice, a quake of a regret. 'You like it here?'

'Truthfully, no. The Pacific Northwest is a fallen dream for me. Donuts, but not enough dough to buy them. Huh. I work sixty hours a week and half my money goes to pay the rent.' He took a long pause. 'Losing Sylvie has brought an end to a chapter in my life. Even the hair salon I used to go to is closing.'

Salon Martin was closing? Maya would have to call Cindy. She kept listening.

'Heck, I'm thinking about moving back to Moscow, where my parents are staying temporarily, although I haven't given notice to my boss at the lab yet.'

What does your boss think about you taking a two-hour-plus lunch period twice in recent times? Maya's worry deepened: Ivan, a suspect, could disappear from her life any day now. Indeed, Ivan, his eyes focused on a far-off point, looked distracted and increased his pace.

She lengthened her stride to keep pace with him. 'You must miss Moscow.'

'Have you ever been there?' At her negative reply, he added, 'They get thousands of visitors from India. Before you and I were born, India and Russia were Cold War allies. The first Cold War, I mean.'

That alliance, however irrelevant it might be in today's world, however fragile in terms of evolving international alliances, might help him open up more to her.

'Well, my mother, who's from Kolkata, talks about the old times, the period after India's independence when the country had a rapport with the Soviet Union,' Maya replied. 'How she would buy translations of Russian classics for pennies from street vendors in what was then known as Calcutta. Tolstoy, Turgenev, Dostoyevsky and many others. Some of her friends would say they were propaganda literature but my mother loved reading them. She regrets that they don't sell those books in Kolkata street stalls anymore.'

Ivan smiled. 'But scientific and cultural exchanges are still going on between our countries. Lots of foreign scientists work in Russia, including many from India and Bangladesh.'

'Oh, do you know any?'

'Yes, I was studying science in Moscow, so naturally I had contacts with the scientists and became friends with several. My best friend, Viktor, a Bangladeshi scientist from Moscow, is here on an assignment.'

Must be the dude Hank had spotted with Ivan. The charmer

she'd made a point to share a table with at Betty's. She wanted to formally meet him. 'He's Bangladeshi? He must speak Bengali then. That's my mother tongue.'

'He's a bigwig where he works and makes a bundle of money.'

She didn't want to seem overeager to meet the man. With a dismissive laugh, she said, 'Is that all you think women want?'

'Pardon me for making such a generalization. I know you're different – you're a serious person.'

'Tell me a bit more about your friend.'

'Full name is Vikram Bhusan Chattopadhya. We call him Viktor. Born and raised in Bangladesh, he comes from the Bhusan Chattopadhya family, affectionately called the BC family. They're wealthy and aristocratic. The lineage has deep roots. From what I understand, status counts as much as money does, if not more, in your corner of the world. And Viktor has status in Bangladesh. He'd be delighted to meet someone as pretty and fascinating as you, who even speaks Bengali.'

She played hard to get. 'I wish I could but my mother's visiting. Thanks anyway.'

'Sure you want to pass it up?' Ivan's smile was charming.

'Thanks, but no thanks. There are plenty of single women around who'd probably love to be introduced to your friend. The bars are packed every night.'

'Oh, come on, Maya. He's a great guy. I'd like to take him out for dinner. He drools at the mention of grilled lamb. Since you're a nutritionist, could you tell me where I could get good grilled lamb?'

'Taj India West is a favorite of mine – it's spacious, elegant and fancy, a special occasion type of a place. I like Chef Arun Singh's style – fusion cooking inspired by Indian spices and French techniques. I'm not a wine connoisseur but they do offer a varied wine list.'

He slowed his pace. 'Sounds divine. My mother has a proverb – appetite comes with eating. You'll enjoy yourself when you get there.'

'OK, then.' The invitation was, indeed, an opportunity. Maya saw herself sharing a table with two suspects in a public place.

Wine would flow; the aroma of grilled lamb would pervade the air. If the situation started to get sticky or worse, she would walk out.

'Is your friend here strictly on business or for pleasure as well?'

Ivan still smiled but his eyes turned watchful. 'A bit of both.'

She felt cold looking at him. Even the purplish-gray clouds in the bruised sky seemed to issue a warning. Rows of tall trees surrounding the lake gave the water an unnatural green tint. 'He's a scientist? I don't suppose he specializes in malaria.'

Ivan shot her a glance. 'He does, actually. He's a honcho in his company.'

A chillier sensation spread over Maya's neck.

'Do you have a business card?' Ivan asked.

She considered, then fumbled in her purse and produced a colorful card from her past that read, *Nourish*: *Eat Well, Live Well*. That was followed by her name, a business phone number and email address.

Ivan gave her an extravagant smile, plucked the card from her hand and scanned it carefully.

Maya was about to turn when Uma swept into her mind. How her wise mother always insisted on finding out about a person's background, including caste and family lineage, questions she felt were perfectly acceptable and which often led to more useful data.

Maya adopted a look of exaggerated interest. 'You can fill me in about Viktor, if you like.'

'He's not at all a geeky scientist. He works out a lot and is an engaging conversationalist. In Moscow, where I met him, we used to run in Gorky Park together. Some of our mutual acquaintances say he's full of himself but I get along well with him. He's as handsome as they come. And if you were to talk about high ideals, he has them. He loves eating out in restaurants, travels the world, likes to dance. Got the dance part from his mother, who danced to Bollywood tunes. He's also down-to-business when he needs to be.'

That description sounded too good to be true; warning bells

chimed in Maya's head. As they walked past a pile of dry leaves coated with mud, she fired another question, as though this man Viktor really intrigued her. 'What town in Bangladesh?'

'You want to check him out? His family is from the Chittagong district.' Ivan gave her a triumphant look. 'He wouldn't mind getting married if the right woman came along.'

She knew zilch about that district. And Viktor's marital status was of no importance to her. 'And, oh, changing the topic, another question concerning Sylvie—'

A touch of fierceness fleeted across Ivan's face. 'You know you might regret . . .'

The sun had vanished; the sky wore an ash-blue mantle. Maya halted, caught by the dark tone of his voice. 'Regret? What? Why?'

He stood, facing her. 'A Russian cousin of mine used to say, "We Russians make good friends and the worst enemies."'

Broad daylight. Two mothers pushed strollers nearby and an exerciser did bar dips. Still, the sky above Maya tilted. She stalled for another instant. Obviously Ivan was warning her, intuiting she had suspicions about him.

Ivan forced a smile. 'Lighten up, will you? I'll call you in a day or two and we'll fix a date and time for our dinner. And don't concern yourself with that crazy message from a stranger.'

Maya waved goodbye and turned toward a trail path bordering a golf course. She could feel Ivan watching her. The lush golf course, the pink roses on the trail's chain-link fence and the white oak towering over the path in a neighborly manner failed to quiet her. That ultimatum came back to her: *Back off or you'll be dead.*

TWENTY-SIX

Standing by the produce aisle in Organics Only the following weekend, Maya watched Uma, who stopped squeezing a kale bouquet and shoved it into the cart. A joyous yet surprising expression on her face, Uma asked, 'Are we having anyone over for dinner tonight?'

Come Saturday, Uma loved to fill the house with friends: the buzz of banter, long, slow meals lasting for hours and the sweet clatter of utensils, all of which she found so energizing. It crushed Maya to have to disappoint her, especially as Uma had wanted to invite Hank over. Here was Maya's dilemma. Ivan had confirmed the dinner date less than fifteen minutes ago, just before Maya left the house. 'Sorry, Ma, I'll be out on a dinner date.'

'And the lucky man?'

'A scientist from Moscow, a member of the aristocratic Bhusan Chattopadhya family of the Chittagong District in Bangladesh, the BC family. Have you heard of the family?'

The glow faded from Uma's face. 'Of course. My mother used to tell stories about them. Although not as famous as the Tatas and the Birlas, they were apparently known in pre-independence India. They lived in East Bengal, which after independence was called East Pakistan. Eventually, after a bloody battle, it became the independent nation of Bangladesh.'

'Give me a minute, Ma.' Maya went to a quiet corner of the store, texted Simi Sen in Kolkata and asked about the BC family, then rejoined Uma. 'While I wait for the official report, will you fill me in on what, if anything, you know about the BCs?'

'At the time I was growing up in independent India, you couldn't help but hear gossip about the BCs, even though they lived at least a hundred miles away in Bangladesh.' Uma grabbed a few oranges and put them in the shopping cart. 'They were rather prominent.'

Maya pushed the cart toward the checkout counter. 'No kidding. They were that famous?'

'Infamous, I should say. Have you accepted the invitation?'

'Yes,' Maya answered in a whisper.

'You did?' Uma's voice rose as she walked alongside Maya. 'Without first checking him out?'

'Will you cool down, Ma?'

Uma shot a few glances over her shoulder. 'It gives me the chills.'

Already mired in doubts about Ivan and his associate, Maya wondered if she'd made the wrong move. She paid for the produce, hastened to the parking garage, helped Uma into the passenger side and plopped into the driver's seat, only then catching her breath.

She merged with the traffic. A blue sedan came terrifyingly close then passed her, took a right turn at an exit sign and disappeared. She got a quick view of the driver, a beefy man of about forty, whom she'd never seen before, and the full license plate number: AMH2647. She'd have to track down the owner of the automobile.

Within minutes, Maya turned on her street and coasted into her driveway. Together, she and Uma mounted the porch steps. Maya glanced around before inserting her key into the door lock. Did she hear a small, crackling sound somewhere?

Once inside the living room, her intestines icy, Maya asked, 'So what's the big deal about my seeing that guy?'

'Does it matter so much if you're dateless on a Saturday night? Are you so bored with me?'

'I'm not bored with you. That's not it.'

'Wait till you hear all the reports.'

Uma went to the kitchen with the groceries, leaving several troubling questions in Maya's mind.

Half an hour later, Maya received a phone call. Simi Sen greeted her from the other end.

'Got something for me already?' Maya asked her boss.

'Yes, we have access to databases and informers and, personally, I know a bit about the BC family. You're going to have your hands full. It's a fairytale and a nightmare blended together. The BC family, those crooks, as I remember from my childhood days, lived in style in a big gated mansion in Chittagong. They were believed to have revived the ancient principle of Sleep Temple, also called Dream Temple, and profited hugely from it.'

'Sleep Temple? Dream Temple? Never heard of either.'

'You're far too young, Maya. A Sleep Temple, a shrine of sorts, was a healing sanctuary where people brought their sick relatives, where you would literally lie down, fall asleep and receive waves of hypnotic suggestions.'

Were drugs part of the equation? 'So it's hypnotherapy?'

'Hypnos means sleep in Greek. So yes, it is, in a way, hypnotherapy. The BC family, going generations back, lived in a village, which at the time belonged to India and is now a part of Bangladesh. Hypnotism was a skill handed down by the male members of BC families from one generation to another. They could make people do things. Some insist they actually cured people of their ailments – mental, physical or spiritual – and they specialized in heartbreaks of various types.'

Were Sylvie and Anna drugged and hypnotized? 'How interesting,' Maya replied. 'How did they manage to cure heartbreaks?'

'With loving, hypnotic words, I believe.' Sen drew a portrait verbally and Maya visualized it so clearly: a tiny chamber in a hamlet, a simple cot covered with a thin mattress, a pillow fragrant with a fresh herbal scent, a lit lantern flickering on a nearby table and sunset outside the window. The patient lay on the bed and took deep breaths, eyes closed and body covered with a white muslin sheet. A priest and his retinue popped in and surrounded the patient's bed. They sang, chanted, recited mantras and beat drums. In a deep, heartfelt, hypnotic voice mingled with the various sounds, a male member of the BC family made powerful suggestions, planting the seeds of healing in the patient's deeper mind. *I'm getting better. My eyes can see clearly now. My legs are strong and supportive. My heart is pure, new. I'm whole and complete and safe, immersed in this ocean of love.* Those positive suggestions enveloped the patient like a warm blanket and even created a hallucinatory effect, until she fell into a deep slumber.

'Do you suppose they administered a few narcotics—?'

'To lower the resistance to getting into the trance state?' Sen said. 'That could very well have been the case. Getting back to my story – night after night, like a puppet, the patient lived in a semi-conscious, relaxed state and accepted the suggestions in her subconscious mind, which supposedly cast out bad influences. If she was at all receptive, those suggestions began to take root. Upon awakening from the trance, she felt better, even though she wouldn't remember much. The symptoms, in many cases, went away. And, supposedly, after a few such sessions, the patient was on her way to getting her life back.'

'I suppose the patients were mostly women?' Maya asked.

'Yes. We ladies give too much of ourselves to those around us and often don't get enough back. It's different with men. Men are like pillars. How many will admit their heart is so broken they can't function?'

'Is there any scientific evidence of such a cure?'

'Aren't there mysteries science hasn't been able to penetrate?' Sen said. 'This is one of them. You see, the cure depends on how suggestible a person is. Individuals differ in that respect. I'm told many patients did reverse their conditions, although they were made to believe a mysterious power had waved a hand and healed them.'

'You don't actually believe people can be influenced so easily, do you, from where you sit?'

'I go back and forth, only because I see instances of such influence every day. A billboard, a television ad or an Internet pop-up does a similar sort of thing when it screams out the name of a product or service. It flaunts before you pleasant, sometimes lurid images of the results you'll get if you spend money on it. If you repeatedly expose yourself to the ad or hear the product name sung to you, you're likely to go for it, aren't you?'

Maya mulled that over. 'Yes, I would. But both you and my mother seem to have quite a bit of hesitation about the BC family.'

'Perhaps because both of us have heard stories about how they misused their talking cure to take advantage of patients, generally young women who had suffered major losses in their lives and were, therefore, vulnerable. They'd get them high and talk them into having sex with the male hypnotist. A remedy of some sort, I presume.'

Maya remained silent and allowed Sen to continue.

'Because the BC family members were such experts at this "cure," it wasn't hard to get the patients to pay through the nose for the treatment, and so, over time, the clan became quite wealthy. That's not a good thing in my book. They claim they use the money for charitable purposes but who's keeping track?'

'Narcotics – that makes sense,' Maya replied. 'But all this was a long time ago. I doubt the family could continue this type of a scam.'

'Don't be too sure. During the troubled days of Bangladeshi independence, those practices stopped or went underground. My guess is they were kept secretly alive by the family members. It wouldn't surprise me if the cheats and puppet masters were again back to their game. To get what they want. Wherever they can find it. And whoever might fall for it. The family is known to be pretty ruthless. Most of the males in the family study either chemistry or medicine. They grow many types of plants in their family home, some of which are believed to be intoxicants.'

'Are you suggesting they smuggle drugs here?'

'No need,' Sen replied. 'You can get plenty there. Let's talk more after your dinner date. Be sure not to lie down anywhere near this guy. Now, I have to go to a client appointment.'

After disengaging, Maya emailed Hank and asked him to research the Sleep Temple concept. Less than an hour later, a reply from him popped up.

'Who came up with this Sleep Temple scheme, you ask? Ancient Indians or Egyptians – who can say for sure? Regardless, it took hold in India. You explained to me once how India tolerates, even absorbs, all sorts of notions, however bizarre they might be, and makes them work. Sleep Temple is a prime example. And that license plate number you wanted me to look up? The car owner's name is Chuck E. Davis. He has no criminal record. That's all I've got for now, Maya.'

Chuck E. Davis – a familiar name. He was a retired policeman, a former colleague of Justin. She'd heard the name from Justin, although she'd never met him. Why would he be following her?

Maya turned, only to see Uma standing at the doorway. She recounted the details, except for the Chuck Davis part, adding, 'Don't concern yourself about my date. We're meeting in a public place, Ma, not a sleep shrine. Other diners will be around. Ivan, too, will be there to introduce us and we have a rapport of some sort. I'll be sure to have an exit strategy ready if I sense something's wrong. I'm not easy to zap – I don't believe in hypnosis. I know better than to drink anything that's not bottled.' She paused. 'Do you have any other friends or relatives in India who I might contact to get an additional scoop?'

Yes, Minerva and Urvasi – you've met both my friends. They still have relatives in Bangladesh and visit them often. They might be able to give you a fuller picture. Let me dig up their numbers.'

TWENTY-SEVEN

The same afternoon, with a few hours to go before her dinner date, Maya received Bill Cameron at her house, Justin's fishing buddy. A gregarious ex-Californian, Bill had a broad white smile and tousled blond hair. Although Maya had met him through Justin, they'd formed their own friendship. Standing in her backyard, Bill asked Maya for her advice on installing an herb garden on his patio. Maya offered her suggestions, then led him into chit-chat, mentioning Justin's name only in passing. Jokingly, Bill said that both he and Justin had been eaten by mosquitoes earlier this summer while fishing in the Sierra. But given that Jennifer worked for a malaria clinic in Seattle, they'd surely be able to get prompt medical treatment, should that ever be necessary.

Malaria clinic, Maya noted breathlessly, put on an innocent look and asked, 'Jennifer?'

'Justin's main girlfriend.'

'What does she do at the clinic?'

'Wish I could tell you, but it has never come up in our conversation. He's rather close-mouthed about her.'

Bill departed but that news, some sort of an anchor, lurked in Maya's mind. Her watch read nearly six o'clock – time to get ready for her date, the butterflies-in-the-stomach moment. In her bedroom, she opened the closet door, spotted a black skirt and a white blouse hanging next to each other on the rod and hastily settled on them.

Uma appeared. 'You're going to wear a job interview outfit on a dinner date in a fancy restaurant? If you want to make it seem to your date you don't have the slightest clue about him . . .'

'You're not suggesting I wear one of your saris?'

Uma smiled sweetly. 'Come, let me show you what I have.'

A half-hour later, wrapped in Uma's shimmering green silk sari and a pair of her own emerald-studded, gold drop earrings, Maya entered through the mahogany doors of Taj India West. Walking past the marble bar and eyeing the women patrons clothed in skimpy low-cut dresses, she felt overdressed and overburdened. She wrapped the embroidered sari train around her chest and scanned the surroundings: a posh, high-ceilinged room, soft leather chairs and fleet-footed waiters. Each table was laid with a cream-colored tablecloth and lustrous silverware. Yellow roses stood fresh and plump in slender crystal vases at the center of each table. Well-placed candles cast warm amber light throughout the room.

A tuxedo-clad maître d' materialized. She mentioned Ivan's name.

'This way, please.' He escorted her toward the far end of the room.

She spotted them at a table for three. Ivan, with his broad face and high cheekbones, sat smiling under a miniature watercolor of a Mughal court scene. Accompanying him was the Bangladeshi man she'd already met, handsome and polished, with brushed-back, stylishly coiffed hair. Both rose to greet her as they saw her approaching the table. Ivan pecked at her cheeks and she smiled widely.

'Oh, it's you . . .' Viktor said, nearly breathless.

Ivan wore a puzzled expression. 'You two have already met?'

'Yes, we shared a table at Betty's.' Maya put on an expression of surprise as well. 'Although we were never introduced.'

'Allow me.' A jovial Ivan made the introductions.

Viktor grinned a welcome, held her gaze and shook her hand, a strong, warm shake. He held out a chair for Maya and all three took their seats. 'So glad you could make it.'

Ordinary words but with high energy behind them, and the voice was silky. And now, once again, Maya measured her date. He was an inch or so shorter than Ivan. Like Ivan, Viktor was virile, personable and forward. The closeness between them was palpable, as though they had a common objective.

'Good choice of a restaurant.' Viktor gave her a smile of admiration. 'Great ambience. You're the first person to suggest this place.'

What he projected was: *I'll make this evening magical for you. As magical as you've made it for me.* Voice inclusive, commanding and even trustworthy, he kept talking and gave the impression of a man comfortable with the opposite sex. There was no twitch of shyness in his body and he put her at ease as well. She came up with answers; he listened intently.

Her gaze settled on Ivan. Eyes sparkling, he watched the two of them. Maya's attention drifted back to Viktor; he was the brightest light in the room. She found herself observing his gestures more carefully. It was then something drummed at her heart – a reminiscence, an edge of fear, a warning that sent a current through her legs.

She'd seen him somewhere. Recently. Not just at Betty's. But where?

She kept her smile fixed, nodded and murmured at his words, and continued to study him, his littlest gestures.

A sinking certainty jolted her.

He was Sunglasses Man.

Spotted at the self-immolation of Sylvie and Anna. Suspected of aiding them. Now he was without his huge, wraparound sunglasses, his jacket and whatever other disguises he'd worn on that fateful day.

Maya couldn't be fooled, however. She recognized the wide sterling silver band on his middle finger and dragged in an uneven breath.

Viktor, either oblivious or playing a similar game, signaled the waiter with just the right tilt of his chin. The moussed-haired waiter drifted over, bowed graciously and poured red wine into Maya's glass. She recognized the bottle as a pricy cabernet sauvignon.

They clinked their glasses. Maya lowered the glass to her lips and inhaled the bouquet. She failed to pay too much attention to the spicy scent and the currant accent, disturbed to be sitting so close to the man who had stood by Sylvie when she'd given her life.

Ivan announced he had a previous engagement and would have to leave. That was to be expected – Ivan would surely want Maya and Viktor to be alone together – yet she acted as though she was jolted.

'Oh, I thought you'll . . .' Accidentally, she dribbled her sip down onto her sari. Oh, no, this was her mother's favorite outfit.

'Sorry, something's come up.' Ivan made an elaborate goodbye, wished them a pleasant evening and swapped a meaningful look with Viktor, then strolled confidently from the room.

Maya turned back to her wine and found Viktor admiring her over the golden glow of the candlelight. She was alone in the evening in a gorgeous room with a deadly attractive stranger. She put the wine glass down and reached for her cellphone. She'd changed purses and forgotten to bring it. Drat. She wouldn't be able to call Uma in case something ugly started to happen. To think she'd be at the mercy of this stranger.

She could walk out. Or she could stay, play along and see where this led.

Viktor's gaze slowly caressed her face over the golden glow of the candlelight. His eyes were large, steady, a deep, rich brown with a gleam that made him seem either like a come-hither hero of a Bollywood extravaganza or a scary dream.

He bowed toward her. 'Pardon me for staring so much. I can't seem to take my eyes off you, Maya.'

She put the wine glass down. A jaded line, delivered in a deep, intimate tone, one that had probably been whispered to countless other dates. Still, she marveled at the way he pronounced her name, with an elongated 'ah' at the end, as though he didn't want to let go of the sound. She smiled awkwardly and pretended she was enjoying this act.

He cupped his hand around the candle flame; his eyes softened. 'Now I can see why my buddy arranged this dinner. I've been here six months. Damn shame we didn't meet sooner.'

'Well, even if we've met before,' Maya said with a smile, 'I'm sure I've seen you somewhere else.'

'Maybe someone who looks like me? I hear it quite often. "Didn't I see you shopping in Renton the other day?" I want to reply: "Do all Bangladeshis – and there are one hundred and fifty-five million of us – look alike?"'

'Please don't put me in that category. My ancestry is similar to yours.'

The waiter was hovering over them. He handed them oversized menus and stepped aside. They studied the long list of choices.

Viktor gave a mischievous smile. 'I'll order whatever you suggest.'

She lowered her voice, bedroom low. 'Grilled lamb?'

He seemed enchanted and, when the waiter reappeared, ordered that dish. Maya chose the vegetarian *thali* dinner, aware that her usually robust appetite had forsaken her. Curious and anxious, she wanted to play the part just right.

He mumbled something about them having many things in common.

'What do we have in common right off the bat?' she asked, giving him a seductive look. 'Perhaps our respective interest in seeing a cure for malaria? I'd love to hear about your work in that field. Nothing would give me more pleasure.'

'More wine?' Viktor lifted the wine bottle and Maya allowed him to refill her glass. 'I rarely meet a woman who would mix a good wine with a deathly topic like malaria.'

'Unfortunately, my mother caught the disease.'

'Sorry. I lost my sister to it. I can well imagine how much your mother must have suffered. How's she doing?'

'She's quite healthy now.'

'MSP, the company I work for in Moscow, will soon offer solutions for certain lethal diseases. Am I boring you?'

'Oh, no, it's interesting.'

'The pharma industry in Russia is still small and we have to import huge quantities of drugs, but there's a growing emphasis on developing our own brands. It's pitiful, the Russian health statistics. Life expectancy is so low that Russians joke they have a "disappearing citizenry." Hopefully my employer will help remedy that. I handle the R and D for tropical ailments – I'm the king there – malaria being top of the list. I'm determined to find a cure for malaria that could be spread worldwide.'

More wine flowed into her glass, poured by Viktor. Had she finished her last glassful? *Take this next glass a lot slower, Maya.* Only now she realized she was holding onto the delicate stem of the goblet. For stability. To touch something. To control her racing mind. What had Viktor said? Something about helping to eradicate a tropical malady like malaria from everywhere?

'Sounds like you're personally dedicated to that cause?' she said, not wanting him to think she'd been daydreaming.

'For sure. My interest in malaria started in the Chittagong District of Bangladesh, where I was born and raised. Have you heard of it? It's in the eastern part of the country, bordering Myanmar, where most of my extended family is settled. The hills there have the highest incidence of malaria in Bangladesh. And . . . it still makes me terribly sad to go back to the days when my pregnant sister caught malaria. We were close.' He took a heavy breath, didn't blink; his mouth softened. 'She died, my kid sister, the sweetest person I've ever known. I couldn't hear her last words. They were a whisper.'

Maya watched as the corners of his mouth turned down. 'I'm sorry,' she said, and meant it.

'It's been a few years, and still, not a day goes by . . . Do you ever get over such heartbreak? I haven't. Neither has my mother. She was such a vivacious woman. She loved to dance. Loved to crack jokes. Loved to throw parties. Now she rarely smiles, hardly ever goes out of the house. So my life's goal, if there's one I'd like to achieve before I die, is to rid my little corner of the world of the disease. I want to be the first, globally. My mother would give me the biggest cheer.'

Viktor's eyes burned with intensity, his passion obvious to Maya. He and Cal Chodron shared the same goal. Whereas Cal had an attitude of serving, Viktor went about it in a more aggressive way, spurred on by family pride.

Her head pulsed and her eyes felt heavy. Still, it pleased her that he'd revealed at least one of his motivations. 'So I suppose working for MSP, you're looking for an antimalarial that could be mass-tested in Bangladesh?'

'Yes, in accordance with FDA standards, which we follow, we'll do a field test there. Foreign clinical trials are increasingly common. With MSP's blessing, I travel worldwide searching for research labs where malaria "weapons" are being developed and assess their progress. I've found nine so far. Often these labs will sell the solution to a pharmaceutical company and collect royalty for years. The lab in New Zealand, which I visited just before coming here six months ago, has been one of the more impressive ones, but they weren't cooperative.'

'What made you come to Seattle?'

'Ivan – we're close.'

'Makes me ask you about Sylvie. I'd imagine she was ahead of the other scientists, as far as her malaria research went.'

If there was a small twitch in his body, he hid it well. 'It's most unfortunate, her death.' Eyes low, he held a neutral expression. 'And if you ask me, in her absence, her project will be abandoned, if it hasn't been already. I keep track of these things as part of my job. Sorry to say the local funding for the malaria vaccine initiative has dried up. The foundation responsible for it is moving on.'

Her stomach soured. 'You mean to say the decade of work Sylvie put in will be useless despite a successful vaccine trial?'

A shudder passed across his body. 'How do you know about the . . .?' His tone had shifted. It had an edge, curiosity overlaid with annoyance, dread even.

The air around her felt dense. 'Oh, I heard it in passing, from Anna's friend. You might have known Anna, who worked in the only Indian sweet shop in town.' She didn't say the rest: *Anna who joined in the trial and didn't get malaria, but who died. Committed suicide, rather. Under suspicious circumstances.*

He didn't meet her eyes. 'Word travels quickly here, doesn't it? In Moscow, you can keep things more hush-hush. Russians don't open their mouths quite so easily.'

She excused herself for the ladies' room. Upon returning, she found her wine glass full again, a pool of light, as it were.

She took the tiniest sip.

Something warned her.

She pushed away from it, a little giddy and somewhat alarmed.

You know better, Maya. The drink might have been spiked.

'You work with herbs?' Viktor reached over and squeezed her hand with his long, tapered fingers, a warm, eloquent touch. 'You'd appreciate my family's vacation home, what we call a *bagan bari* or garden retreat, and where we grow all sorts of flowers, vegetables and herbs.'

'I'd love to hear about it.'

Chest expanded, gaze vivid with enthusiasm, Viktor took her to a Bangladeshi village. To a timber house, with an orchard, a flowering nook, a vegetable patch and a separate plot for herbs, all surrounded by acres of lush forest. Bordered on one side by a serene blue lake and used for vacation purposes, it was a house filled with Viktor's love for his mother, sisters and other members of his family, where he felt fortunate to be present.

Maya listened. A wave of pleasantness passed over her. Her focus narrowed and her peripheral vision became non-existent.

'Although my parents lived in a larger town, my mother went to that little house for my birth.' He spoke breathily, as though drawing emotions from his heart. 'My paternal grandmother, who was also born there, came to be with us. A generational bond must have formed – I can't wait to spend my vacation days there. My family doesn't live there but we have servants to maintain the house and an expert gardener who keeps the landscape lush and colorful.'

'What kinds of herbs do you grow?'

He blinked, swallowed visibly, drank and said, '*Guggul*, *gotu kola* and *ashwagandha*.'

Those are common ayurvedic herbs. You want me to believe that's all you grow? No psychedelic mushrooms?

'When I visit there I rise with the sun and, after a breakfast of fresh fruits and herbal tea, wander in the forest for hours,' he resumed, his timbre richer now. 'It's so tranquil – hiking through the jungle or sitting by the lake, listening to birds and insects and chasing butterflies. I do my best to avoid mosquito bites, of course. Evenings, I stay in the house. I sit in the dark, drink coconut water, read poetry and watch fireflies flash gold like they have a script of their own. "This is where both the sky and the earth greet us and make us whole," my grandfather used to say. I'm an insomniac but I sleep soundly there. Return a new person. See things more clearly. Sense what life is about.'

'I suppose those are the memories that keep you going in Moscow?'

'Naturally. On nights I'm awake, I look out the window, see snowflakes trembling in the air and picture my green, lush *bagan bari*. My life in Moscow is as comfortable as it gets but Bangladesh is where I live.' He focused on her. 'Of course, Seattle is a nice place, too.'

Their orders came. Caught by the colors, shapes and appetizing fragrances, they went silent for a moment then picked up their cutlery. Between not-so-hungry bites, she asked, 'How much longer will you be here?'

'Not much longer.' His leg brushed against hers, a feathery touch. 'But I'm someone who doesn't like to let an opportunity slip through his fingers. Whatever time I have left here, if your schedule permits, I'd love to spend it with you.'

She glanced at her plate; half the food was still there. 'You're leaving soon?'

He sighed. 'In a week's time, maybe two – it all depends on my boss. He'll call me this evening. Will you come visit me in Moscow? Stay with me as long as you like? Mine is a two-bedroom flat with a Euro design. It has plenty of natural light, a balcony with a view of a birch grove and it's a short walk to the Red Square. I know, Maya, we've just met, but it seems like we've known each other for ages. Like we're meant to be together. I knew that when I first spoke with you at Betty's.'

A fast move, obviously practiced over time. A play probably used on Anna, aided by wine, dim lighting, a sumptuous dinner, tales and possibly drugs. Not having been out on a date in a while, Maya didn't have a similar experience to draw from or to be cognizant of when to cut it off. Maybe she shouldn't cut it off. She could see he was attracted to her and that'd be crucial in getting him to confide in her more. She watched the waiter remove the dishes.

'Russians are friendly in an Eastern sort of a way,' Viktor began. 'And if you're wondering about the winters, oh, you get used to them. And there's always vodka – and me – to keep you warm.'

'Moscow? I'll have to think about it.'

'I love being with you. You ask intelligent questions and listen to the answers. I like to talk. With you, I feel open. Like I can go on talking forever.' He patted his napkin against his mouth, leaned over and focused on her face. Speaking breathily, he said, 'Shall we go to my apartment for a while? I have a cozy flat. You don't have to stay long if you don't want to.'

Tough decision. It'd help to see the layout of Sunglasses Man's apartment. So said the investigator in her. Besides, he was drunk. She put her misgivings aside. 'Oh, cool, maybe for a short time. My mother's visiting so I'll have to get back reasonably soon.'

He gave her an effusive, attagirl smile and settled the bill. They walked to the parking lot, where he recited a set of directions to his place. She got into her Toyota and followed him, finding herself invigorated by the short drive. She was feeling fine, just fine, and sort of expectant and a little scared at the same time.

Her destination was a luxurious apartment complex on Roosevelt Avenue. She recognized the pale blue, multi-unit structure as having been renovated for short-term leasing to visiting corporate executives. She found a parking place only a block away. It was so perfect to be out this evening, not a cloud in the sky, not a breeze to mess up her hair, the stars arranged just right. The next moment, she found the perfection frightening, as though things could alter shapes instantly.

Viktor opened the door, welcomed her in and apologized for the mess. The spacious living room, decorated with posh furniture was, indeed, untidy. Books, DVDs and a soiled plate subdued the effect of the fine dark wood floor. An ultra-slim laptop sat open on a desk cluttered with paper. The screensaver displayed the tricolored Russian flag: three equal-sized horizontal bands in red, blue and white.

'I put that laptop together myself in Moscow.' Pride crept into Viktor's voice. 'I do all my work on it.'

Viktor tapped a wall keypad, turned off the dome-shaped ceiling light and turned on the leaf-accented Tiffany floor lamp.

It brought a softer glow to the room and highlighted the ivory walls while lessening the effect of the disorganization.

'It's stuffy in here,' he murmured and went over to open a window.

He had a way of moving through space as though he didn't expect to meet any resistance. As an investigator, she considered that to be a formidable trait in an opponent. She put her purse down on a marble-topped side table and sized up the place. In one corner, on a wooden, filigreed table rested a bottle of premium vodka and a pair of vintage drinking glasses, one of which had lipstick marks. Who did those lipstick marks belong to? She could tell she was frowning at the thought – a kernel of curiosity mixed with dread. On the kitchen wall facing her, she glimpsed a liquor cabinet. Directly below it stood an overfull, plastic-lined garbage pail. A curved-blade butcher's knife gleamed on the counter, as did a sharpening stick.

When she turned, she found him standing behind her, his eyes sleepy, longing and magnetic.

A cellphone sang from his pocket, echoing the disturbance in Maya's heart.

'Pardon me, but I have to answer,' he said. 'My boss – he's in Shanghai this week.'

The phone to his ear, face turned away, he drew back and listened for a few seconds. 'One moment, please.' He handed the phone over to her, whispering, 'It's your mother. She sounds frantic.'

Maya caught her breath. Uma – how on earth did she get hold of Viktor's number? But then, since when had anything been impossible for Uma?

Maya adjusted her sari, exhaled and answered, knowing she sounded bewildered, maybe even displeased.

'Where are you?' Uma cried out.

'In his apartment,' Maya mumbled, hoping Uma wouldn't detect wine in her voice.

'What?' Uma whispered. 'Don't you realize the danger you're in? Leave immediately and come straight home. Tell him I got sick. Vomiting. I'll tell you everything. In any case, it's late. Almost eleven.'

Her hyper mother and her curfew. Didn't she realize Maya was here to work on a case? However, the word danger roiled in Maya's stomach. And she never liked to see herself or anyone else vomit. 'Ma—'

'Yes, right now, split.' Uma hung up.

Maya handed the phone back to Viktor. How quickly the high feelings vanished, replaced by a sensation of stagnancy. 'I have to go. My mother's sick.'

'How did she get my phone number?'

'She has her ways.'

'You said she had malaria?' Viktor stepped closer. 'So sorry. Should I come with you? Be of help somehow?'

Maya shook her head.

'Shall we meet again tomorrow? Promise you'll call me first thing in the morning. I'd like to wake up to your voice.' He handed her a calling card with his Seattle number and escorted her down the elevator to street level, insisting on it for security's sake. Normally, she'd have liked the solid feel of walking alongside a man so late at night. Now her legs froze.

The street was practically deserted, the night drawing out life from the landscape and leaving it bereaved, and yet Maya couldn't have been more awake. In the bluish light of the street lamp, he searched her face. She saw him weaken. She let him give her a kiss on her cheek as she quickly moved her face to avoid his mouth.

In the brown depths of his eyes, she spied passion and a hint of design. She scrambled into her car and drove into the darkness.

TWENTY-EIGHT

Maya reached home, unlocked the front door and heard the murmur of a man's voice. Who could it be at this late hour? She detoured to the dining area, taken by the spicy fragrance in the air.

Parked at the dining table, with a plate of food before him, Cal Chodron – pink hair and all, the Buddha-bright smile fixed on his face – was saying to Uma, 'My sons would kill me if they found out I'm having an authentic *dahl-bhat* without them.'

'It's the simplest meal ever, made with red lentils and rice and a few spices.' With Maya coming into view, Uma surged to her feet and circled her with her arms, joyously exclaiming, 'Thank God you're back.'

Maya threw her hands up in the air. 'Why the drama?'

'You were with a potential killer.'

A flutter of anxiety came back to Maya at this reference to Viktor: how much she still needed to be with him to get the rest of his story and what would happen if she lost the opportunity. Now Cal heaved himself out of his seat, gave her a once-over and boomed a hello. Although Maya returned his greeting, her mind went blank. What was the malaria volunteer coordinator doing in her living room? Until now she'd only seen him in his office on Aurora Avenue.

'Are you all right?' Cal asked.

'Of course I'm all right,' Maya replied.

'In case you're wondering,' Cal said, 'your mother invited me to come over and we're having a most pleasant time.'

So typical of mother to invite strangers, so easy for her to engage them in a dialogue, but how did the two meet? And how did she get Viktor's phone number? Maya held herself still, wishing she had a mint to hide the wine on her breath, and waited for her mother to speak.

'You left your cellphone here.' Uma motioned Maya to a chair and returned to her own seat. 'When it rang, I answered it, guessing it might be you. It was Cal, calling from his office. We got to talking. When I told Cal where you were and with whom, he asked if he could come over.'

How could you trust Cal so much as to include him in this dialogue about Viktor, Ma? Maya silently asked herself.

Uma must have noticed the frown crowding Maya's face. 'Forgive me for ruining your date. As it turned out, Cal had Viktor's phone number, so I rang you up. Before you got yourself in trouble.'

'Trouble?' Still baffled, Maya realized that, pouty, irritated and distracted, she wasn't coming off well in this conversation. She turned to Cal and asked in a neutral tone, 'How did you get Viktor's phone number? How do you even know him?'

Cal leaned back, obviously relishing the fact that he had special intelligence on this matter. 'Well, one of our employees had jotted down two names in her job application as emergency contacts: Ivan Dunn and Viktor Bhusan Chattopadhya. She also, of course, provided their phone numbers, which came in terribly handy this evening. I have access to the personnel files and was familiar with the names.'

Interesting, shocking and ultimately game-changing. Now that the effect of the wine had worn off, Maya saw things more clearly. Ivan, Viktor and Jennifer belonged to the same circle. What did they have in common? A common tongue – Russian, of course – and the tight-knit community they owed their allegiance to, although there must have been more to it, such as a common objective. What if the specimen had been stolen by none other than Jennifer – the tramp, the home-wrecker, the ex-drug-trafficker and a suspicious person?

'Could the employee be Jennifer Marlow?'

Cal's mouth hung open. 'How do you know Jennifer?'

'We've met only once, by chance. What can you tell me about her?'

'Once again, you're questioning me about one of our employees. I'm not authorized to share that type of intelligence.'

'But it might pertain to the mysterious deaths of Sylvie and Anna.'

'What's Jennifer got to do with that?'

'If she has no direct or indirect involvement, then you should be free to talk about her.'

'You don't give up easily, do you?' Cal blew out a breath. 'OK, the women in our office don't like her. They gossip that she's real cunning; call her Ms Rasputin behind her back.'

A dizzy moment. Might there be bigger reasons behind this dislike of Jennifer? 'Looks like you don't like her much.' Glancing at Cal, noticing his evasive eyes, sweaty nose and restless manner, Maya said, 'You probably have your own sources?'

'Yes, lately I've been getting a lot of reports on Ms Rasputin's male companions.'

'Would you care to explain the use of the plural?'

'When her shift ends she's usually met outside our clinic by young men, a different one each time.'

What was Jennifer doing with all these men? Drugs? Prostitution? Was Justin aware of it? A tiny, mean delight percolating in her, Maya directed her gaze back at Cal. 'That in itself is probably not an issue.'

'No. Maybe it's even expected – she's a bombshell.'

A bombshell could be trouble, Maya reflected, a bitter taste in her mouth. It quite often had been in her investigative work. 'I don't mean to pry, but have you observed anything unusual that concerns Jennifer?'

Cal maintained a stony-faced silence.

Maya leaned in closer. 'You might be hiding potentially important data that the law enforcement would like to—'

'If you insist. This is not for public consumption. Jennifer seemed to be doing fine, except . . . a week or so ago, I left my cubicle to go to a meeting. It was cancelled so I went right back to work, only to be surprised. Jennifer stood at my work-station, shuffling through a stack of papers. Though I was furious, I controlled my temper and asked her what she was looking for. She couldn't meet my eyes, mumbled she was sorry and tried to walk away. I stopped her and asked her point blank why she was in my cubicle. She gave me one of her melting smiles, apologized in both English and Russian and promised she'd never do it again. It was obvious she wouldn't admit anything, and I wanted to gather more evidence before recommending to her boss that she should be terminated, so I dropped the whole matter at that point.'

'You dropped it? You must have sensitive data about the malaria trial in your cubicle.'

'Yes, but she didn't get it – all the relevant details are digitized.' Cal gave a snort of anger.

'And that's not the end of it. I bet it was Jennifer who stole the blood sample tube you mentioned to me the last time. Am I correct?'

Again, Cal was silent.

'Come clean with me, Cal.'

'Yes, we can pin it on Jennifer, and that's why we're investigating her.'

'I doubt Jennifer will personally have any use for the specimen,' Maya said. 'But maybe one of her "friends"?'

'That'd be my guess, too.'

A thought sparked in Maya's mind: it would have been easy for Viktor, the charmer, to persuade Jennifer to steal the blood sample tube. But for what purpose? 'Any idea why a person might want to steal a malaria trial blood sample?'

'My boss, Inez, did a bit of digging regarding Jennifer's involvement with the missing blood sample and its implications,' Cal began. 'At one point, she even talked to a scientist in New Zealand.'

It flashed in Maya's mind – Viktor's mention of his visit with a New Zealand scientist who, according to him, had proved to be uncooperative. She now outlined that story to Cal. His eyes sharpened and he leaned toward her in a gesture of cooperation. Maya liked him better now. He'd come over to help her mother. In this homey environment, he acted so much like a family friend.

'And that brings me to my next point.' Cal's expression betrayed a hint of smug self-satisfaction. 'Viktor tried to steal the formula from that New Zealand lab by bribery. He got caught and was shown the door.'

Maya, trying to construct the timeline in her mind, thought out loud. 'Right after that he came to Seattle, where an accomplice was waiting for him – Ivan. The two were already friends from Moscow.'

'Are you saying that, with Ivan's help, Viktor got hold of Sylvie's formula for the vaccine?' Cal asked.

'No, that would have been impossible,' Maya stressed. 'Sylvie had destroyed her hard drive and all backups so no one could get the formula. It had to come from another source.'

'So Sylvie did worry that someone, like Ivan, would steal her research work?' Uma said.

'Right,' Maya said. 'And so Ivan and Viktor sought an alternative. I'm still trying to figure out what that is.'

'Let's look at this from another angle,' Uma said. 'Anna,

the sweet-maker. Why did she take her life? What was her role in all this?'

A strained silence ensued. Maya had no answer.

'Did Anna ever mention Viktor's name to you?' Maya asked Cal.

'It gives me the creeps now,' Cal said, 'but I'd heard Viktor's name – first name only – mentioned by Anna several times when we had coffee together. "Met a most interesting man," she once told me. Then, another time, "Viktor speaks Russian rather fluently." And yet another time, "Finally met a guy I really like. Victor is cool, suave, good-looking and generous, with strong family ties." She began seeing that rascal regularly and fell for him. He kept her on a leash. Poor girl – she was totally devastated when she realized she didn't mean anything to him. That broke her. Ultimately, that's what did it. He lost interest in her or perhaps he'd never been in love with her. Smart as she was, she lost interest in living.'

Maya sighed. 'Maybe temporarily, but that doesn't mean she'd want to commit suicide. She must have had help. And since—'

'I'll never forgive that sonofabitch, that scoundrel.' The light in Cal's eyes flared. 'Makes me both sad and furious.'

Sad and furious – that also described Maya's current state of mind. How similar their stories were – Sylvie's and Anna's. Both of Tibetan origin, both jilted by the men they loved, Ivan and Viktor. Maya wanted to shout at both of them: *How could you be so vile?*

'I had a gut feeling Viktor would turn out to be an evil character,' Uma said to Maya. 'But I couldn't really stop you from going on a date with him. You're a big girl.'

Maya took a second to steady her nerves. 'Well, I wouldn't have uncovered this much if I hadn't—'

'My darling daughter – she doesn't mind putting herself in harm's way in order to break a case wide open for her client,' Uma interrupted.

On the sidewalk outside, a passerby whistled a tune. Cal lifted his shirt sleeve and peeked at his watch. 'Goodness, I had no idea it was this late. I have to go. Anything else I can do for you, ladies?'

Maya visualized Viktor's apartment with all the messiness. He wasn't who he seemed to be and she needed to collect much more proof for the police. 'For my next visit to Viktor's apartment, I'll need to figure out an escape route for my use, in case I need it. You have rental agency contacts, don't you?'

Cal looked thoughtful. 'Yes, let me find out who Viktor's landlord is and check to see if he'll cooperate.'

'And if it's necessary to pull some strings with the SPD . . .?' Maya asked.

'My boss Inez could help us with that.' Cal got to his feet. 'Her father, a retired cop, knows the ropes.'

Cop – an image of Justin flew into Maya's mind's eye. Still seated at the table, she glanced at the centerpiece, a fruit bowl consisting of an appetizing mélange of pears, apricots and red grapes. As she gazed at the rich colors of the arrangement, she had an interesting thought. Jennifer, a recent hire at the clinic, hadn't used Justin as a contact person in her job application. Why not? With residual feelings about Justin still bubbling inside her, Maya recalled how, only the other day, Jennifer had called out to him in a seductive voice. She would only get him in more trouble. *Oh, Maya, why concern yourself? Why not let him go?* Mentally, she cut the fragile threads of their bond and was swept up by a feeling of relief.

While Uma showed Cal out, Maya used her cellphone, which was lying on a living-room table, to Google MSP. What she found: a conglomerate whose U.S. headquarters were located in Los Angeles, MSP developed, produced and marketed pharmaceutical products. The company had a poor reputation and was not well regarded by the regulatory agencies but still had a banner year. As far as clinical trials go, it was believed to lack transparency. To think Sylvie's research would end up there, Maya mused bitterly.

She also went over the details of the evening in her mind. It occurred to her that Ivan, the man responsible for Atticus's beating, had tried the same tactic on her by attacking Uma. The rock that was thrown was either him or one of his boys. Yet Ivan must have realized that it had not been enough to stop her. He knew Maya was still trying to unravel the real cause behind the two suicides and now Ivan didn't want her to be scared; he wanted her to be gone. Her date with Viktor had been a setup. Ivan had brought them together and assumed an attraction would develop between them from the way they looked at each other. He'd wanted Viktor to stop her, tame her, use her and now probably murder her. Fortunately she'd seen through much of it.

The puzzle pieces were beginning to fall in place. Yet, instead of making her happy with the progress she'd made, they choked her chest.

After closing the door, Uma stepped in and resumed her seat. 'What a nightmare. You got out in time – I'm so relieved.'

'Hard for me to admit this, Ma, but only a short time ago I realized I must have been hypnotized by Viktor. I was very definitely under his influence.'

'How did he do that?'

'He's a pro but he doesn't require that you relax, close your eyes and concentrate on what he's saying. No lecture. No Zombie eyelids. No loss of consciousness. Instead, he flattered me and looked deeply into my eyes. His voice was so deep and rich; I couldn't get enough of it. His speech had a certain rhythm that lulled me. Then, when the time was right, he described his home and family in a gentle, loving way. I couldn't help but think of him as a nice man who doted on his family. I relaxed and listened, enchanted. A pleasant sensation spread through my body. By the time the phone rang, I'd snapped out of it. It was you calling to warn me, just in time. I think you may have saved my life.'

'You did speak and act funny when you came in, my dear,' Uma said. 'Cal also noticed that. He said so on his way out. "She's acting like Anna. Like she'd do anything he says. Do keep an eye on her tonight."'

Acting like Anna? Recalling the last glass of wine poured by Viktor earlier in the evening, Maya said, 'You know, Viktor might also have slipped something into my drink when I went to the ladies' room. It didn't smell or taste any different. If there was a color change, I didn't notice it. But my muscles seemed to let go, which was a warning bell, and so, after one small sip, I put the glass aside.'

'Why did you go to his place then?'

'To play along. I was well aware of his intentions. Being alert, I got the lay of the land.'

Uma smiled. 'Good, I don't have to deprogram you.'

'Let me tell you what else I've figured out about Viktor. On this, my second meeting with him, I had the strangest, scariest feeling I'd seen him before. Then it dawned on me. He's Sunglasses Man who pushed Sylvie and Anna to suicide. On that day, he wore a disguise.'

'What? If he's Sunglasses Man and if he assisted Sylvie and Anna to die, then he's evil and could face charges.'

'You know what, Ma? I'm having a wild, what-if moment. What if Viktor, the scientist from the BC family, with an agenda of his own, hypnotized and drugged Anna and instructed her to burn herself? He could have easily done that, since they'd spent so much time together.'

'What would be his motive?'

'Let's deconstruct that,' Maya said. 'The BC family has no particular interest in Tibet's freedom, I don't think. Sylvie and Anna have advanced the cause for Tibet by sacrificing their lives, but for Viktor, the scientist, there has to be a pay-off for leading an innocent woman like Anna to kill herself. And I believe it's the malaria cure he was after. That was his motivation.' Maya gave Uma an account of their conversation, how he yearned to find an experimental vaccine to take to Moscow and then to Bangladesh to conduct a trial of longer duration with more participants. 'I'm still not sure what purpose Anna served in Viktor's game, why she had to die and why Jennifer stole Anna's blood sample. I need to figure it all out.'

The corners of Uma's eyes crinkled. 'If you're thinking of seeing Viktor again, I will not let you go. That'd be insane. He's ruthless and you're on his murder list – the woman who figured out too much.'

Maya had to go all out this time. 'Please, Ma, he's a killer but I'll have to see him one more time, to make him talk. I'll wear a bodycam – a copcam, which I'll have to get from the SPD. I promise I won't get myself killed. And, next time, I'll make him tell his whole story and record it for the police.'

'How will you do that?'

'He likes to brag, especially when he's had a few drinks.

He might even give the game away now because he thinks I've fallen for him.' Maya paused and thought of Uma's malaria physician in Kolkata, recommended by no other than Sylvie. Perhaps he could help decode a few issues related to her malaria research. 'One more thing, Ma. I need to speak with your doc.'

'That's easy. I can arrange a call to Doctor Palas. But it'll have to be tomorrow, my child. Now, I insist you get some sleep.'

Maya rose and smiled. Her kind-hearted mother, always thinking of her daughter's needs. It had been so great to have her around this last month or so.

TWENTY-NINE

The soles of Maya's favorite walking shoes had worn out and needed to be fixed. The next morning, the first item on her agenda was a trip to the cobbler for a tune-up. At around nine a.m., carrying the shoes in a plastic bag, Maya walked into Sole Survivor, a shoe-repair shop located about half a mile from her house in a busy foot-traffic area.

A ruddy-skinned, sixty-something man, who was working with industrial equipment in the back of the room, hastened to the counter. He had the appearance of being overworked and exhausted. 'May I help you?'

It came to Maya with a jolt. She'd seen him at Sylvie's self-immolation. Eyes closed, his boxer's nose catching a ray of sunlight, this man had chanted as a part of the prayer group. She'd been trying to trace him or, as a matter of fact, anyone from that group. Now, finally.

'Do you have a moment to talk?' Her voice wavered in anticipation. 'Didn't I see you at that suicide scene a few weeks ago? Weren't you one of the chanters?'

He stood still, his eyes widening in horror. Without warning, he burst into tears, mumbling, 'So sorry, so very sorry.'

Maya reached into her purse and handed him a tissue, feeling a deep sorrow within herself, and stayed open to listen to him.

He took a few moments, wiped his eyes and shuffled his feet. 'If only I had the sense to read what was going on. I'd have punched that guy and dragged the two women out of there. I could have saved them, you know, I could have, but I was crazed.'

Maya clutched her bag to her chest. 'That is one of the biggest regrets of my life as well. I just happened to be walking by. I, too, had no idea what was going on. I didn't realize Sylvie, a friend . . . I saw her but didn't see her – know what I mean? What took you there?'

'I answered a casting call for extras on a website.'

'A casting call? You really thought they were—?'

'Yeah, the website said they were filming a violent cable movie. They paid well, even for background roles. No prior experience required, no physical danger, but confidentiality was asked for.'

'How did you learn to chant?'

'I'm a musician in my spare time. We were given a link to a recording which showed us how to make the sounds. And we were told to clear out as soon as the police showed up. That'd indicate the end of the scene. The whole thing would take only a few minutes. I said to myself, why not?'

'Can you give me the link?'

'I'm afraid I lost it. My brain's shrinking. They tell me I should eat more greens but I positively hate kale.'

'Any idea of the motives of those who hired you?'

'Who looks for motives when you're trying to make a fast buck? Not a boozer like me. Here I make the minimum wage. It did smell a little weird but I was paid in advance and I like to keep my nose clean. Only later that morning did I find out it was real fire and real people perished from it. Oh, bugger. How could I not have been man enough to stop it?'

'There were no cameras anywhere and you still didn't suspect anything?'

'Again, I didn't pay attention. Getting old, I suppose. And I'd drunk a little too much the night before. A guy has to have a vice.' Voice turning jovial, he winked at her. 'A few minutes into it, you tried to peel off my jacket, you feisty lady, and I wouldn't let you. I figured a little tussle with a lovely woman would make me look good in the film, even if it wasn't a part of the script. That's how blind I was.'

'You didn't go to the police station?'

'I suppose I should have.'

'Will you do it now?'

'Why don't you tell the police to pay me a call? I'll talk to them, clear my conscience, sleep better.' He handed her the store's business card. 'My name is Clark S. Sutter.'

'Maya Mallick.'

'Now I have to get back to work. Do you have shoes that need resoling?'

Maya handed him the shoes and they discussed the date of delivery. She'd just turned when she heard his voice from behind.

'Don't go looking for trouble, Maya,' Clark said, sounding as though he meant it. Maya cringed involuntarily.

Once outside, she called Hank on her cellphone, a routine check.

'Ivan's bolting,' Hank said in an urgent manner. 'He's stopped coming to the gym – end of my swimming lessons, end of my keeping track of all the hot women he was bedding.'

Veen's face flickered in Maya mind – Veen, who never danced around things. 'Let's touch base later in the day,' she said to Hank.

At a few minutes to nine, Maya sat on a bench in Meridian Park, a stone's throw from the skeletal survivors of an old apple orchard. Wild flowers were sprinkled across the grass at her feet. A sliver of weak sunlight shone over the large playfield in front of her like a distant dream. Despite the morning's hospitable temperature and the scenery, she remained wary. The sound of traffic behind her on the vehicle-choked Northeast 50th Street hummed in her chest.

Veen, dressed for work in a camel-colored cardigan and a matching A-line skirt, was perched beside her. Except for a thin gold chain at her throat, accentuating the roundness of her face, Veen looked severe and in control. Yet she sounded chirpy as she asked, 'Hey, what have you been up to?'

'Oh, I'm seeing someone.' Maya pictured the mirage that was Viktor: attentive, smooth-talking, drug-dispensing hypnotist and literal lady-killer. 'Had a date last night.'

'No wonder I haven't heard from you lately.' Veen's voice soared. 'So what time did you get home?'

'Must have been close to midnight.'

'He must be hot stuff. You have dark circles under your eyes. How did you meet him?'

Maya flinched. 'Actually, I met him through Ivan.'

Veen sat, her eyes lowered and chillness embalming her face, surely unaware that Maya had suspicions of Ivan being implicated in Sylvie's death. 'What was he like?' Veen asked.

Maya reviewed the details of her evening with Viktor – mainly the glossy part: the wine, the spicy fragrances and the soft light. She spared Veen the details about his questionable background. Maybe another time.

'How romantic.' Veen gave her bangs a flip with a not-so-slender wrist. 'Is he someone our mothers would call a "suitable boy"?'

'Your guess is as good as mine.'

Veen laughed uncomfortably. 'Hey, you said Ivan introduced you to Viktor? How did you meet Ivan?'

'Long story. Let's talk about that another time.' Maya took a deep breath. 'Oh, since we're on the topic of dating, can I ask you a sensitive question? How well do you know Ivan?'

Veen's eyes grew cold. 'What the hell do you mean? What's that got to do with the price of coffee in . . .?'

'Quite a lot, actually. It's been bugging me ever since the day Sylvie died.' Maya allowed a sigh to escape her. 'Somehow I got the impression, gathering bits and pieces here and there and putting them together, including hints I got from Ivan, and I'm still not completely sure, but I've seen signs that suggest . . .'

Veen's cheeks turned a shade of mauve. 'What are you hinting at? That I was intimate with Ivan? That's absurd, a lie. Just because I helped you dig up some dirt about Justin doesn't mean you have to retaliate.'

Aware of Veen's volatility and seeing her face turn red in anger, Maya considered dropping the topic, saying, *forget it* and apologizing. But Veen was staring at her with tight-faced vengeance. However shaken inside, Maya opted to continue.

'Please calm down, Veen. I'm not trying to retaliate. I put our friendship way above that. This issue stands on its own. It's part of the puzzle as to why Sylvie died and so, in my opinion, important. I've wanted to ask you this for weeks now but I never could. I didn't want to hurt you, make you uncomfortable or ruin our friendship, and—'

'Cut out the crap, Maya. Cut out this amateur detective stuff.'

'Amateur, I'm not. You don't know this but I'm now employed as a P.I. I'll talk about my new profession another time. We have an important matter on our hands. I've gathered quite a bit of vital information about what went on with Sylvie before she made up her mind to—'

'What fucking business is that of yours, for heaven's sake?' Veen yelled. 'She's *my* sister.'

A tallish dog-walker wearing shorts shuffled past them. In the quiet surroundings, Veen's voice must have sounded like a siren. The woman turned and gave both of them a piercing look.

Maya collected herself. 'Look, Sylvie gave her last breath for the masses. We owe it to her. And, as someone who saw her end her life, I—'

'You asked once why Sylvie threw her bracelet to the ground. Do you still wonder why? It was because she loved her family.'

Maya hated to be so direct, so point-blank, but she figured that, with Veen, that was the best way. 'My guess is she sent a message through her bracelet to one member of her family – her mother.'

Veen's face twisted, perhaps from the knowledge that she was about to be found out. She stayed silent.

Her voice choking, Maya got the words out, but only partially. 'It's hard for me to ask this, Veen, but I wonder if you ever were in an affair with . . .'

Fury rippled across Veen's features like lightning. 'Are you accusing me of driving Sylvie to suicide? What a schlock job of "investigating." You make me want to laugh and, at the same time, you disappoint me, both you and your mother, all sweet talk and samosas—'

'Why bring my mother into this?'

'I'm not going to listen to your fucking bullshit.' Veen consulted her watch and jumped to her feet. 'I have to get to a meeting.'

'No, sit down. Call your office and say you'll be late. Sylvie is far more important than your meeting.'

Veen flopped back down on the bench again. 'What business is it of anybody's that Ivan and I were together for a while?' Her voice took a shrill edge. 'I hate myself, I so hate myself, but he's the best fuck around.'

'You hated yourself but you didn't break it off soon enough.'

Veen fired her a hateful glare. 'Was that even up to me? No – he fucking ditched me. "Go on, get lost," he said because he was seeing both Sylvie and me and couldn't handle it. And I'm the one who had to go. I was so mad.'

The drumbeat of Maya's heart drowned out all ambient noise. The picture wasn't complete, although a few more puzzle pieces were in place. 'But you—'

In one sharp movement, Veen shouldered her purse and scrambled to her feet. 'Are you trying to say I was complicit in my sister's death, you fucking whore? Yes, I screwed Ivan. Yes, I knew he and Sylvie were an item. She didn't jump off the bridge on the day she found out. My sis . . . I tried to speak with her on the phone but she cut me off. She wouldn't see me, either. Ivan and I were through by then.'

'But he's visited you recently, hasn't he? Asked you to tell me about a phone call from a woman called Lola. It's a made-up story, designed to put blame on the guru. Am I correct?'

'Don't even think of blaming me for what happened to Sylvie, Little Ms Detective. I could make trouble for you.' Veen stood up. 'And don't call me ever again.'

'Veen, please—'

'Go fuck yourself.' Veen stormed away, her hair flying in the wind, one hand drawn up to her face, presumably to wipe away a tear.

Maya sat stiffly on the bench. A deep sense of remorse rising in her, she questioned herself. Had she treated Veen too harshly? Knowing it would devastate her yet still pressing? Veen had been against Maya's investigation from the beginning, what she'd considered a personal family matter. Had Maya's efforts prevented Veen from expressing her grief the way she wanted to? Maya would forever regret that.

THIRTY

Maya had difficulty sleeping that night. The next morning, she retrieved a message from Viktor on her phone: 'Darling, please call me as soon as you can.' There were two more messages from him with similar content.

She'd wait a little while to call him back. She stepped through the door of the living room, only to find Uma, serene-faced, dusting the bookcase. She must not have heard Maya's footsteps. Uma retracted an oversized tome on home decorating from its standing position, held it like a treasure box, wiped it with a rag, then slid it back.

'Leave the drudgery for me, Ma.' Maya could tell her voice was a trifle off.

Uma threw the dust rag in a corner, pointed to the sofa and smiled. 'What a scoop I have for you. My friend Urvasi has an update about the BC family. You know how some of our boys go abroad, date every girl in sight, then go back home so mommy and daddy can find them a virgin bride?'

Maya nodded, fully aware of where this was going and yet eager to listen.

'Well, our Viktor-Babu is no angel.' Uma added the affectionate suffix with thinly veiled sarcasm. 'He's engaged to a stunning doctor who practices pediatrics in Dhaka, a match made by his mother about a year ago. The wedding will take place in a few months. It'll be the wedding of the century. At least a thousand people will be invited, a who's who of that city. Urvasi laughed and said that the BC family calls the doctor a virgin, "a pure girl who's never looked at a man." Everyone else smiles.'

'So he was playing Anna but had this marriage in mind all along.' Maya, suddenly sickened by the episode of Anna's death, shuffled over to the window and parted the curtains. A blue sedan cruised by. When she turned, she saw Uma standing by her.

Uma patted her shoulder, her hand veined but elegant, her touch a mantle of comfort. 'I touched base with Doctor Palas in Kolkata. He didn't mind being awakened by my call. Expect a call from him any minute. He'd like to speak with you. Cal will also be here a little later.'

'I'll ask Hank to join us. He's looking up a few things for me.'

'Let me prepare refreshments.' Uma departed.

Maya's gaze traveled to the sliver of bluish-white sky and the distant green of a slender pear tree visible through the curtains. That glimpse, that timeless scenery cleared her mind like a deep breath of fresh air would have.

An hour later, Maya found herself settled on the sofa. Uma, Cal and Hank sat in a semicircle around her. *Chai* and hazelnut shortbread were spread before them on the coffee table.

'I had quite a time this morning speaking with Doctor Palas, Ma's astute physician in Kolkata,' Maya began. 'Briefly, I presented all the facts. How Anna was vaccinated against malaria using an experimental drug whose formula is still a secret, as part of the Phase One-A trial for the vaccine. How the doctor at the malaria clinic here did a series of blood tests on Anna to evaluate her immune response. Then, for reasons no one in the clinic could figure out, one of the blood sample tubes disappeared. After that, both Anna and Sylvie self-immolated.' Maya looked around, noticed the rapt attention from her audience. 'I asked Doctor Palas the question that's been bugging me: why on earth would anyone want to steal a specimen? What good could it do?'

Cal rubbed his forehead with a hand. 'Yes, why?'

Uma nodded thoughtfully, as did Hank.

'There are two possibilities,' Maya replied. 'First, the specimen could be useful to a rogue scientist who wants to obtain the formula for the vaccine for personal gain, given that there's no low-cost malaria vaccine available in the world market. The second is an altruistic scientist, someone who wants to make it a low-cost cure and spread it.'

Uma cocked her head. 'You mean in either case they could get the vaccine without having to do a decade of research, like Sylvie did?'

'Precisely. Before the vaccine has had a chance to break down, a scientist could analyze the blood of the vaccinated subject, do a bio-chemical analysis of the vaccine structure and reverse-engineer the formula. I asked Doctor Palas how long the vaccine stays viable in a person's blood. He said that it varied with the disease and the vaccine.'

Cal nodded at Maya. 'How clever. The scientist has to be highly motivated to go through all this and also have someone who acts on his behalf. Who is it?'

'Viktor. Last night he told me that he wants, in the worst possible way, to acquire a malaria vaccine. His sister died from malaria. Being in the field, he could have the specimen analyzed and then reverse-engineer the vaccine formula. Once he had it, he'd conduct a bigger trial in Bangladesh. If all went well, he'd eventually break into the world market with that vaccine. But first, Bangladesh – a family pride sort of a thing.'

Uma held a strained expression. 'It's also Viktor, the bad boy, who hypnotized Anna and made her fall madly in love with him, with a barbiturate to help him. Would you agree with me on that?'

Maya nodded.

'Oh, what a pity. I was the one to get Anna on board for the vaccine trial. For that and other mysterious reasons, she had to die. That infuriates me, devastates me. And Viktor, that psychopath – I could break his neck.' Cal sucked in his breath audibly, folded his arms and closed his eyes. 'Please forgive me, infinitely kind Buddha.'

'Well, Anna had to die so no one else can analyze her blood and get the formula for the vaccine,' Maya said. 'It'll be Viktor's alone. So the woman, who had passed the vaccine test, had to be eliminated. Viktor manipulated her to commit suicide. "Anna's blood was that precious," Doctor Palas said.'

'Original but crazy,' Uma said. 'So it was Viktor's evil plan, with Ivan assisting him?'

'Yes,' Maya said. 'Ivan came to Seattle, got employed as a junior scientist in the same lab as Sylvie and got to know of her research. His twisted mind was working. He saw the potential for a commercial malaria vaccine and profiting from it. He started seeing Sylvie. He also contacted Viktor, who was in Moscow, and asked him to join him here so together they could carry out their plan of stealing the vaccine formula. They couldn't get it directly from Sylvie. So they got it from the blood specimen of Anna, the trial participant.'

'How horrible.' Cal looked bewildered. 'And what did they do with the specimen?'

'Doctor Palas said there's a lab in Seattle that could do just what we're discussing: take the vaccine formula apart from the blood sample and put it back,' Maya replied. 'I got the most important part. Doctor Palas said something like, "Using a specific chip, malaria protein microarray will be performed." Seattle apparently has a protein chemistry research lab. Scientists from various disciplines, such as immunology, work there. I've written down the name of that lab.'

'Let me have it.' Hank rose from his chair. 'I'll look it up.'

Maya handed him a Post-it note. 'Doctor Palas mentioned that this new technology could change the market.'

'Now I see it – why both Ivan and Viktor have stayed in Seattle these many months,' Uma said. 'They waited for the lab to finish its work for them.'

'You told us about Viktor's motivation but what's Ivan's interest in this?' Cal asked Maya.

'Money. It really comes down to that. Ivan is broke, broke, broke. Viktor will pay him handsomely, or so Doctor Palas guesses.'

'I'll second that,' Hank said. 'Ivan also hinted to me at the gym that, with the association he has, meaning Viktor, he could easily get a job in Moscow if he were to move up there.'

'But who's the accomplice?' Uma asked. 'Who actually stole the specimen and gave it to Viktor? Who enabled it all?'

'It has to be Jennifer Marlow.' Maya turned to Cal. 'Am I correct?'

'I'm afraid so.'

'Jennifer is the missing piece of the puzzle, the person we've been looking for,' Maya said. 'It's still not clear to me why she did it.'

'I'm not sure, either.' Cal's voice was firm. 'But Jennifer's history as far as our office is concerned. And now that we're finding she's complicit in what might prove to be a homicide—'

'It's urgent that we go to the police,' Uma chimed in. 'Ivan and Viktor are biding their time here. Now that they've pretty much accomplished their objectives, they'll surely flee.'

'Yes, Ivan told me he's getting ready to fly to Moscow,' Hank said. 'He still has no idea who I am and what I do.'

'But first we need Viktor's confession,' Maya said to Cal. 'For that to happen, I'll need his landlord's assistance. Do you happen to have his number?'

'I sure do. His name is Joe and as it turns out I've known him professionally for years.' Cal prized his cellphone out of his pocket and recited the number to Maya. 'I've already told him about you. He's ready to offer any help you need. You might want to slip him a few dollars.'

'No problem.'

Maya excused herself, went to the kitchen and called Joe. The man gave the impression of being middle-aged, organized and efficient. Maya could see him as part of the team.

'Have you noticed any patterns in Viktor's coming and going?' she asked him.

'Yes, ma'am, I'm keeping an eye on him. The dude's not home much during the day. Drinks his evenings away. The maid regularly finds several empty vodka bottles in his garbage can.' Joe revealed more: Viktor had already given him cash to cover the rent for the month and the fee for breaking the lease. He would check out this weekend.

A little tremor passed through Maya's body. So little time left. She'd talked about working out an escape plan from Viktor's apartment during her visit there should she not be able to slip out the front door. 'Is there a back entrance I could use?'

'No, but his bathroom has a big window that's always open,' Joe said. 'I'll have a coil of rope attached to the window frame outside, which you'll be able to use to get yourself down to the deck. A fire escape ladder, a few feet away, will lead you to the alley behind the building. Be careful of your steps on the ladder. You could fall and hurt yourself.'

'Sounds like a good Plan B.' Maya cut the call. Returning to the living room, she explained about her conversation with Joe, adding, 'Now I understand the urgency, why Viktor left so many messages on my cellphone. But we have to have proof for the police. For that I have to speak with him before he leaves town.'

'You're not going to visit him at his place, are you?' Uma asked.

'Yes, Ma, I'll have to. Hopefully this evening. Not to worry, though. I'll be OK. With the escape plan Joe has worked out for me I'll be able to get down to the alley behind the building.'

Cal said, 'I'll wait there for you in my car.'

'I'll come with you, of course, otherwise I'll be in a tizzy,' Uma said to Cal, who nodded.

'You two are such a formidable team,' Cal said. 'This is my small contribution. Anything else I can do to help, ladies?'

'Yes, there is,' Maya said. 'I also need to be wired up.'

'Wired up?' Uma said.

'Yes, with a wearable body camera, like the police do when recording covertly.' Maya further explained the features of this contraption. A shirt-button-sized clip-on enclosed in a metal shell, also called 'military tough,' was an on-the-go, high-definition video camera used by the law enforcement. The battery lasted about an hour. 'The body-worn camera sees more clearly than we do in dim light. It's a digital police.' She turned to Cal and asked, 'Could you perhaps—?'

'Yes, I'll get Inez to help us with that,' Cal said. 'I sort of expected that you'd want to see that bastard one more time. Now if you'll excuse me, I'll go get the copcam.'

'A gadget geek, I never was, but this one sounds cool,' Hank said to Cal. 'Maybe I should come with you and together we can get the copcam from the police? I'm curious about it.'

Cal nodded at Hank. Both rose. Uma showed them to the front door.

When Uma returned, Maya mumbled a few words of gratitude for her help.

'Jaa.' Uma made a dismissive gesture with her hand. *No need to thank me*, she indicated, like she always did, and left the room.

Maya picked up her cellphone and keyed in Viktor's number, chewing about the challenge ahead of her. She got him on the line.

Coquettishness in her voice, she cooed to the phone: 'Free this evening?'

He gave an enthusiastic yes and she acted jubilant.

The pretense took a bit out of her – a natural reaction, Maya guessed, to what might turn out to be a life-and-death situation. Only hours from now.

THIRTY-ONE

It was evening. The weatherman had predicted a storm later that night. Maya's heart wouldn't stop thumping as she shared the same couch with Viktor in his living room. She'd never feared so much for her life. Like she could be gone in a second, become a blank space in the eternity. Each moment felt interminable. Each breath carried the same question: might this be her last?

They had had dinner earlier and he'd drunk more than the last time. She'd made a point to go to the ladies' room, ever aware that he could spike her drink with a 'club' drug. Once she'd reclaimed her seat, her heart thudding, she'd switched their wine goblets without him noticing. He'd finished his wine, totally unaware, and quite possibly drugged himself.

Now he half-sat, half-reclined, his heavy eyelids masking the shrewdness ever-present in those eyes. Her formidable opponent, none other than Sunglasses Man. A shock of a black curl fell over his eyebrow. She was equipped with the copcam – a hidden gadget attached to a button of her shirt to record their conversation, turned off for now.

He brought his face closer to her, so close that she caught the smell of his cologne, which somehow agitated her. Her head buzzed with a warning: she mustn't fall for the rich timbre of his voice, soft gaze or the aura of confidence he had about him.

Clasping her hand, he kissed her lightly and murmured something about her full, luscious lips. The bottle of champagne, which he'd opened earlier with a ceremonial flourish, stood on a side table. He reached for his glass and took a long, leisurely sip. 'Been missing you these last few days,' he said wistfully. 'I was on the go but you were on my mind constantly.'

An electric current passed through her, as though he'd spoken the truth for a change. He'd fallen for her, which had made him weak. She sank deeper into the couch, even managed a smile.

A smile bloomed on his lips as well. His hand gently moved up between her slightly pressed legs. She casually cupped his hand in hers, then, in one smart move, eased his T-shirt up over his head with the other hand. She was only playing a role in which she had to perform her best. Do or die sort of thing.

He laughed from the surprise of it, albeit with a hint of embarrassment, and fell back, glanced at his bare chest proudly and winked at her. 'I like an aggressive woman who's also gentle. Shall I take my jeans off, too?'

'There's no rush.'

He struggled to his feet, laughed at himself. His legs came out of his jeans; thin underwear barely concealed the bulging private parts. Although paler than the rest of his skin – lack of sun in both Moscow and Seattle – his legs were well-developed. He could outrun her, no question about that. She heard the clang of the elevator and muffled voices in the hallway. Could it be Uma, accompanied by a friend, checking up on her daughter? She could derail Maya's plan. The voices soon faded.

'What a switch.' He laughed again, falling back onto the couch next to her, and nuzzled her neck. 'A man showing off his body. Now, it's your turn.'

She drew back slightly. His gaze tracing her body, she wiggled out of her jeans. Her limbs were stiff. *Don't be afraid, Maya. You're only setting a trap.*

His feverish eyes flashed at her bare legs. 'Beauty and smarts and a healthy libido. Do you know I've been waiting for you all my life?'

'I'm actually quite—'

'Shy?' His voice turned silky, intimate. 'Shall we go to the bedroom, darling?'

Here was a man engaged to be married.

'Well, not yet . . .'

'We can lie on the bed and talk.'

'I want to know all about you before we become more intimate,' she said. 'Will you be my Scheherazade this evening?'

'Oh, the male version? If that's what it takes, darling. Come. I'll be your Scheherazade in the next room.'

It was the perfect opportunity to execute her plan. She followed him to the bedroom, to a king-sized bed covered with luxurious white cotton sheets. He curled on the left side of it. Her breath ragged, she plumped a pillow behind her and sat beside him. He reached for her, obviously intending to stroke her face. His clumsy hand banged against her chin.

He smiled sleepily, the insomniac. 'Shorey,' he said.

Sorry? She didn't look at him strangely, just smiled. His fatigue and the effect of the spiked drink – she was almost sure he'd spiked it – would be a real help. Playing to his vanity might also get him to open up to her. Then she heard drunken voices outside and became aware of the passage of time. She needed to do what she'd come here to accomplish and get out before he succumbed to sleep. She started to give him a hand massage by placing his hand in hers and using her thumb to apply gentle pressure all over.

'You're beautiful,' he mumbled and winked at her.

'As pretty as Anna?' she cooed into his ear.

'Anna? Oh, no, no comparison. You're a knock-out and you know how to please me. She wasn't wife material and I was so tired of her neediness.' He paused. 'I feel so relaxed. It's your wonderful touch, sweetheart. Don't stop.'

The light had changed outside, the train of time rushing away from her. She almost laughed when this confident man, a lady-magnet, an accomplice in a double murder, gave her a grin in return. *He doesn't realize what he's in for, this braggart. It's copcam time, Maya.*

She pressed a knob to turn on the wearable camera clipped to the button of her blouse, aware that the conversation from this point on would show up on the video footage, covering him from the waist up. He glanced up and gave her a leery look.

'But first,' she said, 'I want to hear Anna's story.'

'Why her?'

'Because of her death. You must have been good in bed, so good that she would rather die if she couldn't have more of you?'

He chuckled.

She caressed his manhood, felt herself blushing in embarrassment, but this was the only way to get him to confide.

'Ah, keep doing that, darling. You don't know how good it makes me feel.' He paused. 'Anna also had a little help.'

She fought a little nausea. 'What secret power you must have.' *Not to mention narcotics and a friend like Ivan?*

His chest puffed up. 'My secret skill, or whatever you call it, was handed down to me by my grandfather, who got it from his father.'

She made her voice clear and words distinct; she kept her fingers working. 'A form of hypnotism?'

'Yeah, although I hate that word – it's cheap. Did I use it to put that stupid sweet-maker under my thumb? You better believe it. I'd only been seeing her for a few weeks when she started hinting that we should get serious. At first I thought she was kidding.' A pause. 'Feel so good. It's your wonderful touch.'

Maya thought of Anna; a wave of sadness washed over her. It was as though he was saying: *How do you get rid of a woman who falls for you so quickly, except by persuading her to kill herself?* He was, indeed, a psychopath, as Cal had suggested. She became aware of the insinuation that he'd try to do the same with her if she demonstrated any more interest in him.

A thrill of terror ran over Maya's body; her breath caught in her chest. Even though a gut-level instinct told her to flee right now, she wouldn't budge, not until she got him to confess the rest.

'Come on, my Scheherazade,' she said. 'There's more. Anna passed the trial for malaria. Her blood specimen, I suppose, will be useful to you in recreating the vaccine?'

'Ah, keep doing it. You're the best.' Viktor's glossy eyes popped back open. He moved his head a little. 'Oh, the specimen you're asking about? Of that lab rat who wanted to marry me? I'll tell you. We've done some work here on the specimen already, analyzed and reverse-engineered. Just finished, actually. It's done. The results have been shipped to Moscow. We'll get a malaria vaccine out of it for the next stage of the trial.'

'And if Anna died by fire . . .'

'Don't you get it? Then no one else could have her blood and, by extension, the vaccine formula. Sylvie, malaria queen who came up with the formula, wouldn't be there to claim it. She'd have died by fire, too. The formula would be mine and MSP's. We'd dominate the world market.'

'And Ivan would get a huge finder's fee?'

'Yes. He's the one who put me on to this after he'd met Sylvie. I was in Moscow then. Once he got a whiff of how valuable her research was, he got back in touch with me. But that's all in the past, darling. Now it's just you and me.'

He raised his head and kissed the air, and she was sure he believed he'd kissed her, as though he'd been overcome by an unquenchable thirst. Her temperature dropped. She pictured Anna and the way she might have felt during her last tryst with him. Anna's hopes had evaporated. In the dry, barren landscape where she stood, her footing unsteady, she could see no one.

Maya glanced at her watch and became aware of how little time she had left. She must formulate her remaining questions carefully to get the last bit of the narrative out of him.

'Did you consider using any mood-altering pills with that "lab rat," to loosen her up a bit?' she said in a controlled voice.

'I did, even though my power was perfectly adequate for the job.' He smiled faintly, smugly and put a finger through his tousled hair.

'You fascinate me, you arouse me.' She breathed those lies

in his ear. 'Tell me more – I want to experience it. Once you'd gotten Anna into that state of mind, I suppose the power of suggestion took her down the desired path?'

'Yes, dear, and a noble path, too, I insist.'

'Help me live it, or maybe we should live it together?' Again, the lies popped out of her mouth. She even managed to look at him with feigned pride. 'Your skills are terribly sexy, by the way.'

'I'm not really that sleepy, you know. This evening I'll give you the kind of pleasure no man has ever given you.' He sounded euphoric. 'Since you asked, purification was the process I advocated to Anna.'

'Anna, being a Tibetan, was familiar with the concept, wasn't she? Dance with fire, in God Agni's presence, to sanctify the cause of Tibet – am I correct?'

'Yes, you burn yourself to ashes, turn into a beautiful pile of nothing.'

He doesn't get his hands dirty. His victims die of their own volition. 'Only then, I suppose, can you make a lasting statement to the world about the suffering of Tibetans and help break China's domination of that country?'

'You said it all. In the end, I managed to focus Anna on the benefits of what she was about to undergo. She was totally convinced. She even thanked me.'

Maya felt oppressively hot. Sweat accumulated on her temples, as though she, too, was on fire. An image of Sylvie bubbled up in her mind. Along with the recollection of the video titled *Burn Give Live*, which the guru had lent to Sylvie and which had glorified the same concept Viktor had employed to bring Anna to ashes. Still, to get him to spill out more she had to show she was on his side.

'Sylvie – what about her? Why did she choose the same path?'

'What are friends for?' he said boastfully with a chuckle. 'I use all the tools at my command. I leave nothing to chance. That's why I am who I am.'

'I still don't get why a smart person like Sylvie—'

'Oh, Sylvie was the easy one. She couldn't live without Ivan and she couldn't have Ivan. She didn't need much convincing from me. As far as she was concerned, her life was over. A romantic fool, she was. She lost all faith in people after she found out her sister was sleeping with Ivan.'

Maya took an uneasy breath. 'Makes you wonder if Ivan did that intentionally to hurt Sylvie, to get rid of her.'

'Yeah, you could say that. It wasn't for Veen, certainly. I've seen a photo of her. That fat slut, that bitch – she killed Sylvie if anyone did. I only helped Sylvie by giving her what she wanted . . . a beautiful ending.'

Get them high and talk them into burning themselves. Make them believe it's a beautiful ending.

Again, he gave a smile of self-importance. 'You're not upset, are you? I assisted Sylvie with the mechanical part of the act, to put her out of the misery. Mine was an act of compassion, sweetheart. What a glorious way to die.'

The mechanical part of the act? How cold-blooded that sounded. How it tallied with what Maya had come to believe regarding Veen's involvement in the love triangle. Veen, also, had been used by these men, manipulated and blinded to reality. Maya's heart felt crushed. Now she saw what the guru had also suggested: the fine demarcation between life and death, a fragile line in the sand. Pursue the wrong partner, lose your head, get so obsessed that you sever yourself from the real world and soon you're standing on the wrong side of that line.

'Oh, about Atticus,' she said. 'Did Ivan send those gangsters to beat him up?'

'Now you're asking about that stupid accountant?'

'It'd really help if you just told me.'

'Yeah, he was too chummy with Sylvie and we didn't trust him. He'd have gone after Ivan for having a fling with his wife. He'd have foiled our plans.'

She threw in her last but one question: 'How does Tara Martin fit into all this?'

'The crazy head. We didn't trust her either, not knowing what Sylvie had spilled to her during those salon visits. She took almost no convincing.'

'Aren't you proud?' After a pause, she slid in another important question. 'What about Jennifer?'

'Jennifer, the ravishing beauty, made it all possible. We couldn't have done it without her. But maybe now we can.'

They were planning to do away with Jennifer.

Still lying on his back, Viktor rubbed his eyes and blinked a few times. 'Have I talked enough? I'm yours. I'm all yours, darling. I want to dance with you. Dance naked. Dance all night. Dance under the stars. Shall we?'

'First, let me get more champagne.'

He propped himself up on the pillow, then again fell back on the bed. 'Don't be too long. I'm ready.'

Acting as though she was light on her feet, she danced out of the bed, tiptoed into the living room and found her loafers but not her jeans. She was breathing hard. Had he hidden them? No time to look, but she couldn't go out the front door dressed like this. How fortunate she had a plan B worked out with Joe. In the bathroom, she locked the door, her heart hammering. What if Viktor rolled out of bed and came chasing after her?

She opened the window wider, took a deep breath. Outfitted in her blouse, underpants and walking shoes, and standing on top of the toilet tank, she grabbed the top of the window frame. She put her head through the window, saw the hanging rope. Grasping it, her lifeline now, coercing her legs after her, she wriggled out onto the open steel gratings of the fire escape deck.

A furry hand feathered her bare legs.

Her scream froze in her throat.

It meowed.

Chest heaving, she groped her way a few feet to reach the ladder of the fire stairs, a contraption that had probably never been used.

She heard Viktor's faint bedroom voice. 'Darling, where are you?'

That gave her the jolt she needed. She descended the three flights of steel-grated stairs as fast as she could, grasping the iron railing for balance and still feeling nearly out of control. Panting, she reached the retractable ladder at the very bottom of the escape and slipped down it, dropping the last two feet to the alley.

Solid ground. How good it felt on her feet. And that light breeze.

Once her eyes adjusted to the dimly lit yard, she looked around frantically.

Cal's metallic gray Hyundai was waiting. 'Get in,' he said urgently, poking his head out of the driver's-side window, then leaning to his right and unlocking the passenger door.

She snatched open the passenger door and somehow managed to put her seat belt on, disregarding the odd look Cal gave her for her scanty outfit.

By now Viktor had figured out Maya wasn't returning to bed. She imagined him cursing her, looking for her and frantic to catch her. What if Viktor took the elevator and came downstairs? He'd kiss her hard. He'd use his honey-smooth voice and his scent to talk her into going back to his apartment.

A light flashed somewhere. Did she also see a shape?

'Quick.' Maya's heart surged in her throat. 'We must get out of here fast.'

Cal gunned the engine and the car shot out of the alley; tires squealed.

'Are you all right?' Uma cried out from the backseat.

Maya gave an embarrassed, 'Yes.'

'But your clothing?' Uma passed her shawl to Maya, saying, 'You can tell me later.'

Maya wrapped the shawl around her. She absorbed its warmth, got a grip on herself.

Cal turned onto Roosevelt Avenue. 'We're heading straight to the police precinct. They'll have a search warrant to go to Viktor's apartment.'

Uma said to Cal, 'Do you suppose the arrests will happen soon?'

Cal nodded and maneuvered the car around a slow-moving pickup truck. 'Everything will happen quickly now, ladies. Don't worry. The men will be locked up. Jennifer, too.'

Uma passed a bottle of water to Maya. 'Drink, my child.'

After a few sips, Maya got her natural rhythm back, although a deep sorrow blew through her for the women who had died. A cold hand feathered her neck as she pictured Viktor flinging his clothes into his suitcase, searching the Internet for an earlier flight and making a call to Ivan. He'd formulated a plan to take revenge against her – try to relax her guard and seduce her. Her only hope: in his drunken state, he might not be able to trot out too far.

She thanked both Uma and Cal for their help, adding, 'I'll have plenty to say to the authorities. With my copcam being on, the police will also have a chance to watch the camera footage of Viktor's confession. I only wish it wasn't such a sordid tale.'

THIRTY-TWO

Maya dropped Uma off at the airport a few days later and returned home, still weepy from the farewell. The living room was empty, shadowy and lifeless; the windows were blank. She heard footsteps on the porch and looked through the peephole. There stood Justin, out of the blue, weary-eyed and denim-clad, his shoulders hunched.

She opened the door. 'Hello,' she said, if a little unenthusiastically.

'Hope you don't mind my dropping by. May I come in?'

Once they were seated on opposite sides of the coffee table, Justin said, 'I'd like to talk with you. It's long overdue. I apologize.'

'It's not really necessary.' Her voice was level, unemotional, with a finality to it.

'It *is* necessary, Maya.'

'You may not realize this but I know everything because of Annette.'

'You don't know everything because Annette doesn't know everything.'

'So what's left to tell? Isn't it enough you cheated on me, betrayed me and didn't have the decency to—?' Maya stopped speaking, her voice clogged with resentment.

'You have every right to be furious. In fact, you've shown more restraint than most women would under similar circumstances.' Sadness and remorse dulled his features. He looked plain, ordinary, confused. 'You see, when I was investigating the drug case involving Jennifer's boyfriend, she began to lean on me. I was seeing you then and at first I tried to keep our contact businesslike. But she was so young, so vulnerable, had survived so much and had no one to turn to. And I . . . I got caught.'

'Couldn't you have told me this sooner?'

'I wanted to. It was a difficult period of my life and I failed miserably.'

Maya turned her face away and silently weighed several other aspects of this case: Jennifer stealing the specimen, being in cahoots with Ivan and Viktor and being complicit in Anna's death. She said out loud, 'Why did she do it?'

'What you might not know is that Jennifer has a rare disease, a hereditary neuropathy inherited from her mother. Jennifer has been on strong painkillers ever since I've known her. I felt so sorry, I had to be there for her. Other symptoms also presented themselves. Because of her own medical condition, Jennifer grasped Viktor's urgency in getting hold of the malaria vaccine. Then there was Viktor's persuasive power. And her attraction to Ivan. Before long, she got caught in their plan. Maybe she didn't care, knowing she didn't have much time left. Maybe she thought she'd be able to get away with it. I might never find out the real answer.' He took a long sigh. 'I still can't believe it . . . but Jennifer and I have split up. She's met someone else.'

After all that? Maya could see how much this fall-out had hurt Justin. Head bowed, lips pressed against each other, he fought the mist in his eyes.

Maya sat with this extraordinary confession. 'You, as a police detective—'

'I'm clearing out my office desk.' His voice broke. 'Devastated as I am, my career is over. I knew that Jennifer had stolen the specimen, but just couldn't . . .'

She felt herself softening toward Justin, knowing how much that detective position meant to him. It defined who he envisioned himself to be: dutiful, efficient, serving his employer and offering help to the community. 'What's next for you?'

'Oh, I s'pose I'll mow the lawn, prune my cherry tree, fertilize the flower beds and plant some herbs. How many times did you ask me to do all those things? And I'm trying to get custody of my son. He's the sweetest boy. He'll keep me on my toes if he comes to stay with me.'

She pictured the boy with pudgy cheeks, how he'd reached for her with his little hands, how he could quickly turn on a full, silly smile. 'You'll do a good job of raising him, I'm sure.' And she found she meant this. She bore no ill-will.

'I also need to look after my yard. Would you have time to give me a hand?'

It startled her but didn't move her; too late now. The excitement with which she might have greeted such an offer in the past had vanished. Now she regarded herself as a different person, one who'd outgrown her fantasy about Justin, and she stood on a different shore. Her ability to follow through on her beliefs, willingness to put herself at risk and to jump into actions when necessary had helped bring her to this point.

She shook her head and said softly, 'I'm sorry.'

How light her shoulders felt. How easy it was to breathe. She looked toward the sun-splashed street outside the window, heard piano music floating from a neighbor's house.

'Oh, one more thing, Maya. You came to see me several times at my house to talk about Sylvie. You probably got the impression I was brushing you off – I acted so curt toward you.'

'Well, yeah, I thought you didn't want to have anything to do with me.'

'No, Maya, that's not it.' Justin's voice was thick. 'I dearly love you; I was concerned. I didn't want to see you get hurt.'

He'd never spoken so openly about how he felt about her. Nor had she ever heard so much emotion in his voice. 'What do you mean?'

He turned his face away for a moment, then spoke again. 'Those criminals would have been at you. I wouldn't have been able to bear that. You're probably still scratching your head over a whole host of incidents. Allow me to shed light on a few of them. That blue sedan belongs to a friend of mine, Chuck Davis. You figured that out, didn't you? I knew, sooner or later, you would.'

She nodded and smiled at the man who had been her

guardian angel. Her heart filled with gratitude for others in her circle who similarly cared about her. Love and care at unexpected times from unexpected places. How the very thought brightened the room for her. Sylvie dawned in her mind. Lovely and talented, Sylvie had been adored by many. Pitifully, she'd signed off without that awareness.

Justin broke the silence. 'And, oh, that elderly woman who followed you to the grocery store? She's Jennifer's multilingual grandmother. A former stage actress in Europe, she now lives in New York and is quite a prankster. She loves Jennifer, came to visit her on vacation. It's probably no surprise that Jennifer is jealous of you. You two met at the flea market. Later, Jennifer asked me if I knew you and I had to tell her the story of our relationship. We weren't getting along well and she felt even more insecure because of that. In order to keep you away from me and scare you off, she recruited her grandmother. That old lady could have hurt you. She had a knife with her. She didn't quite pull it off, but still, it must have left you wondering why she came after you in the first place. You know, Maya, I'd have stopped the whole thing, except I didn't hear about it until after the fact. That led to a big disagreement between Jennifer and me, the beginning of the end of our relationship.' He paused. 'My apologies to you.'

Back off or you'll be dead. Jennifer wanted Maya to stop her visits to Justin. Simple as that. Maya had misunderstood that warning. She took a deep breath. 'I have something to disclose as well. I'm a licensed private eye now, with this case in my portfolio.'

'Really?' He gazed at her proudly. 'How did that happen?'

She sat back, felt the plush rug under her feet and gave him a rundown of how she'd proceeded, what she'd found, all her struggles, fears and setbacks and a few triumphant moments.

Justin's face relaxed into a hint of a smile. 'Congratulations. Look, if you ever need to brainstorm another case, you know where to go.' Slowly, he got up. He seemed to have difficulty getting the words out as he said, 'I'll always love you, Maya. Hope someday you'll be able to forgive me.'

He started for the door, turned back and gave her a wistful look.

Maya heard the click of the door. She remained seated; her memories swirled around their time together. At one point, she wondered if Justin had ever loved Jennifer. She answered that question herself. That tramp was trouble and, as a dedicated cop and a decent person, Justin doted on that aspect of her character. He'd stayed with her, giving her the support she needed, hoping to alter her behavior. Somehow Maya would have to let go of that painful realization along with the push-pull of old memories.

She rose and rearranged the furniture in the living room, lifting and dragging, taking into consideration the best-lit spots in the room and areas of shadow. The sofa was now placed against the wall that faced the door, which seemed like a more inviting arrangement. And now, without the sofa blocking the window, more light poured into the room. She put a crystal vase on the coffee table, which accommodated a bunch of pink coneflowers that harmonized well with the red throw pillows on the sofa and added to the overall effect.

Time to check her messages. She found a text from Hank saying he was cutting out early to have dinner with Sophie. She could almost see his eyes, alive with excitement as he danced out of the office. She sent him a congratulatory note: GLHF (Good luck. Have fun.)

Now in a better mood, she went to the mailbox that hung on the patio railing. Among overly cheerful junk mail and a stack of boring bills, she found a personal letter addressed to her – a five-by-seven-inches cream-colored linen envelope. A bit on the pricy side, it exuded a mild lavender scent, the penmanship unknown.

She checked the top left-hand corner. Atticus Biswas' name was scribbled on it, but no return address. With the letter in hand, she exited through the back door, eased into the yard and pulled up a patio chair. There, surrounded by the red carnival of *nicotianas*, she tore open the flap. Inside rested a sheaf of fine yellow paper written in longhand.

Dear Maya,

By the time you get this, I'll be sunning myself in Bora Bora. No joke, I really am flying out there for a vacation.

After a week or so, I'll head on to another equally sunny pasture. After Guru Padmaraja's death I couldn't eat or sleep or work and opted to take a long break.

I must thank you for all you did for me. You pinned it down: the gangsters who'd beat me up were Ivan's buddies. In fact, you exposed a much bigger crime involving both Ivan and Viktor that explained our loss of Sylvie.

Please allow me to make a confession right away. You asked me more than once, I so painfully remember, if the man in sunglasses had given me a warning and if that's why I prevented you from rescuing Sylvie. You were correct. I'd lied to you. But please consider this transgression from my perspective. After getting my leg broken by those goons, I couldn't take another chance. I had to go along with that nyet *in order to protect myself. I had to play nice. As a result, I'll forever have to bear the burden of my duplicity. Please forgive me if you can.*

Incidentally, it was I who had asked Arthur, the derelict poet (who dedicated his latest poem, 'Tax Shelter', to me), to watch out for you. Whenever you showed up in his part of the woods, he was to make sure you were safe. How do I know Arthur? I met him through Cal Chodron. You see, I do Cal's taxes. Seattle is still, in many ways, a village of like-minded people.

You've already figured this out but please allow me to repeat it. Our guru, although falsely blamed by Ivan, had no direct involvement with Sylvie's suicide. The police are still investigating, but my suspicion is Ivan or an accomplice is responsible for the hit-and-run that took away our guru's precious life on this planet. I found out after the fact that Ivan did have an appointment to meet with the guru that evening, which was what led him to that challenging intersection. And Samuel, the guru's dedicated assistant, betrayed us. He'd been bribed by Ivan to make that appointment. Samuel managed to leave early that day at short notice, leaving the guru protection-less.

My heart aches as I write this. I am trying my best to forgive myself; that's what our guru would surely have wanted. When I return to Seattle, I'll reopen the meditation center, take over its operation and resume the classes. The guru would have liked to see the center continuing to operate in his absence.

It was my good fortune that our paths crossed, even though it was under terribly dark skies. You're an able private investigator and I see you catching many more perpetrators, doing good for us all.

I hope to get back in touch when I return for old times' sake. Let's talk over chai.

Ever yours,
Atticus

Maya stuffed the letter back in its envelope and placed it on the patio table. She could see and hear Atticus: his odd behavior, mathematical humor and protective fatherly ways. It'd still take her a little time to get over his lies.

Her eyes swept the yard. This summer had been a season of many tears and disappointments but also a few gains. Autumn was just around the corner. But before she could welcome the new season, she'd have to take care of that which had sustained her in the past. The overgrown, silvery sage needed to be controlled, the daisies were waiting to be dead-headed, the fuchsia had to be trimmed back before the onset of cold weather. Only then would she be able to till the soil and plant new seedlings for the next season. And that forlorn, single-stalked snapdragon – come next summer, she'd replace it with a cluster of cosmos.

Meanwhile, she'd look for a suitable case to work on. She'd also try to rebuild her social circle, one friend at a time, knowing loneliness would often haunt her steps. Another visit from Uma would be welcome, this time with her gentleman friend, although Maya understood someday that would end as well.

The summer, still lingering in all its magnificence, reassured her. She marveled in its form and rhythm, drank its goodness and rejoiced in its strength. Then she rose, readying herself for whatever challenge awaited her.